The Point Where the Ocean Ends

Siobhan Murphy

Cover design: Miladinka Milic - Milagraphicartist.com

Formatting: Cate Ryan - CateEdits.com

Editing: Bryony Sutherland

Author website: Siobhanmurphyauthor.co.uk

For the people who've stayed by my side
And the people who've allowed me to fly

For the people whose light still shines
And the people taken too soon

For the people who blaze like fireworks
And the people who feel like home

PROLOGUE

MOONLIGHT AND STARDUST

You once told me, as the cool dark silky water lapped over our toes, that the mood of the ocean reflected the mood of your soul. And I told you in return that I had been born at the wrong time. A couple of decades too late, to be precise.

I believed that for a long time. I was born in 1967: the 'Summer of Love', which was fitting for someone with the soul of a hippie. I like to think I'd have gone to San Francisco with flowers in my hair and danced barefoot under the stars at Woodstock.

But now I realise I was born exactly when I was supposed to be born. Born on a date that ensured my path crossed with yours. By some miracle, the universe conspired to put us under those same stars, in that exact place, at precisely that moment in time.

Two adventurers from opposite sides of the world; wanderers looking out at the same horizon, watching the moonlight shimmer across the ink-black ocean. Strangers who talked for hours about fate and destiny, infinity, and stardust.

I have always been drawn to wild, passionate dark-haired souls; you were no exception. Later there would be others who reminded me of you. Complex, inspiring drifters who left a gaping hole in my world when they moved on. All unique in their way. Unforgettable, even. Forces of nature. Authentic free spirits. Each one of them appeared unexpectedly, lighting up my world, then all too soon travelled elsewhere. Part of my world lost its luminance when they left. And part of my heart left with them.

But none of them were you.

The Celtic circle tattooed between your shoulder blades was the first thing I noticed, even before you turned and smiled at me. Then I took in your sleek dark hair, drenched from the surf. Your deep tan and toned arms resting on your surfboard. A silver letter R on a braided leather neck cord glinted in the blazing sun.

Two souls fated to meet.

I felt the most exquisite thrill as I watched you through my lens. I saw an alternative lifepath, a previously unimagined future. Those mesmerising eyes met mine and I clicked the shutter.

PART ONE

LEAVING THE HARBOUR

DECEMBER 3RD, 2020

CIRCLES OF STONE

It's pitch dark. My husband's car is in the driveway. I realise I
have been gone for hours. Yet I dither, collecting snack wrap-
pers from the car, getting my camera bag out of the boot. A gust of
wind picks up a disposable face mask from the passenger seat and
rolls it along the pavement. I chase after it and manage to retrieve
it. I pick up a few pieces of rubbish that have blown in front of the
door and turn the key in the lock. This kills time, but I can't put off
the inevitable.

Despite the fierce breeze rushing off the surface of the ocean,
today was mild. By contrast, the cottage is bitterly cold. Cold in its
very bones, even though the fire is full of glowing orange embers.

And the two of us are cold. Emotionally cold. Cold towards one
another.

There's a distance between us now that we can't reduce. A gap
that seems impossible to close. We move in a constant repeating
circle where he tries to draw closer to me and I try to maintain my
distance. Normally I am the one who holds on too tight, never
wanting to experience loss of any kind. My unpredictable moods
frustrate him. Sometimes they sadden him. At other times, like
today, they make him angry.

'Where the hell have you been?' He's sitting at the table in the kitchen, his hand clenching a bottle of beer, the dog at his feet. 'Honey is starving. I'm starving. There's nothing here to make for dinner, you said you'd sort it out.'

A chill around my neck. A slow sensation of dread. I remember now. I promised to make a special dinner, told him not to bring food home from the farm shop. I've forgotten, again.

'I'm sorry, I lost track of time. I needed to go somewhere ... somewhere away from here.' My hand gestures vaguely round the room. 'Just for a while. I drove over to Bodmin and then I—'

'For Christ's sake, Kerensa, it's been hours. Everywhere's a mess as usual. The washing machine hadn't been unloaded since yesterday. The clothes stunk of damp, so I had to run it again. Your phone was switched off. I've told you to leave it on when you are in the middle of nowhere.' His piercing green eyes flash at me.

'I know, I'm sorry. The battery ran down. I needed space, I thought—'

'You don't think I need some space? That I might need to get away too? I had no idea where you were. I was getting your voicemail for hours. You can't keep thinking of yourself and forgetting everyone else.'

He drains the beer bottle and grabs another from the fridge, slamming the fridge door. The noise makes Honey whimper and she runs over to sit by my feet.

'I got caught up. I had this idea for a new series of photos, maybe an exhibition. I was shooting ... thinking. Wandering.'

'Another idea you'll abandon,' he mutters.

'What's that supposed to mean?'

'Nothing. Forget it.'

The criticism hits me; my heart starts to pound. Usually so supportive of my work, lately he's dismissive. Worn down. I take a breath, try to calm my words.

'Look, I had to get out this morning. You wouldn't understand. Sometimes just being stuck here is too much for me.'

'And it's fine for me, is it? You don't think I get sick of these four walls too? It's so typical of you to think you are the only one struggling. The only one who deserves time to themselves. All the time in the world to just swan off and indulge whatever idea randomly popped into your head today.'

I fetch wine from the fridge and pour a huge glass. 'I thought if I was somewhere else then I'd feel different.'

'Yeah, because that's the magic solution.' He laughs, but it's hollow, derisive. 'If it was, don't you think it would have worked by now?'

The second bottle of beer is already empty and his face begins to soften a little. Honey has moved back over to sit by his side. Sighing, he reaches over and rubs the top of her head.

'I've said I'm sorry.' I walk over, lean down, and hug him around the shoulders. 'You know how I've been, feeling frustrated and exhausted for months. I can't even remember when I last picked up the camera. I had this idea about circles and repetition. Stones. Shapes. I just wanted to create something again. I got completely absorbed.'

'Okay. okay. Can we just leave it for now?' He leans back on the chair, stretching out his back. 'Look, I'm stressed out. Work is killing me.' He pushes both hands through the top of his hair. I've always loved his hair. It's still thick, but what was blond is now grey.

'Grab another beer. The pub is doing takeaway tonight, I will fetch us some seafood. We can relax, maybe watch something together.'

'Sure,' he replies, in a resigned tone.

I walk back up the hill from the pub, dinner warming my hands. I hadn't planned to take photos today, a serendipitous accident, the camera shoved in the car as an afterthought. I wandered round and round a stone circle on Bodmin Moor. Thoughts whirling in my head, feet circling the stones. Each movement attempting to keep pace with the other, ideas flowing at top speed until one took over Finally, after months of stagnation, I was inspired again. But now that exhilaration, that seductive creative high from earlier in the day, has drained away.

He doesn't know the real reason I was awake before dawn. The reason I had to get out of the house at four o'clock this morning. Why I walked round and round like a lunatic on the moors in the early hours. Why I didn't return until dark.

He doesn't know why I needed space. He doesn't know about the email that appeared without warning last night. The shock as it landed in my inbox, stirring up feelings I had suppressed for decades.

An email that was like a portal to another existence.

WANDERLUST

Ten months. Ten long months of sameness, boredom, predictability. Ten months during which I haven't slept properly. Forced to stay in one place, my standard crutches have been removed and my freedom curtailed.

The realisation dawns that I only cope with life by escaping from it.

I needed space today but truthfully, I have always needed space. Always felt trapped. Trapped inside my own head, battling against my own thoughts. Fighting the never-ending loop of emotions that rushes around my mind. I have always felt this constant restlessness gnawing away at me. Always longing to be somewhere else, always seeking out the next destination or the next chapter of the story.

I took my first solo flight aged seventeen, only my second time abroad without my family. The first was a school trip to France which led to my first fleeting teen crushes; one a breathtaking olive-skinned boy named Olivier, the other my French exchange partner Monique, a girl so sophisticated she could have stepped straight from the pages of a magazine.

But then I fell in love properly.

In love with the elegant streets of Paris. I strolled along wide leafy boulevards and down quaint meandering lanes. I sat at stylish roadside cafés, watching impossibly chic women dip buttery croissants into huge cups of coffee. Those teen crushes happened from a distance, were entirely unrequited, and only lasted until I returned home a week later, but my love affair with Paris never ended.

Now, as with all love, I can see the imperfections. The dark, seedy, unpleasant side as well as the polished, charismatic surface. But when I was young, Paris could do no wrong: with its winding riverbanks and shabby charm, the city was perfect in my eyes.

But Paris represented the faded glory of the old world, and my plane was heading for the shiny splendour of the new world. New

York City. Home of iconic skyscrapers and bright yellow taxis. New York, New York. A place that exuded the kind of glamour I had only ever seen on TV. A place that didn't seem real until I landed there. A place where a stretch limousine collected me from the airport, and I saw my first heroin addict shooting up in a corner at an outdoor Frank Zappa concert. I didn't even know who Frank Zappa was at the time. I'd grown up in a house filled with Fleetwood Mac, John Denver, Neil Diamond, and the Carpenters. I was obsessed with Madonna, Kate Bush, and the New Romantic bands.

My mother embarrassed me by crying at the airport when I left. Many, many years later, she told me that standing in that airport on that day, she knew she would spend her entire life watching me leave on planes while wondering if I would ever come home again.

She was right.

December 5th, 2020

A nother restless night. I haven't slept well for months. The uncertainty in the world causes my mind to spiral more than usual. So this morning at dawn I walked around the garden in my bare feet. The last traces of autumn have disappeared and taken my favourite colours with them – the russets, ochres, and deep reds have all faded. Leaves have detached and floated away.

In the cold misty sunrise, as the icy wetness seeped into the soles of my feet, I travelled back in time. Back to my mid-twenties, to my garden in Nairobi. A garden where I often walked barefoot on rain-soaked grass after the same bird woke me every morning with its irritating, monotonous chirping. A tropical garden filled with banana trees, orchids, and lush green leaves. A place that exists a whole lifetime away, yet I can still conjure up the smell of the earth after the rains have come.

Rain mixed with hot dust.

A fragrance so comforting. A fragrance deeply entwined in my memory along with so many others. Fresh pineapples and papayas. Kerosene. Jasmine plants. Woodsmoke and nyama choma cooking on the stove. Signature scents of a place that is forever ingrained in my heart.

11

Stretching right across Africa and the Middle East is the Great Rift Valley. A landscape formed by plates separating from one another and pulling apart the earth's crust. It snakes its way through Kenya with stunning lakes dotted all along its valley: Naivasha, Elementaita, Nakuru, Baringo, Bogoria. Lakes teeming with pelicans and flamingos that turn the surface of the water pink. Lakes where hippos wallow, partly submerged, observing the world around them. Lakes that go all the way up to Turkana in the north.

Turkana is like nowhere else in the world. A place on the edge of existence. Spectacular, yet desolate. A deserted moonscape, a land shaped from dust and lava. The lake is a surreal jade oasis in the middle of an intensely hot, dry desert.

In the end, I didn't get to see Lake Turkana. Our trip was cancelled due to political instability in the area. A trip my boyfriend and I didn't rearrange because by then things between us were starting to unravel.

Those early years we spent together in Kenya were magical, at least for some of the time. A sprawling house full of guests, bronzed feet in flip flops, the high-pitched giggles of children leaping gleefully into the pool. Splashing water and flying braids. A CD player on an extension lead dragged into the garden. Slices of seared meat, piled up high on the barbecue grill. Boxes of empty Tusker bottles. Dusty desert boots. The waft of skin smoothed with cocoa butter, the crack of an ice cube being dropped into a gin and tonic. Smoke and laughter, entwined and floating up into the dusk sky. Sundowner cocktails in luxury resorts and writhing bodies in sweaty nightclubs. A joyful convoy of jeeps heading off on a weekend safari.

In time, deep cracks formed. Forces beneath the surface erupted and, like the Great Rift Valley, the ground between us fractured irretrievably. Eventually, it began to pull us apart.

December 8th, 2020

Sand in My Shoes

L ying on our backs, eyes squinting at the sunshine overhead. Intense heat. Heat from the sand, from the air, from the rays of the sun. Heat from unfamiliar skin. Intoxicating. Thrilling. Wild emotions tinged with an edge of danger and a sense of fate.

Hours pass; a balmy breeze begins to waft off the ocean. It tries to cool us down, calm the adrenaline, steady our breath, and soften the electricity between us. Two people on a collision course of lust, fascination, surprise. It all happened so fast. With such force. Almost like a form of addiction. A form of madness. Reality was slipping, time falling away.

We caught a glimpse of forever. Or so we believed …

The Long and Winding Road

The email derailed me. Physically. Emotionally. It jolted me straight back into the past. Seeing those photos of you … photos of us, after all this time. I had packed my thoughts of you away into a box long ago, just as I had packed away all of our photos and all of our letters. The boxes are still there, in the loft, just as they were. Kept closed for so many years now. I cannot bring myself to look inside.

To read the thousands of words across the pages, see the shape of your handwriting and hear the sound of your voice.

Letters feel old-fashioned now; modern life moves too fast for them. Everything is so fleeting – texts, thirty-second videos, emojis, voice notes. Communication no longer feels solid and enduring. There is something almost meditative about writing a letter by hand. My mother still receives one every Christmas from a cousin in Australia, written in exquisite handwriting, with a pressed flower tucked inside. I pressed flowers myself as a child, placed them lovingly between pieces of coloured paper. Delicate pieces of nature's beauty became little hints at immortality.

Forever preserved, forever young.

A letter arrived this week too, but it is not written with love, not penned by hand. It is the opposite. Hospital letterhead, computer-generated, clinical, and abrupt. It was expected, but I still procrastinate, not opening it for several days. Possibilities I don't wish to contemplate flash through my mind, so I shove the contents back into the envelope and pretend the words do not exist. Instead, I reach for my diary and I picture different words. I visualise old travel journals. Page after page filled with scrawling descriptions of intrepid adventures. Recently, I realised there was a point when I stopped writing and only took photographs. When I began to view the world entirely through a lens. Framing decisive moments. Immortalising people on glossy paper.

Freezing time.

But those images of us on the screen transported me back. I yearned to hear voices from the past once more, to relive long-ago moments. Most of all, I craved words once again, so I picked up my pen and began to write this diary. Trying to make sense of my thoughts before responding to the email, I suppose.

And strangely, after all this time, when I started to write, I realised I was writing to you.

I think you will be surprised that I returned to England, but not that I live by the water. I settled on a rugged section of the North Cornish Coast, where salt fills the air, and the wildness of the sea is right within my reach.

A tiny white-washed cottage on a cobbled street. Outside, a rose garden and an old stone wall. Inside, a whole raft of stories. Stories that pervade every inch of this house. Each candleholder, soapstone dish, wooden carving, and piece of art has a story. Each photograph. Even the magnets that pin childish notes and funny cards to the fridge have a tale attached.

Stacks of journals, old magazines, and untidy piles of notepaper are spread across my antique desk. A forgotten cup of coffee. Numerous pens that no longer work. Above the desk, a framed photograph. The recipient of my very first press award. To the side a bookcase with a handful of battered first editions and beloved novels from quaint, dusty bookshops. They have leather bindings and broken spines, brown-edged pages that exude the fragrance of old love stories, of moments buried forever in the past. In this corner I can always see the flowers in the garden, I can always see the sky, and, most importantly, I can see the ocean. Here, with Honey curled around my feet, I switch off the phone and the computer, and I write with an ink pen. This allows me to time travel and frequent other lifetimes.

Books and music comfort me, but there are times when memories overwhelm me, when they seep from the very walls of this house. Walls that feel so claustrophobic after the last year and force me outside, whatever the weather, almost gasping for air. Some days I drift into gentle daydreams of the past and find no words at all. At other times, I barely pause for breath; my feelings spill furiously onto the blank page. But always, I find myself picturing your face as I wait for the ink to dry.

Because there is so much you don't know. So much I never told you ...

I have no idea how long I've been sitting here. How much time has passed. The silence unnerves me. For so long I needed peace, but now I crave noise again. Unpredictability, surprise, a touch of madness.

Have I outgrown the tranquillity of this place? Is this serene bubble no longer enough? What if nothing is ever enough?

Counting my breaths, my heartbeat slows as I read the email

through again. Twice. I wait for the water to boil and allow the words to sink in.

The kettle clicks off. A loud echo in the emptiness of the kitchen. I wonder again why it is so quiet. No one replies when I call out, so I sit with my coffee at the large wooden table, its surface a mess of envelopes and papers, folded bills, and junk mail. I put the coffee mug down. On a recycled envelope in the middle of the table is a note, next to a flyer advertising window cleaning. A note scribbled with a biro that was running out of ink. The writing tails off and fades at the end.

I've sent you a text. You probably won't notice it. You didn't even reply earlier when I tried to talk to you, so I'm leaving a note.

I can't do this right now.

I'm going to stay at the farm for a while. Think we could both use some space.

How long has the note been there?

How long has his car been missing from the drive?

When did I stop seeing him?

How did we reach this point … again?

December 9th, 2020

The Things We Treasure

The house is such a mess. I seem to create even more clutter whenever I try to tidy it. Today I can't face it: even working out where to start feels too much. So I ignore everything, promising myself I will sort it out later. I was the same as a child, leaving utter chaos in my wake, causing my mother to shout all the time. I think my brother was similar.

'Finn O'Connell, clear this lot up. *Now*,' my mother yells at my older brother.

His football cards are scattered all over the carpet. He collects them avidly, different players, different teams.

'And pick up these bloody marbles, the pair of you. Talk about a death trap.'

It's the early seventies and both of us collect marbles, but the ones strewn over the carpet are not mine. I hold on tight to mine, keep them in jam jars, and protect them like the treasures in Aladdin's cave. At school we swap them with other children during playtime. My brother's figured out that he can sell the special ones and make some money, but they are my favourites. Like the inside of a kaleidoscope. I hold them up to catch the light and gaze endlessly at the swirling colours. Little circular rainbows.

My Irish grandad collects darts trophies from competitions. We often drive to their bungalow in Hampshire for Sunday lunch, and I run my hand across the plaques engraved with his name. In the afternoon, we have tea and cakes served on the fancy china from the glass cabinet. Battenberg cake and French Fancies, with a ball of fake cream on the top under a covering of coloured icing. Even though we are only sitting in the lounge, my grandad is dressed in a suit with a waistcoat and tie. He even has a tie pin. He is a story-teller. I listen to his gentle, lilting accent as he spins tales about the 'little people,' the fairies and leprechauns. He believes in other-worldly things. In ghosts and pixies. I beg him again and again to tell me about the banshee, the female spirit who appears before someone dies. I know this story so well, but he smiles, and he tells me again anyway.

'Well now, darlin',' he begins as he strokes my hair, 'sure I heard the wailing and the screaming and I promise you, no word of a lie, I saw the banshee there. Right on the fence. The following morning now, we heard that our neighbour was dead. Taken in the night, so he was.'

Grandad's wife refills the teapot, asks if anyone wants another cup or more cake. I always want more cake.

'I'll have a second cup of tea, you know me,' my dad replies.

Dad's real mum died when he was young, and my grandad married again. It's strange but we don't call her Grandma, maybe because my dad calls her by her first name, even though she's an O'Connell like the rest of us. Even though she's been there our whole lives. When we leave, Grandad gives my brother and me a £10 note each. He has them folded up ready and slips them into our hands when she isn't looking. He stands on the driveway and waves us off. Won't go back indoors until our car has disappeared. I always look back and see him standing there in his smart suit, getting smaller and smaller. Eventually, he becomes too frail to come out and wave us off, and our visits end. I can still picture him standing on that drive, waving. As if time never moved on.

My other grandparents live in a tower block in London. The lift is always broken, and the stairs are getting harder and harder for them to manage. They are always kind to me and my brother, but sometimes when we visit them, my mum and my grandad have rows. The reasons only make sense to me when I'm older.

'Oh here we go, Dad, you don't seem to like any of the neighbours,' she says impatiently. 'What's wrong with these new people now?'

'Well, you know love, they're foreign,' he replies in a strange, hushed voice. 'They're ... they're *black*,' he whispers.

'Honestly, Dad,' she snaps.

But he just shrugs his shoulders.

London gets too busy and noisy for them; they say it's changed too much. There are too many of 'those foreign people'. They decide to move to Wales, back to where my grandmother was born. A little terraced house, nestled on a street in the Rhondda Valley. The broken lift and stairs are replaced with a steep hill up to the shop and the working men's club. My grandparents spoil us by taking us on trips to the beach, two kids with white-blonde hair jumping through the waves in the freezing cold sea. They buy us ice creams and sweets. So many sweets. Big plastic shopping bags full of sweets.

'Your grandad likes to buy you all these things just because he can,' Mum tells us. 'Food was rationed for a long, long time, you see.'

'That's right,' Grandma agrees. 'You kids don't know you're born.'

In the room where we sleep, there is a cupboard full of sugar. The bags are rock hard, they've been there so long, but my grandad keeps them anyway. The house is only small, so a few years later, after my younger brother Gareth and my baby sister Alanna come along, they sleep in the room with all the sugar, and Finn and I camp out on the sofas. There's a strange painting at the top of the stairs, a head and shoulders portrait of a crying boy. I find it creepy, but my mum tells me they are popular. I learn later there are stories of houses burning down around these paintings and that they are the only thing to survive the fire unharmed.

As soon as we cross the bridge into Wales, my mum starts talking in a Welsh accent that she doesn't normally have. We always visit her aunt, uncle, and their two poodles. They live at the top of another steep hill and give us glasses of 'fizzy pop' from bottles delivered by the milkman. My grandparents have swapped a skyline of London tower-blocks for a skyline of collieries. The shapes of the head frames over the mine shafts and the chimneys are everywhere.

The tragedy of Aberfan still haunts the valleys. An avalanche of coal slurry, which slid down a hill onto a school, killing nearly all the children in the village and their teachers. Some of my mum's family were there that day, trying to save people, trying to dig them out. It happened the year Finn was born. The same year that England won the World Cup. Over time the engines ceased, the pits closed, and the collieries became part of the past. Shafts were filled in and new structures were built across the land they once defined. My grandparents have been gone for a long time, and so the Wales I remember as a child is a landscape filled with ghosts.

THE DARK ROOM

'Kerensa, it's me. How are you?' My sister has somehow heard what's going on.

'I'm fine. Honestly. My stomach is uncomfortable, but I've felt like that for months now.' I try to sound upbeat.

'I'm worried about you.'

'Alanna, it's fine. It's a routine hysterectomy. They knew about the fibroids, but it turns out there's an ovarian cyst making things more complex. They just think it's easier to take it all out. It's not as if I need my ovaries now, is it? Too late for all that.'

'Don't be flippant. You obviously aren't fine. I can tell from your voice.'

'It's not the surgery, it's the recovery. I'm going stir-crazy here as it is and they are insisting I rest for about two months, six weeks at the very least. I can't stand the thought of an even slower existence than the one I already have. It feels excruciating. Walking Honey and going running are the only things keeping me grounded. Oh, by the way I'm taking photos again. Did I tell you? It's a project, well, it might be, I'm not sure yet. It's about stone circles and pathways. Did you know there's a place in Oregon with stone labyrinths on the beach? I want to go there sometime. You can walk through them, it's living art really, it's meditative and—'

'Kerensa. Stop rambling and tell me what's going on. You sent me a WhatsApp message.'

'Did I? I don't remember, I've been working on the images all day. I wonder if I can get my old editor interested in an article or—'

'Yes. You did. You sounded worried. When is he coming back? Where is he, anyway?' She's trying to be supportive but sounds irritated.

'He's staying at the farm. Saves him driving back and forwards for work at least.'

'How long for? Has he been in touch? What did he have to say for himself?'

'He called last night, but we ended up arguing. I couldn't hear him properly. It's in the middle of nowhere. The reception kept dropping out.'

'No, I'm on the phone. Go and ask Daddy,' she shouts. 'Sorry. I'm listening.'

'I only got odd bits of it. Said I'm "selfish" and "guarded". That I never communicate or let him in. Said he needs a break, space to think.' I grab another tissue and try to stifle a sob.

'What does he mean you never communicate?' she snaps. 'What a load of nonsense. Of all the times to decide he needs space, why now? Unbelievable.'

'Well, I haven't had a chance to tell him about—'

'It's probably a fuss about nothing, stress. All of us are struggling one way or another. Mind you, it's not like he hasn't done it before. Hopefully he'll pull himself together before your operation. He is coming back for that, isn't he? I can be your official person if not. I'll come down there, be part of your bubble.'

'But Alanna you can't,' I struggle to get a word in. 'You have far too much—'

'Don't argue. We're family, that's within the rules. The kids will be fine. They have a home-school routine now.'

'It's not necessary, I'm not alone. I have—'

'Well, I want to help. You aren't the only one that could use a change of scene, you know. I can work from your place. The last year's been hell, and I'd love a bit of sea air. Is your Wi-Fi still crap? Never mind. We'll sort it all out. Thank goodness you got a surgery date reasonably quickly.'

I've barely pressed end call when my friend Bernadette calls.

'Darling, got your message. Listen, let him get it out of his system, he'll be back.' She has a habit of cutting to the chase. 'I insist you don't stew on it. In the meantime, I prescribe a large glass of wine, and a mindless film on Netflix.'

'Thanks, I know you're right, it's just—'

'Sorry darling, sorry, got to go, the damn cat just dragged in a half-dead rodent.'

Laughing as I end the call, I take her advice, pouring a large glass of wine and switching on the TV.

I wanted to write something light-hearted to you today, something to make you smile, but the weight of the world felt too heavy earlier. We had a blazing row. I tried to pretend with Alanna, told her everything was fine as I always do, but she could tell. She always can, even on the phone. She wants to come and help. Being her usual practical self, she is busy working out all the logistics.

He doesn't know I have my operation date. I haven't told him yet. I guess it's fair of him to say I don't communicate. I'm just so exhausted with it all. Even taking a walk feels impossible. Sinking into the warmth of the sofa with a blanket, lighting the fire, and reading a book are all I can manage. Yet even that hasn't worked. I can't concentrate, reading the same sentence four or five times. Distracted, catastrophizing. Thoughts and fears battle for space in my head.

Images of you flash through my mind like a reel of film negatives, faster and faster. I close my eyes and try to breathe. And they begin to slow down. Floating in a chemical bath, the pictures take shape on the paper, rising through the haze. I imagine hanging them up to dry. One by one. Rolling waves. Soft sand. Sunlight dappling the surface of the ocean. Palm trees in the distance. Your hand trailing in the water, the tips of your fingers lightly brushing the foam as the boat moves along. The blazing heat of the afternoon softening into the sultry warmth of the evening. Sunset. Snatches of sounds filtering in: the rhythmic swell of the surf, your infectious laugh, a clinking of cocktail glasses. Tracy Chapman's 'Fast Car' drifting over from the nearby bar. The natural light fades and lights from the town replace it in the background. Soon the moon will bathe the ocean in swathes of silver.

Suddenly, abruptly, there is darkness.

December 12th, 2020

Sunsets Like Fire

You would hate winter in England. I can't bear it myself and I grew up here; I always wish I could hibernate. The government guidelines actively encourage this as the pandemic rages on, but I still need air.

So I am trying to embrace winter. Appreciate the changes in nature during this unforgiving season. I take long walks as the frost creeps in, breath hanging in the air and boots crunching through the leaves. I imagine thick blankets and huge mugs of hot chocolate awaiting me, warming my hands as I thaw by the hearth. I gaze at the fire, spending hours lost in the flames. I imagine long-ago campfires and stories born of warmth and memory. The crackling sound of the logs soothes my soul, the woodsmoke comforts me. I savour these moments of beauty even more as each day passes.

I feel unbalanced. Unsure of the future. Nature is out of balance too; parts of the world are on fire. A friend in Australia sends me photos. Raging fires on Fraser Island, catastrophic walls of flame ravaging the sand-dunes and forests. It's a place I remember as a total paradise, seventy-five miles of pristine beach that I drove along in a four-wheel drive with Alanna and two of her closest friends, all of us carefree and laughing. They were on a gap year after university; I was on a gap from life in general. I wore my hair in two French braids. It made me feel ten years younger than my real age and look more like all the younger backpackers. On Fraser Island I floated in a swirling turquoise lake, unburdened by the troubles of life. Yet now it is burning ...

The sky above Port Isaac bay looked as if it were on fire earlier, one of those spectacular sunsets that sneak up and surprise you on a dull grey day. You know the kind. Like a fiery, passionate love affair – magnificent, overpowering, all-consuming, and then the sun disappears below the horizon and the splendour is gone as quickly as it came. Nothing remains to show that something so intense and blistering ever existed.

The East African sunsets were often like fire. Blazing palettes of red and gold. Kenya was a country that existed a whole world away from the life I knew when I was young. Somewhere I never dreamed I would visit, let alone live. At dinner when we were kids, my dad would say, 'There are starving children in Africa,' if I left food on my plate. He would make me sit there and eat it all. My mum would tell him to let me get down; I was stubborn, but I was also tiny. I didn't eat much. She knew that no matter how long I sat there the plate would not be emptied.

I knew nothing about Africa apart from the narrow stereotypes on TV. Films like *Zulu* came on every Christmas. Michael Caine on the screen in a red uniform and white pith helmet, rows of chanting warriors with big oval shields. Violent battle scenes I would hide from, diving behind pillows on the sofa. Just as I did when the daleks were on *Doctor Who*. Later it was *The Flame Trees of Thika*, a gentle story of a British family moving to Kenya and setting up a coffee plantation. Gorgeous scenery and a plot I don't remember. Of course, when I grew up I realised these depictions were all clichés, a glorification of a shameful colonial past.

Years later I headed to Kenya to see my friend Cara, the first of our group to fly the nest. She was teaching in Nairobi. Ironically, her privileged expat life felt pretty similar to those old colonial narratives I watched as a child. The first night we drank Tusker beers in a big, gated house, attentively waited upon by Kenyan house staff. We watched *Out of Africa* on an old video recorder – Meryl Streep and Robert Redford – in yet another story of a coffee plantation and colonial settlers. The next day I sat on the terrace of

Karen Blixen's former home, taking in the panoramic views of the Ngong Hills. I imagined her drinking gin and tonic, watching fire-coloured sunsets and waiting for her great love, Denys Finch Hatton, to return in his plane.

'I've got so much planned,' Cara tells me as we drink gin on her terrace. 'I've booked you a safari in Samburu and of course the Mara. The tented camps are incredible, and you can't beat sundowners watching the animals. You'll hopefully get to see the Big Five.'

'It all sounds amazing.'

'Then we'll do a trip to The Ark. It's shaped like Noah's Ark, and you stay up all night watching the animals at the watering hole. Then the coast, Malindi, which is stunning. My friend Rhys is coming too. He has a customer down there so he's meeting us for the weekend. You'll like him, he's Northern too. That's how I met him. He heard my accent and made fun of me.'

The safaris were like nothing I'd ever experienced, and Malindi was perfect. Luxury hotel, blazing sunshine, cold beers and wonderful food. Snorkelling. Swimming in crystal-clear waters and revelling in the sight of the pure white sand. Halfway through my trip and the start of something new, an unexpected whirlwind of a romance. Rhys and I clicked. It felt as if I'd always known him. He was almost a male version of Cara: his voice, sense of humour, his hair colour. He was new and intriguing, yet somehow familiar. Hand in hand, our feet firmly planted in that perfect sand, we stood on a beach that felt like paradise and looked like something from the Bounty ads I watched as a child. He was accustomed to the beauty surrounding us, almost taking it for granted, but I took nothing for granted. Truly awe inspiring: a beach that made every other beach I had ever seen feel like a poor imitation.

Later, as the sun glare softened, the breeze grew stronger and gradually lessened the heat of the day. We curled up together on the sand. Its powdery softness felt so luxuriant as it streamed through my fingers and I laughed, remembering the rough pebbles on the freezing Welsh beaches of my childhood. We waited for dusk. Waited for the moon to rise over the ocean and we waited to see what lay ahead for the two of us …

Of course, Kenya was not all paradise – no country ever is – but

I was distracted by the intensity of this new love, so I tried not to notice the sprawling slums, or the begging street kids. I watched crimson sunsets, bathed in moonlit water, and tried to forget that these blissful days of passion would come to an end far too soon.

But life can surprise you and soon I was on my way back to Kenya, aged twenty-four, about to move in with someone I barely knew. I threw myself into this so ferociously, partly to help me forget you. It was reckless, impulsive. But I had a friend who was there to catch me if I needed it. Eventually, I would need it. But at the start it was all dizzying excitement. Getting on the plane was daunting, thrilling and in its own way heartbreaking. Mum wasn't the only person crying at the airport this time. The tearful faces of my family followed me through the departure lounge, onto the plane, and haunted me until I finally fell into a troubled sleep.

In the years that followed I lived through astonishing moments: wild camping trips in the game parks, close encounters with magnificent animals, dangerous off-road driving experiences, frightening plane journeys, sundowners in idyllic locations, and once in a lifetime moments in nature.

And as for the romance, well, while Kenya was sunny all year round, our own relationship mirrored the more distinct seasons. We had languid, happy summers and we had tough, biting winters.

And we had sunsets that looked like fire.

SHAPED BY THE SEA

I have spent so much time alone this past year. Locked in. Cocooned. Not yet able to emerge butterfly-like into the new world that exists. Even when I am with others, I feel alone.

Despite pushing him away, the space I thought I wanted feels too big. He has only been gone a week, part of me worries about a future without him. None of us can predict the future after this last year, but I fear it may be forever changed. I walk along the beaches and search for sea glass. Much easier to find after storms, I spot these little gems of glass amidst the ordinary grey stones. Tiny unwanted pieces of waste that tumble around the ocean as they travel from place to place. Rough surfaces are smoothed, sharp edges become rounded over time. Finally, they return to the beach as items to be treasured.

It is 1975 – I see myself as an eight-year-old scouring the beaches in Wales, collecting seashells and pebbles from the water's edge. I see myself collecting books, like my parents. My childhood home is a world of overflowing bookshelves. Books in every room. Books piled onto bedside tables. None of these are given away: instead, my dad simply puts up more shelves.

Alongside all the books are photographs. It is later now – 1990 – photos are scattered throughout the house. In frames. Propped onto shelves. An entire photo wall runs along the hall corridor. Photos going back years: Mum in a miniskirt and a beehive hairdo; Dad smoking a pipe, wearing flares and John Lennon glasses; wedding photos; school photos; old colour-tinted baby photos. A touching black-and-white photo of my grandparents dancing in an old dance-hall. Embarrassing photos with bowl cuts, curly eighties hair and dreadful mullets.

There are boxes and boxes of older black-and-white photos and Polaroids of my parents when they were young. Some are creased and the people are starting to disappear from existence, like that scene in *Back to The Future*. My mother inherits even more photos after her parents die. Time-worn. Sepia-coloured. Formal, stiff-looking images taken in photographic studios and unsmiling men in uniform. Names and dates are marked on the back in fading ink. Words to identify people now that everyone who knew them is no longer here.

The faces of people who are long gone. The treasures of lives that are long past.

By the year 2000 some of my photos are on the wall. Prize winners and images from successful exhibitions. A large photo of the first grandchild takes pride of place. My dad hangs it next to an old photo of me on safari. I have a battered film camera in one hand, my other hand shading the sun from my face, as I lean against a dilapidated Land Rover, laughing. The dry, sweeping land-scape of the Maasai Mara stretches out in the background.

My grandparents are all gone now, but there's a family group photo, from the farewell dinner just before I left England for Kenya. The dinner where my Welsh grandparents and my grandad's wife finally asked the question they had been worrying over for months. They asked my parents whether the man I was going to live with was black.

'Oh no,' Mum told them. 'He's blond. He's from Manchester,' as if the whole of Manchester was white. Their relief was palpable, and I remember feeling fury, disappointment, and disbelief, all rolled into one.

'Don't make a scene,' Mum hissed under her breath. I could tell she was stressed; everyone was putting a brave face on my imminent departure, but they were all sad in their different ways. As I helped Mum clear the table and carry things to the kitchen, her tone became more defeated. 'Don't mind your grandparents. It's just their generation, you know how they are. They won't change now.'

Like the sea glass, my grandparents had been shaped by the world they inhabited. A world that had tumbled them around the depths of its waters. My Irish grandad was also shaped by the past. But he was formed in a different way. Softer, more translucent. He existed in a world where the veil to other places was much thinner. I remember he took my hands, held them tight, and told me he was proud. Proud of my adventurous spirit, proud that I was heading off to see the world.

'Ahh now, take no notice of them.' His eyes twinkled at me. 'Sure, you love whoever you want now, my darlin' girl. Just go and find your stories.'

So I did. I tried to find all the stories that I possibly could, from every single country I could possibly visit. Life is just a collection of stories when you think about it. We all weave our individual tales. Paint pictures of our lives for ourselves and for others. Our tales are like the delicate threads in a swatch of cloth, intertwining with other people's and forming a pattern. A pattern that is striking and complex or perhaps it's gentle and muted. In my mind these patterns resemble the brightly coloured woven blankets piled high in Peruvian markets or the bold graphics printed across fabrics worn by Kenyan women. Fabrics sewn into stylish headwraps or made into kangas and used to carry babies.

We tell so many different stories, both real and invented. Stories that we believe define us, until we realise they are just stories. We keep telling them until they become suits of armour. We are scared to step forward without their protection. We cling to these stories from the past just as we cling to the person we were in the past, a person who is long gone. Creating new stories is thrilling, but we fear it. Our old stories are so familiar; we know we can handle them.

We aren't sure if we can handle new ones.

December 13th, 2020

A beep on the phone. An email comes through. The date for my pre-op is confirmed for early January. I'm fortunate, there have been so many delays. There's a reminder of all the safety precautions to follow in order to minimise infection risk and a mention of the biopsy they will do as standard following the procedure. My tough core shatters and reality bites. I want to talk to him, but he is not here. Once I tell him the date, he will feel obliged to return out of guilt and I will feel as if I've given him no choice. That I've clung on too tightly when he's specifically asked for some time and space.

Despite all our years together we were moving around each other so awkwardly, he and I, even before he left. The strangeness between us has been going on for months. Even with all we've been through in the past, being forced together during lockdown without respite, without real freedom, has taken a huge toll. But deep down, I know that it's because I have never opened my heart. Not completely.

He doesn't know that you are one of the reasons. But I know he has always sensed there were parts of me he couldn't reach. I miss him now, though. I miss his solid presence. The way he is able to calm me down. Music can calm me most days, assuming I find the

33

right song to suit my mood. I often return to the eighties – transported back to those days when I danced in my room. 'Tainted Love' or something by Kate Bush blaring out at full volume. But today I listened to *Parallel Lines* on a loop, one of the first albums I ever bought on vinyl, using my birthday money. I was obsessed with Blondie back then – was I a little in love with Debbie Harry? Or did I want to be like her? Maybe it was both. I had forgotten how much I adored that album, so many superb tracks: 'One Way Or Another', 'Fade Away And Radiate', 'Heart Of Glass'.

I wonder if he finds comfort in knowing he cannot break my heart again. That it is no longer a thing to be shattered.

December 15th, 2020

The Wilderness Behind the House

I've been putting it off, but I finally call my husband with the dates for my operation, and we try to iron out some of our recent issues.

'I can handle most of your craziness' he tells me. 'I mean, it drives me up the wall, but I'm used to the mess and your chaotic way of doing things. I even quite like your impulsiveness at times. But it always felt manageable in the past and, well, lately you seem to have gone somewhere inside your head. Somewhere I can't reach you. As if you don't register anyone else's needs, that you don't see either of us. By the way, you are feeding Honey, aren't you?'

'Yes, of course I'm feeding her.'

'Alright, sorry. What I'm trying to say is that I think it might be time to try another therapist. They all operate remotely now. It doesn't matter that we live out here in the middle of nowhere.'

I know he's right. I'm too tired to argue with him. Usually, my hackles would be up immediately, hypersensitive reactions would kick in, but instead I feel numb. Things that have always existed within me seem amplified. I'm not sure if it's the lockdown restrictions taking their toll. Or a fear about the operation. There is nothing on my scans to indicate problems beyond those they already know about. Biopsies are standard practice with fibroids and cysts, but it must be natural to feel worried?

'I'm sorry. You're right. You are. I'll do a bit of research. I promise. See if I can find one that feels like a good fit. I just need to get this operation out of the way first. They've confirmed 4th of January, so fingers crossed it's not cancelled.'

'Look, are you sure you don't want me there? It seems crazy your sister driving all that way.'

'She wants to help, needs a break from the kids I expect. Paul can manage for a week. And neither of you can come in with me anyway with all the rules. We can decide nearer the time.'

I switch on off the phone, cuddle under a blanket and stare at the fire.

There are so few memories of the house where I was born. A flash of the bunk bed, in the room I shared with my brother. A snapshot of the stone fireplace, where I fell and cracked open my head. That shiny scar across my forehead, the one you once ran your finger over so gently, is the only evidence now that it happened.

Finn and I would wake early, while Mum and Dad slept. We'd sneak out of the house, through a gap in the fence, into the woods behind. Our secret wilderness. I would follow, never questioning, as he led us on an adventure. We were pirates and stowaways, cowboys and Indians. We were jungle creatures and fugitives living off the land.

Much later we moved to another house beside an enormous park. A child's paradise with a river and an old canal running through and woods that sprawled for miles. There too I was always looking to escape into an imaginary world. Hanging off branches. Building dens. Conkers, wellies, and mud. Sunshine and bare feet. Leaning over the bridge playing Poohsticks. Wading through a stream. Water rushing down a weir. When it snowed, we would sit on a rickety old sled and crash down a hill, tumbling into the muddy snow at the bottom. Red-cheeked and sweating, we would realise we were hungry, that hours and hours had passed. Time to head back to a home that always smelled of cooking and the warmth of a fireplace I didn't associate with an accident. A fireplace where, no matter how old I get, I think of crumpets and love.

A couple of years ago, I passed near that first house. Drawn irresistibly down a street to a vaguely familiar turning and echoes of forgotten childhood laughter. And there it was, a tiny house I only remembered from photographs. I looked for my wilderness, for the forest that contained all my memories. But it wasn't there, I couldn't see it. I wondered if new houses had covered it. New houses with new memories for other children.

But then I saw it.

Where once had been a wonderland of surprise, danger, exhilaration, and daring, was now a bit of scrubland between the houses, some scraggly bushes, and an old wire fence. The person I was a long time ago smiled once more, as I ran my much older hands across it. A fence with a gap just big enough to allow a tiny dreamer to squeeze through.

THE ROAD TO EVERYWHERE

I was always a dreamer, it was on every school report I ever received. Right now, the dreamer in me is working overtime, her wanderlust muttering ever more persuasive arguments into my ears. If ever there was a time I needed to get on a plane and run away from reality it is now. But the strangeness of the world has made this so difficult. Other people are travelling now, as some have been all along, but I am being forced to stay in my safe little corner of the world.

Unable to travel to exotic new places, I find comfort in fictional ones. In books that are familiar.

Books are powerful, don't you think? The good ones never leave us. Like dear old friends, we find ourselves turning to them again and again for comfort. When I was young, my dad talked about Jack Kerouac's book, *On the Road*. It gained a cult following when it was published and he read it before I was born, when he had long wavy hair and a big scruffy beard. When he wore moccasins with holes in and was arrested for protesting in favour of nuclear disarmament. In the days before he went to night school, got a degree, and wore a suit to work every day. Years later, I borrowed his tatty paperback copy. A copy so well-thumbed that some of the pages fell out. A story of friendship and restlessness. The pull of hitting the road for the sake of it and seeing where it might take you, that youthful feeling of being invincible, bulletproof. It's a feeling I remember so well when I think of you. We were so similar, you and I. Our thirst for adventure, our need for freedom, our desire to squeeze every drop of beauty from this world …

I didn't care much for the characters, but certain lines leapt off the page. Descriptions of small towns across the miles and miles of endless dusty road. The vibrancy of the Mexican streets, the 'mad ones' burning with passion for the things they wanted from life. The exquisite pain of saying goodbye to people on the road, of seeing someone special heading in the opposite direction. Like the characters in the story, I tired so easily of people and places and looked for new ones. Always trying to outrun something. To escape.

And I did escape. For years. I travelled to different countries; slept under different stars, in different hemispheres. Yet, I was finally called back here, to this village. To Cornwall, the place where my name originated. A kind of homing instinct. Did I tell you my name is Cornish? It means 'Love.' My mother read it in a book two days before I was born.

So here I am. Closeness to the sea gives me peace, but I am still searching for something. Staring at the ever-moving horizon. Wondering if that thing I seek is out there, in the far, far distance. It used to be a faint whisper in the background, but it's getting louder now. Telling me that my stories need to be immortalised while all the colourful details remain clear in my mind. Stories that were stepping stones from one place to another. One life to another.

Incredible moments in magical places and ordinary moments on normal days.

I think we can heal by telling our stories. Eventually, we will tell them when the time is right.

December 17th, 2020

'Everything is getting on top of me right now. I've got no headspace,' I told my sister earlier today. 'Worrying about the surgery, the future, work, my marriage … Not to mention my mental health is in bits. All of it.'

'That's understandable,' she reassures me. 'It's a lot to take on at once.'

'It's like … if I could stand under a massive waterfall, and have it wash all the fears away, I would totally do that right now.'

It has been years since I left Kenya, but this evening I felt like watching *Out of Africa* once more. Alanna agreed and watched simultaneously from her house, while we chatted on FaceTime all the way through. A habit we formed during lockdown since she's the only person who likes the same films as me. Alanna was very young when I lived in Kenya, but she visited some years later, when her friend's husband was posted there. The film makes us both nostalgic, but as ever, I am the one who cries. I start sobbing as soon as Robert Redford takes Meryl Streep on a journey in his two-seater plane. He pilots from the back seat, and they fly across the country, over the Great Rift Valley, and over the plains of the Mara and the hordes of migrating wildebeest. They fly over a majestic

39

waterfall that tumbles to the ground via two huge drops at the top and bottom and a smaller one in the centre.

Rhys and I found that waterfall once, while staying in some fishing lodges one weekend and hiking in the Aberdare mountains. A deafening roar of water passed through the trees as we stumbled across it quite by chance. The movement of a thundering waterfall contains all of nature's immense power, I always think. There is beauty, vigour, and strength in the water as it moves with such force. The spray from so many different waterfalls has drenched my skin over the years. Tropical spray in the Bali heat, icy cold spray in the wilds of Patagonia, and many places in between.

Back in the film, the plane glides over the vast pink blanket of flamingos at Lake Nakuru. No talking, just the beauty of the film score, the sunlight shimmering across the lake and the sound of me sobbing. As the plane swoops through the air, the birds take flight en masse. Then, there's a glimpse of Mount Kenya through the clouds, as Karen reaches back to hold Denys's hand. As she closes her eyes.

Later there's a scene by a river. Denys washes Karen's hair and quotes poetry, while a hippo watches nearby. It's an unassuming moment in the film, but there's such palpable chemistry between them. I had my hair washed for me once, in a little hotel in a Cotswolds village, mid-winter with no heating and a broken boiler. The area was completely flooded, but of course there were no hippos. Just the water from a kettle poured gently over my hair, my neck leant back over the sink in the freezing bathroom. Later we huddled under the duvet with a fan heater, laughing and sharing a bottle of champagne. There was no poetry, but it was romantic and intimate in its own way.

I keep experiencing these flashes. Piecing together moments from my life. Do you ever think that life is like a jigsaw? That we take all the pieces, and we slot them together without thinking? The final picture is smooth, no pieces missing. We copy the image on the outside of the box, just as everyone else does. And we get the image the world insists we should want.

But what happens after we've created this perfect picture and it looks exactly like the one on the box? Perhaps we love it. Maybe we keep it, display it proudly. Let other people admire it.

Or maybe we get to the end of recreating that image from the outside of the box and we realise that we don't want it anymore.

So, we rip the whole lot apart with our hands.

Something that took hours, even years, to build can be destroyed in an instant ... or it can be slowly taken apart in a series of small, separate, defining moments. Once we start to dismantle it, it falls apart so easily and the picture transforms into a pile of unidentifiable shapes. Where once something colourful and vibrant existed, now there is nothing.

And we put the lid back on the box.

December 19th, 2020

The Pain of Saying Goodbye

Today the weather has turned, and the harshness of winter has set in. I feel the cold deep in my bones, even though Honey has snuggled herself alongside me, trying to lend me additional warmth. Dogs are such special creatures. They know when we are not well, they sense these things, so she is spending more time by my side.

There is a particular kind of dampness to the English weather, something I never feel in other countries even in their harshest winters. A sense that summer will never return. That true warmth is out of my reach.

I felt this so keenly when I flew back from my Kenyan holiday leaving literal and metaphorical sunshine behind me. My London life felt so flat, somehow. The city itself felt vacuous. I found myself craving wide open space, sandy feet, and the scent of campfires. Dreaming of cold pool water that never fully warmed up, even on a day where you felt you were melting, and a dense shimmering veil of heat sizzled above the earth.

I have never managed goodbyes well, least of all when I travelled. I think the greatest gift of travel is meeting new people and the greatest sorrow is having to say goodbye to them. We agreed on that, didn't we, you and I? I've always marvelled at the unlikely odds of crossing paths with someone, on a particular day, in a world so extraordinarily immeasurable. Someone who can alter the trajectory of your life. Loving each moment spent with someone yet knowing you may never see them again. Simultaneously intoxicating and agonising. It makes me think of the tragedy and comedy masks from the theatre.

At that point, I had no idea that my life would turn on its head and I would go back to Kenya to be with Rhys. Outwardly, I chalked it up as 'one of those things'. Pretended it was nothing special, a fling, a holiday romance, ten days of magic that could never become anything more. But then he visited. For one whole blissful week.

After an emotional journey to the airport and a tearful goodbye, I went to my parents' house. Bereft, a mess of noisy tears. My mother knew immediately. My hands were shaking as I boiled the kettle. Hoping as we British always do that tea might fix everything.

She took over, poured the tea for me. 'So, what will you do now?'

'I'm moving to Kenya,' I replied, avoiding eye contact, and speaking so quietly that I could almost pretend it wasn't the truth.

She nodded. 'Yes. I suppose you are.'

I don't think I had ever seen her look that sad.

December 20th, 2020

The First Cut is the Deepest

Growing up in the seventies, the world was quieter. The constant noise of our modern existence had not yet revealed itself. We didn't have much. A few gifts in a stocking for Christmas, hand-me-down clothes, simple birthday celebrations with sandwiches and homemade cake. The occasional treat or day out. But one thing we did have were gorgeous songs on vinyl records. They filled my head with beautiful melodies and my heart with pure poetry ... lyrics that stayed with me for years.

Diana Ross, Marvin Gaye, Fleetwood Mac, The Eagles, Carly Simon, Roberta Flack ... such powerful songs. Songs that planted intense feelings in my mind. I made mixtapes of love songs. 'Touch Me in the Morning', 'The First Time Ever I Saw Your Face', and 10cc's 'I'm Not in Love.' Songs I listened to with a broken heart.

Those heartbreaks of my late teens and early twenties still feel so real. Young love is somehow much more heightened. In the run up to Christmas 1984, I met Peter at a party. 'The Power of Love' by Frankie Goes To Hollywood had been at No.1 for most of December and we danced to that song over and over.

Peter with his scruffy fair hair and sparkly green eyes. A friend of a friend. Outdoorsy, a venture scout. We were together for eight months until I left for university, and he took a job in Norfolk.

Short-lived, but intense. We went our separate ways, but it was a connection that never severed.

Time has moved on and the world has continued to turn. There are people who form the absolute bones of my story, the foundations that keep my life in place. Others, once so close, have now melted away, the casualties of a busy existence. I've learned that a shared history is not always enough to sustain friendships through the storms of life. Some, at one time so daring and vivacious, now seem ordinary. Random details of their lives float across my social media feeds, but in truth I don't know who they are any more.

So few of us are still the people we used to be.

I often think how life would have turned out if I'd chosen differently. On the bad days, the days when I feel reflective, I switch on the projector of my imagination, and I run those images like an old-fashioned cinema reel in my head. The images of those unlived lives. They run clear as day, in glorious technicolour … until the spool ends, the screen goes black, and the world is eerily silent.

FINDING THE LIGHT

The photos of us attached to the email were phone snaps. Only you and I had actual copies. As far as I knew, we were the only people who ever saw them. The originals are still buried in those boxes I cannot bring myself to open, boxes marked with an 'R'.

When I was young, I adored the idea of painting and drawing, but I had no talent for it. When my imagination gets the better of me, I picture myself in a manicured garden painting a gentle water-colour. Protected from the sun by a parasol, I wear a long romantic lace dress, my curls falling to my waist. Or I see myself as a tortured artist in a dusty Parisian atelier, surrounded by empty bottles of wine and overflowing ashtrays. A world of creative chaos; half-finished canvases, covered with violent brushstrokes depicting anger and fury.

Always extremes, even in my dream life.

But I found I could create art with a camera, inspired by nature and its ephemeral beauty. Later, I became fascinated by the diversity of people across the continents. Different cultures, customs, and ceremonies. Small details of traditional clothing, bustling markets, and sumptuous-smelling foods and spices. I thrived on the chaos of those countries, the lack of order, the glorious blend of ethnicities, and the sheer colour of other people's lives. I had begun to visualise every aspect of life as a photograph, contained within an imaginary frame and frozen forever in time.

Photography is all about the light: we can always find it, if we know where to look for it and if we know how to use it. But we still need the shadow. The shadow shapes the image, giving it depth. Photos that are flat and one-dimensional will have no impact, elicit no emotional response. Life has been rocky in places, but it has always contained far more light than it has shadow: more joy than pain, more adventure than boredom, more fun than disappointment, more love than heartbreak. But we always need both. We need to experience one to truly appreciate the beauty of the other. If we live too cautiously, life lacks vibrancy and magic. When our time comes, we may leave behind a photo album filled with safe, neutral shades, instead of a riot of dramatic colour.

I never wanted that.

December 22nd, 2020

A Home by the Sea

We have an awkward conversation about Christmas.

'No, I totally understand,' I tell him. 'I mean, obviously I would prefer you to be here, but it's complicated, what with the latest government guidelines.'

He doesn't sound bothered either way. Or perhaps I'm reading too much into each word he utters at the moment.

'Look, I know we need to talk,' he says. 'Properly, I mean, and we need to try and figure things out. We are both testing negative but still, with your operation coming so soon I don't think we should risk it.' Then, in a quieter voice, 'I could use a bit more time away, to be honest and you did say Alanna wants to be there after new year.'

I agree without complaint, which surprises him, I think.

I recall those early days, of when I first fell in love with him. How exhilarating it was. How 'right' it felt. I have fallen in love with so many people around the world, in the same way I have fallen in love with so many places around the world. And so, I fell in love with this place before I moved here. I had always rented before, kept a semblance of transience in my life, the option to escape. But I decided I would buy this cottage, realising it was time for a sense of permanence.

I can't imagine living anywhere else now and yet I am not rooted down. Perhaps I thought marriage might fix me. Fill a void. But despite having all the things I wanted in my younger years, I remain unfulfilled, as if I finally realise society's version of 'everything' doesn't mean much after all.

Other people find it so easy to settle in life. To stay somewhere forever. Maybe that's the jigsaw they created. Part of me is jealous of their certainty. I have spent large parts of my life sitting outside of myself. Almost as if I am looking through a pane of glass at some imagined existence elsewhere. Waiting for something to begin. For so long my wanderlust felt like a search for home, so here in Cornwall, I tried to tell myself I was home. But over the last year, being forced to stay in one place, being unable to run, has challenged my concept of home. On the toughest days I watch the sunrise on one side of my cottage and the sunset on the other. I walk for miles along cliff paths. I try to feel comforted and renewed by the breeze from the ocean. Grounded by the weight of water that surrounds me. Reassured by the dependable music of the tides.

The Paradox of the Ocean

'Well, you've always been the same,' Alanna tells me. 'Volatile. Fiery. All your relationships have been emotional rollercoasters.'

She says this as if it's blindingly obvious. And perhaps it is.

I was the same with you, I suppose – such extremes of emotion. So, she's right as always. It's probably the reason he and I are clashing now, the reason we always did …

Do you remember that perfect night at the water's edge? That's when you told me that raging storms could cause you inner turmoil and calm waters could bring you serenity. You said you were inextricably bound to the tides. I didn't fully understand at the time, but I do now. I wonder if I am the same. My feelings have always come and gone in such intense waves. Almost as if I only exist at certain times. I am there and I am not there. High tide and low tide. It's as though my personality dissipates for days at a time, becomes lost in the swell of water and then, from nowhere, it surges back again. Violently and without warning.

Human nature and mother nature are so similar in that way,

don't you think? A duality at their core. Opposing forces in one place. On one planet. In one body.

Chaos and calm. Familiarity and unpredictability. Rocky shallows and unfathomable depths. Quiet, peaceful ripples and enormous crashing waves. A vast expanse that is both gentle and dangerous, welcoming and cruel. Elements that cannot be controlled and wild, destructive, addictive beauty.

It is true of the ocean, and I have discovered it to be true of myself. We both contain extremes, secrets that lie undiscovered, mysteries not visible from the surface. But we also contain complementary forces, co-existing side by side. Dark and light, positive and negative, yin and yang.

As the moon affects the tides, so are our internal rhythms affected by external powers. I struggle so much with the ups and downs of my mind, with the ebb and flow of the tides, but I am trying to surrender to these emotional polarities. To allow the mood of the ocean to reflect the mood of my soul.

DECEMBER 24TH, 2020

SILENT NIGHT

The fire is raging and yet the world is quiet. A lonely, eerily calm Christmas.

'Look, are you absolutely sure you're okay?' Alanna keeps asking, despite me telling her repeatedly that it's fine here. Different, but fine. It's not as if we have a choice anyway: families are not able to be together. 'It feels weird for me too,' she insists. 'None of the usual O'Connell noise and insane amounts of food.'

'At least you'll have the mad present opening and squealing kids,' I reply. 'I've never spent Christmas in this cottage – isn't that mad? Always been at Mum and Dad's place or abroad somewhere.' I ruffle Honey's fur absentmindedly. 'It's so quiet here, but it's actually nice just the two of us, like the old days.'

In the past my parents loved to be the hosts at Christmas – children, grandchildren, chaos. Everyone together under one roof. They are finding this harder as time goes on. All of a sudden, my parents are old. Of course, it's not all of a sudden at all, but it feels that way. They take all kinds of medication between them. Boxes of pills sit on either side of their bed filled with different coloured tablets; the days of the week written on the outside. Nothing prepares us for seeing the gradual yet inevitable deterioration in the people we love. People who have always been strong for us, acted as our protectors.

So much about my childhood home is still as it has always been. Paint colours on walls change, kitchen cabinets are updated, bathrooms modernised, and sofas replaced, but the fundamental things remain the same. The ancient tongs and the poker by the fire. The copper coal bucket. The old-fashioned, handwritten address book by the phone. So many numbers and addresses have been crossed out and rewritten now, it would be easier to buy a new one, but they haven't. Old paintings on the walls, ornaments kept for sentimental rather than aesthetic reasons. The cut-glass sherry goblets, a wedding gift from almost sixty years earlier. Wonky bits of pottery we made as children. A baby shawl, hand-crocheted by my great-grandmother, laid lovingly on the arm of an old rocking chair.

The same decorations I remember as a child are lifted carefully from a special box and placed onto the tree each year. New ones have been added over time, but so many are original. There is no stylish colour-coordination, nothing matches, but each piece has a story. The Father Christmas who sits at the top is the same one I placed there when I was a little girl. When my dad lifted me up so I could reach. These familiar objects never change or age, but with each visit my parents seem frailer, smaller. Even the youngest grandchildren are now too heavy for them to lift up to the highest branches of the tree. Each passing Christmas is now more poignant than the last.

There is something so soothing about waking up to Christmas Day in your childhood home. A sense that nothing bad exists in the world. And yet this year, of all years, we all know that is not true.

THE SPIRIT OF ADVENTURE

I often wonder where my spirit of adventure comes from. Is something we are born with, like a personality trait, or something that develops over time? Nature or nurture? My parents were not particularly adventurous, and yet, just before Christmas in 1974, we went to the USSR, as it was still called then. A flight to Moscow on an old Aeroflot plane with dodgy seatbelts, surrounded by strange accents and cloying smoke from strong cigarettes. We were supposed to go to Cyprus that summer; I'd been told about moving walkways across the floors at the airport. But a military coup happened in Cyprus and we couldn't go. The travel company offered alternatives and strangely my parents chose Russia. We had to make a special trip to London, in search of coats to withstand a Russian winter. Mine was pale blue suede edged in white fur, with a fur-trimmed hood. I adored it and can still picture it. My mum stitched gloves on strings to each armhole of the coat, so my hands would never be cold. And so we ended up at a different airport, at a different time, for a different holiday. Here the floors were normal.

Children no longer have gloves on strings; lost belongings are replaced without a thought. But in the seventies, it was all 'make do and mend'. My dad was born in 1939, grew up with rationing, remembered bomb drills, and being evacuated. As a child, he played on the remains of blitzed London buildings with his best friend. In our home nothing was ever wasted; clothes were passed on or worn until they were threadbare. Objects could always be fixed or kept for years in case they came in handy one day. I learned the importance of holding on to things.

The holiday to Russia felt so different, intrepid even. I discovered when I was older that my mother is a nervous traveller, always imagining unlikely scenarios of doom. She has never understood my lifetime's obsession with seeing the world. Abroad was a novelty for us. A winter holiday was a novelty too. Normally we went to Wales in the summertime, where I ran across windy beaches, cut my feet in jagged rock pools, and got horribly sunburnt. Mum and Dad didn't bring sun cream. Or they forgot they had it with them and didn't make us use it.

In Russia we went to the Bolshoi Ballet. Lots of escalators and ice cream in the interval. We walked through Red Square in the deep snow, the winter sun glinting on the brightly coloured domes of St Basil's Cathedral. My dad bought a Russian hat made of rabbit fur. He wore it in the winter back home to defrost the car, and it made him look eccentric. My parents still talk about the Moscow Circus, where there were real bears on ice skates, but I just remember I felt sick in the middle of the performance and my mum had to take me to the toilets. The Moscow underground was nothing like the one in London. People polished the tracks and the walls early in the morning, so the whole place shone.

I don't remember our hotel rooms, but do I remember the never-ending corridors and clunky lift that played music. I remember a massive dining hall with a dance floor and my parents eating something bright purple in bowls. I found out later it was borscht, a traditional soup made of beetroots. They made friends with two men from Colombia and watched some Russian dancing. My dad was told that if you see people queuing, it will be for something worth having. So, he joined a queue in Leningrad and stood in it for what seemed like hours. Road sweepers were making the streets look tidy while people queued. In the end he came away having bought a volume of Lenin's *Selected Works*. It was the third volume in a series, and it was all in Russian. Even though he couldn't read a word of it, he kept it on one of his bookshelves.

My parents bought me one of those Matryoshka dolls that fit one inside the other. I still have it all these years later. The colour is completely worn on the outside, from where I took it apart so often. I loved to look at the dolls getting smaller and smaller. Like one doll living many different lives ...

They stayed in touch with the Colombians for years. After the holiday, there was a party in their flat, somewhere in London. Wild, noisy, and full of smoke. My brother and I were put to bed in an upstairs room while people danced, drank, and sang loudly downstairs. For some reason I remember that their fridge was covered in some plastic patterned stuff that looked a bit like wallpaper.

After that, we went back to having nearly all our holidays in Wales again.

December 28th, 2020

Pictures of You

I haven't responded to the email yet. I still don't know what to say. That photo I took of you, one of those attached to the email, was the image that kick-started my career, even though I didn't know it at the time. A photo that ignited a lifetime's passion.

That was the first time I realised I had captured something ephemeral on film. The pure essence of another human. A soul, not merely a body or a face.

There were others. People I met on my travels. People I photographed on assignments or by chance. Others I befriended, or I fell a little in love with. People who had something of your spirit, your wildness, your indescribable magic. Those dark-haired free spirits.

In Kenya, at the start, I was seduced by the landscape and the animals. On my first ever game drive in the Mara, I felt like a child again. Seeing the animals in the wild, tearing across the plains, was overwhelming. A baby elephant lolloped along, trying to catch up with its mother. Baby lions wrestled in the dust like naughty domesticated kittens. Majestic giraffes strode across the savanna, silhouetted against the sunset alongside the acacia trees.

I stare at that first award-winning photo on my wall. The little toddler dancing outside the makeshift health clinic in Tanzania.

That was the moment I began to truly capture people. I realise with a jolt that my work in recent years has become about the earth, the elements, the water. I realise, once again, I have stopped capturing the intangible core of what makes us human.

WUTHERING HEIGHTS

I am in that strange lull between Christmas and New Year. Alanna is arriving on New Year's day, so for now I am retreating into someone else's world. Curled up in front of the fire with a book, I lose myself in the world of *Wuthering Heights*, reading it again for the first time since I was a teenager. I loved the Kate Bush song when I was young, but the lyrics and the video seemed so peculiar until I read the book. Until I entered that dark, tragic world. Such awful characters, yet so unforgettable and a story that is so bleak. Obsession, torment, and hatred. Love that is inextricably linked to pain. I expect it's the creative in me, the chaotic soul searching for meaning to the world, who was so drawn into this story. Drawn into this wild love that transcended death. I wonder if it will enrapture me again now that I have lived through my own painful love stories?

I finally visited Haworth with my husband a few years ago. To follow the paths the Brontë sisters had walked and see the landscapes that inspired the books I loved. On a warm, clear day we set off from The Parsonage, across the bracken-covered moors, then black clouds rolled in without warning, drenching us in torrential rain. Biting cold lashed across our faces; early summer felt like the depths of winter. But it turns out I am married to a man who had brought a survival tent with him, in a day pack, for a short ramble. The moors are so exposed it was a blessing and we huddled under it for over an hour, laughing, protected from the harsh rain. I would never have thought to pack such a thing. I don't even own such a thing. I take a chance if I'm going for a walk, much as I take a chance on most things in life. But his nature is the opposite. He's a protector, hooked on adventure but always prepared in case harm is lurking around the edges of our lives. Had I been wandering those hills alone there would have been no survival tent. In fact, in centuries gone by, I would most likely have needed rescuing from the rain-soaked moors by a ruggedly handsome passing horseman. A Willoughby from *Sense and Sensibility* perhaps, or a Ross Poldark. I'd have caught a chill that within hours turned into a life-threatening illness. I'd have lain in a grand four-poster bed, a servant stoking the fire, being nursed back to health by my saviour. I imagined him at my bedside, brooding by candlelight, holding nighttime vigils until I was out of danger.

Back in the real world, we waited for the rain to ease and warmed up in the nearest pub. The moors were as desolate as I expected them to be, wild and unsheltered. The kind of place I would go to contemplate the enormity of the things we cannot control, to feel emptiness and loss of hope. Somewhere I could imagine screaming my pain into the wind with no one there to hear me.

After that I sought out so many stories of intense passion, unrequited love, wild romance, and star-crossed lovers. I suppose when you grow up devouring stories of extraordinary love, love filled with pain and drama, then perhaps gentle love is too quiet by comparison. Too uncomplicated, not dangerous or thrilling enough. At least that's how it was for me. I craved all the drama. I often created it. I think a small part of me still craves it ... I have never entirely adjusted to the beauty of ease.

December 31st, 2020

Notes on a Half-Century

Another New Year. A turn of the page. Another chance to look back, reflect, and begin again. I turned fifty not so long ago …. well, you know that. An age that seemed ancient when we were young, yet here we are. And it has happened so fast. The speed of life never fails to surprise me.

Of course, I don't feel any different inside. But we never do. My dad often says he still feels young in his mind, but there is an old man looking back at him in the mirror. It is so true. My reflection in the mirror has changed so much, I have experienced so much and yet I feel I have barely started on all the things I want to do in life.

After that first trip to New York, it was as if I had discovered my own personal magic beans. Over the years they grew and grew. They spread their twisty vines far and wide and called my name. Loudly. Insistently. From across the continents. So, I followed them.

I have managed to fit so much into my years on this mysterious and ever-surprising planet, but still there is so much more to do and see. So much more to discover. Inevitably though, I will run out of time.

I suppose we all run out of time in the end, regardless of how long we live. Time is never quite long enough.

January 1st, 2021

Echo Beach

It's 1985 and we are heading north on the motorway, a car full of bedding, books, and random belongings to make my room in the university halls feel homely. In the rear-view mirror, aside from the top of the duvet that's stuffed in the boot, all my dad can see is a mass of backcombed hair. I am wedged in the middle of the back seat between a suitcase of Madonna-inspired clothing and an enormous box filled with alcohol and tea bags. Having said a final goodbye to Peter yesterday, I'm desperately trying not to ruin my thick black eyeliner with more tears.

'Tell people you have booze, it will help break the ice,' my mother assures me.

I nod in reply and clutch the two cuddly toys and huge biscuit tin resting on my lap. These are for personal comfort, not for attracting new friends. Mum notices my nervous expression, my slightly nauseous pale face.

'You'll be fine.' She smiles reassuringly. 'You'll meet people quickly.'

I don't remember choosing to go to university; I think people expected it of me and handed me the relevant forms to fill in. I've spent the whole of my childhood and most of my teen years with my head in a book, so studying Literature makes sense. Earlier today Gareth and Alanna gave me big hugs. They squeezed so hard, sad that I was leaving. I realised I would never be at home with them again in quite the same way and my eyes filled up again.

My parents help me carry all the boxes to my new room. Then they leave me to start the next era of my life, my mum tearful, my dad keen to get ahead of the traffic. Alone in this room, I put my biscuit tin, kettle, and tea bags on the side. I attach a poster to the wall. It's Kate Bush's *The Whole Story*, a beautiful black-and-white shot of the album cover. After that, I'm not sure what to do next, so I check out the communal kitchen.

A girl sits on the kitchen counter, a baseball hat pulled down over her eyes not disguising her bored expression. Absentmindedly banging her DMs against the cupboards, she glances up at me dismissively, then carries on rolling a cigarette. She is nothing like the girls from the school I just left.

'Hey, I wondered who was in here,' I say, my words tumbling over each other. 'I'm Kerensa … I'm studying English. I'm just down the hall, Room 12.'

'Nadia,' she replies with a wary look. Lighting up her rollie, she leans back. Smoke curls from her lip as she looks me up and down.

Unsure what to do next, I blurt out the words, 'I've got vodka.'

'Cool, lead the way.' She jumps off the counter.

'Nice one, Mum,' I mutter under my breath, and we head off to my room.

I was soon immersed in a world of lectures, parties, and books. Mostly books by dead white men, as the joke goes, but I managed to find one module full of women writers – Toni Morrison, Alice Walker, and Margaret Atwood, among others. Powerful, memorable books. Books that stayed with me for years and changed my perception of the world. I remember throwing myself headlong into Maya Angelou's *I Know Why the Caged Bird Sings*. I think we always want to find ourselves in other people's stories no matter how different our lives may be. Enter their world, breathe the air that they breathe, and try to understand their lives. It was impossible to walk in Angelou's shoes – my life was so privileged in comparison – but something about the image of the bird in the cage ... a bird that continued to sing ... resonated so much.

Of course, in this new life of mine there was no cage. There were no curfews. No alcohol restrictions. No veiled disapproval of tops that were too tight or skirts that were too short. I didn't require permission for anything. I was still mourning Peter in my own way, but I soon locked eyes with someone new in the Union Bar. A place where we bought plastic glasses full of beer and cider for £1 a pint. Where the song 'Echo Beach' by Martha and the Muffins seemed to play all day long, blasting from an old-style jukebox.

Years later I was on a beach in Bali. A haven of peace filled with surfers, dreamers, and insta-glamourous people filming videos for social media. A place called Echo Beach. Some signs suggested it was the beach from the song, but it wasn't. The one in the song wasn't even a real place, more of a concept. A vision.

But this beach planted that song in my head and took me back anyway. To the Union Bar and the carefree days of the past.

To another place in the memory banks of time.

January 3rd, 2021

Protection from Danger

The pre-op was yesterday. It was fine. However, I'm surprised to realise I feel nervous about tomorrow.

'I've been doing the home Covid tests wrong,' I tell Alanna, trying to keep everything light. 'The nurse put that cotton bud so far up my nose it touched my brain.'

People think I am fearless. I'm not. But they look at the things I've done, places I've been, and assume that I am brave. Right now, I don't feel brave. I feel like a small child.

My mother relates a story about me as a toddler. In the late sixties, when there were few health and safety measures and no seat belts in the backs of cars, I climbed over the front seat and jumped out of the car into oncoming traffic. This sounded fantastical when I was young. I thought she exaggerated it for storytelling effect. But one day, a toddler I was babysitting climbed out of a window and I realised kids are utterly fearless. We only learn about fear as we age. In the same way we learn about hatred or mistrust. We are not born with these feelings. The toddler was normally in bed when I arrived, but on this particular night he was awake. He waved goodbye to his mum through the window of her bedroom then I put him to bed in his nursery, pulling the door almost closed. Later, something made me glance towards the window of the

67

lounge. A little pair of feet were dangling there. He'd climbed out of his mum's bedroom window. I ran upstairs, leaned out of the window, and grabbed him from where he was hanging onto the guttering, smiling. I didn't even know he could even get out of his cot; he was only eighteen months old.

When his mother returned, she said, 'Oh he loves to climb, I should have told you.' The following week, she had roped all the doors along the corridor together by the handles so he couldn't get into any of the other rooms. It was only then that I noticed there were bars on the window in his nursery.

A decade later I was living in a house with bars on all the windows and huge security gates. On holiday, distracted by love and excitement, I hardly focussed on these details. I think we only see the things we want to see. But once Nairobi became my home, they were all too obvious. They were a constant reminder that it was not safe, that danger was never too far away, and that fairy tales, without exception, always include villains.

Our house had an askari (a twenty-four-hour security guard) and a back-up emergency call system. Armed robberies were common, even the occasional machete attack. I had only been in Nairobi a few days when, alone one evening after dusk, hair dripping from the shower, I inadvertently pressed the panic button instead of the light switch. Oblivious to my mistake, I was shocked by the confused shouting and loud tyre noise that ensued, by the pickup truck full of security men with AK-47s that screeched into the compound minutes later. I stood nervously at the door in my dressing gown, surrounded by towering men who were brandishing guns. They were kind and understanding as I answered their questions. I confirmed there were no intruders and that it was just a mistake, and reassured them that I was fine. It wasn't the first time, and it wouldn't be the last. Drunk people often pressed these buttons at parties.

This was one of many unsettling times over the years that followed. Times when I felt out of my depth, a fish out of water, an outsider. Kenya was not my country and yet I was treated as if it was: I was afforded a position of superiority purely because of my white skin; a position that I was never comfortable with and should never have been given. These are the strange remnants of colonialism that have irretrievably entered the culture, including the ability to speak English and be understood by most people, paying for things in shillings – still referred to as 'bobs', just as Grandad used to say. I found myself feeling simultaneously lost and at home, living a life that was both familiar and foreign.

After a while, the window bars became a way of life, the fairytale lost its charm, and seeing men in uniform carrying assault rifles became normal.

January 4th, 2021

Potholes

I am sitting on the ward, waiting to be taken down for surgery. It's so silent without visitors. I look at people in the other beds, at the nurses, and wonder what is going on in their lives. What exists behind the masks and the facades we create. We know so little of other people's lives. We all curate a surface image that hides the things beneath. Each seemingly quiet and ordinary life has stories hidden beneath its surface. Incredible stories. Unthinkable stories. Stories that rise to the surface when they are ready to be told. But some are never ready – some remain hidden forever and die with the person that knew their words by heart.

I haven't led a particularly extraordinary life. My stories are not that special, merely a selection of vignettes from a life anyone could have lived. A charmed life in many ways. Inevitably, pain has crossed my path, but it has been the sort of pain we all expect to face during our lifetime. Manageable pain. The kind that did not destroy me.

In truth, I have simply encountered a few potholes in the road.

On my travels, however, I encountered perilous roads. Both the random off-road routes and the badly damaged main roads. Some vehicles survive this terrain far better than others. Sometimes I was driving, sometimes other people were. You can try to go slower, weave around the potholes, and prevent too much damage being done to the car, or you can crash on through, with no regard for the damage that may arise. Years ago, negotiating a road in Cambodia, there were dips, troughs, and massive potholes. The driver ploughed on, smiling. He smashed in and out of the craters, while we were thrown around the inside of the vehicle. Our guide laughed throughout. He called it a 'dancing bus'.

Some people have many regrets about their decisions and choices. They feel they were never in control of their own lives. Whatever lies ahead, one thing I am sure of is that I have been in control of my life.

As they wheel my trolley towards the lift, I close my eyes and picture that journey in Cambodia. I remember the camaraderie, the laughter. And I try to remind myself that I have always been the person driving the dancing bus.

JANUARY 5TH, 2021

THE FEELING OF BEING CAGED

I wake in a total panic. I vaguely remember coming round yesterday, but not returning to the ward. I gradually realise I am in a hospital bed. That I cannot move. I have a catheter and I am attached to IV drip dispensing painkillers. I have no idea of the time but assume it's early. An exhausted-looking nurse smiles with her eyes over the top of her mask and makes a 'T' symbol with her fingers. I nod and wonder how I will manage to sit up to drink it. I feel as if I've been run over by a truck. And I feel trapped.

For so long I felt as if an invisible cage surrounded me. I experienced a constant, almost visceral need to get out. To escape, to be somewhere else. You felt the same and so you understood. Of course, I was never trapped and nor were you; we have always been free.

Even before I lived in Kenya and I saw the animals roaming wild on the plains, I was never a fan of zoos. As a child, I despised the thought of such remarkable creatures being restricted, caged, unable to be their natural, wild, most primal selves.

This last year the cage began to feel physical, the size of my world diminished. The virus, the lockdowns – all of it took its toll on my state of mind. So, the storm clouds have gathered. Never more so than now. They said I would probably need to stay in for two nights at least. As I digest this reality, the cage constricts further. The painkillers are strong and I don't remember finishing the tea. Later, I wake up propped upright against the pillows and someone brings me dinner.

Whenever I feel trapped, closeness to extreme elements helps me feel more alive, so I usually spend large parts of my day by the sea. Harsh breeze invigorates me and strengthens the core of my being. But the sea is not always enough.

I thrive on constant change; I feel the need to look at different views. So, I seek out variety in my days. The simplicity of following a river's path or sitting beside a lake. Occasionally, I will drive to Bodmin Moor, walk up to Colliford Lake, near the old smuggler's haunt Jamaica Inn, a place made famous by Daphne Du Maurier's novel. Normally filled with visitors wanting to experience its haunted rooms and ghostly history, it is so quiet now. We are all staying at home as much as possible. Bodmin is steeped in mystery and ancient legends, while Colliford Lake looks supernatural at times. Dead trees are submerged, forming a lost, petrified forest. Their branches stretch upwards, reaching out of the cold dark water like the arms of swimmers drowning in its depths.

On other days I walk the windy paths across the open moors. Paths dotted with old mines and tors, straggly yellow gorse bushes, and ghosts of the past. I pass carefully through lichen-covered granite rocks, rocks patterned with greys, whites, and greens. Nature's own version of camouflage cloth. I wander amongst the stone circles – places like The Hurlers, and I imagine the people behind the legends. Those men, it is said, who were punished and turned to stone for playing a game of hurling on a Sunday. Or I walk up to The Cheesewring, a strange, stacked rock. Legend has it this was created by giants. Up there, looking across the moors, the pounding wind feels relentless. Making me weightless, as if I could be swept up at any moment, lifted high on the blustery air and then cast down. Smashed against the jagged rocks like an old tall ship being wrecked against the coast.

Whenever I need to taste freedom, I go outside, to feel the wildness of nature, to feel battered by the breeze. I walk or I run. I don't time my run, or care about the speed; I simply run. I sit and stare at the water when I am finished.

Some days when I can't sleep, I drive to the moors in the early hours, and I walk through the woodlands along the River Fowey as the sun rises. A river where the last King of Cornwall was drowned in strange circumstances and a wood where a ghostly old man is said to wander during the full moon. Before the world is too full of people, I wander along moss-covered walkways past emerald-coloured trees wrapped in ivy. Sometimes I go to Golitha Falls.

It is often icy on the paths this time of year. I won't be able to venture out for a while, but normally in winter I take extra care. As I wander, I take pictures of extraordinary things, like the morning sunrise streaming through a veil of cold fog. Freezing leaves scattered on mossy rocks, the ice forming sugar crystals around their edges. The rays of winter sun that try to break through the branches as a deep mist rises from the water. The gushing, cascading falls after the rains. But mostly I take pictures of ordinary things, like ivy. Ivy has its own simple beauty. Curling around fences and gate posts. Adorning trees in interweaving patterns, creating endless pathways ... and yet it is one of the most destructive plants that exist. It's invasive, it can burrow into walls and weaken buildings, it can rot and damage fences. Nature has a way of giving the world both good and bad, sometimes disguising one as the other, much like life does.

Damaging thoughts and fears are just as deceptive as ivy, burrowing into my subconscious, destroying the good and making me unable to see the beauty. These days I can usually spot these thoughts and then try to defeat them, but still, sometimes, the ivy wins, and it takes down the building ...

On difficult days, I seek solace in nature, in the same way I have always done. I look for the light, find comfort in simplicity. During that unsettling first lockdown, I took pleasure in the increased volume of birdsong while there was less traffic, the clear skies while there were fewer planes in circulation. I relished the quiet of the coastal villages without the onslaught of tourists, marvelled at the clarity of the stars with the reduced pollution. The world looked as if it had been upgraded to a newer, higher-definition version of itself.

Normally, I try to do as I did during the darkest days of that first lockdown. To go outside whatever the weather, brave the elements on the wilder days and look for the light.

I realise I will have to be patient for the next days and weeks. This pressure weighs heavily on my mind, and I resolve to do as best I can. I remind myself there isn't a cage surrounding me at all.

January 6th, 2021

Driftwood

The past two days have drifted past in a haze of painkillers. A nurse removed the catheter and I managed to walk slowly to the bathroom. If all the checks go well, they will discharge me later this afternoon. I've spoken to everyone in my family over FaceTime and I am ready to leave now.

I feel I've been existing in a dream state while I've been here. Moving between sleep and wakefulness. Hardly registering the comings and goings.

My search for love made me drift for years. From country to country, bar to bar. From cocktails in Manhattan to homemade beer on plastic baby chairs in Vietnam. From cheap wine in boxes on the beach to Tequila Slammers round a campfire in the mountains. Trying to find a fellow nomad. A deep thinker, an adventurer, a lost soul. Trying to find someone like you …

I was not alone in my tendency to roam. My husband did the same thing for a few years. Then, when the time was right for us both, we crossed paths again. He recognised the value and the beauty in the driftwood, and he picked it up off the beach.

He does the same thing now. Collects me from the hospital and takes me home, where he and Alanna fuss over who is in charge.

Tucked up in a blanket by the fire I listen to the noise and activity in the kitchen. The two of them squabble as they make enough food to feed an army and we all have a meal together.

January 8th, 2021

Stress. Fear. Adrenaline courses through me. It's unlikely anything is wrong, yet I am panicking. With Covid delays I must wait at least four weeks for the results of the biopsy, six weeks until the post-op check. Everyone is taking care of me. Endless phone calls and video calls. Mum and Dad, Gareth and Finn have all checked in on me since I got home. I speak to friends and watch films, yet I feel so stuck. I drink endless cups of tea. I have too much time to think.

As if on cue, Alanna's voice drifts in from the kitchen. 'Another cup of tea?'

'Sure,' I reply, 'actually no, black coffee would be good. Not too strong.'

She brings it through and sets it down, stroking my arm as she does so. True to her word she has stayed here in my bubble. Dropping her commitments to come and look after me. I pretend to be completely immersed in something on my screen so she cannot see my tears. After such a strange year, spending this time with Alanna is priceless.

Adrenaline often comes from fear, but it can also be about excitement and feeling indestructible. The real adrenaline junkies crave danger and high risk. I have a little of that embedded within

79

me, but not the life-threatening kind. The exhilaration of moving at top speed, for example. Not in a car, not limited by the road, something more open. Being on a boat in high wind, or speeding across the water on a jet ski. The kind of speed where there is nothing blocking your path. Nothing but endless space, fresh air, and pure freedom.

When I was young I was a sprinter, an excellent one. Over short distances I could run incredibly fast. I still run, not as fast these days, but that feeling is still there. That feeling of invincibility, of the world dropping away. Throughout my life, I have had vivid running dreams. I still get them. In fact at the moment, they are coming so much more frequently. In these dreams I run faster and faster, I feel lighter and freer until eventually I take off and I'm flying. Soaring through the air.

Maybe that's why I am so fond of airports. The anticipation of taking off …

SHOULD I STAY OR SHOULD I GO

It's 1988 and we are about to head south on the motorway. The end of my university years, it feels as if barely three months have passed, rather than three years.

'Are these the last few bits?' Dad asks. He is scientifically packing the car to within an inch of its life. 'There are a couple of spaces left. I can squeeze the odd thing in.' I hand him a rolled-up poster. The famous Athena 'man with baby' poster that has been on my wall for months, the old picture of Kate Bush long gone.

We are about to drive away from this house for the last time. A house I lived in for two years after spending my first year in halls. A house that had ice on the inside of the windows in winter and glistening slug trails across the carpets. A house with seven women and one tiny bathroom. Never enough hot water, but plenty of bitchy arguments. I was leaving behind memories of getting ready for nights out, drinking before we left the house and dancing to 'Don't Stop Me Now' by Queen (our 'going out' anthem). I gaze around my room with its old gas fire and ugly wallpaper. All my things are gone. The room is empty, yet it is full of ghosts. Two years' worth of ghosts, faces, and feelings: Falling deeply in love then suffering the pain of a heavy breakup; obsessing over someone new; running freezing cold in a towel from the bathroom at the top of the house, down to my room at the bottom. Sitting shivering in front of the gas fire, trying to warm up again. Drained from crying and unable to get out of bed.

As I pick up the last bags and head for the door, images flash across my memory. Tears. Shouting. Hangovers. Getting stoned. Sitting on the kitchen floor, helpless with giggles, surrounded by empty crisp packets and the occasional slug. Stressful weeks of exams and thrilling encounters with men that would never last. But mostly, the endless nights of laughter. Memories that are embedded in every inch of this grubby, run-down terrace house. But the harsh realities of adulthood are beckoning now. It feels hard. Transitioning to any new phase of life is hard. The world is waiting with all its pressures, career decisions, and parental expectations.

And it was too soon. I wasn't ready. Are any of us ever prepared to face the serious parts of life? Those years of working and taking on responsibility? I was not ready then. I didn't want the last three years to finish. I wanted to delay the inevitable for a little longer.

And in those last six months something unexpected had happened. Or someone unexpected.

Peter.

He came back into my life after I went home to a friend's twenty-first. Those few months we had together were comforting and thrilling rolled into one. He should have made leaving university easier, yet he made everything more complex. I had to choose, to toss a coin. Stay in the nest or spread my wings ...

I chose not to stay. I told Peter I needed to go. The official summer graduation ceremony was right around the corner, but Nadia and I jumped on a plane, and we missed it. There was a smaller ceremony in October, not much of an event in comparison. By then I was a completely different person to the girl who left at the end of term. I collected my degree certificate with a deep tan and hair that had been bleached by the Californian sun.

Because that is where it all began ... that first long hot summer in America.

JFK Airport. The first time I landed there, a chauffeur in a stretch limo drove me across the bridge to my friend's house in

New Jersey. This time there was no limo, no welcome party, no one to help. We took the airport bus to the Port Authority Bus Station in the centre of Midtown New York ... dirt, noise, people sleeping rough, and hundreds of bus listings. Exhausted from the flight, we were overwhelmed. People rushing, pushing past, knocking into us. A low hum of anger and frustration, no one who had time to help. Then there were men who looked as if they had all the time in the world, men who made me feel uncomfortable deep down, men whom I knew instinctively would be bad news. A couple approached us, but we brushed them off. We sat on our rucksacks on the filthy concrete floor, away from a couple of vagrants, and we waited to board our bus.

Summer camp in Pennsylvania. Eight weeks of sunshine, a huge lake with water skiing. Daily swimming. Activities like softball, tennis, drama, and art. 'Boat race' drinking games in local bars. A weekend off in Atlantic City. Competitions, events, and practical jokes. Long sun-soaked days and nights out in rough local bars. People sneaking across the grounds at night. Clandestine meetings between couples and incredible friendships with counsellors from all over the world. I met Cara here, among others. It was over in a flash and six weeks of travel time lay ahead.

Cara joined Nadia and I and we chose the West Coast – California. There was no plan, only vague suggestions: take a road trip, visit Vegas, travel up the famous Coast Road. California, Oregon, Washington.

'We could start in San Diego. See what happens?' I suggested.

No one had any better ideas so, with old Beach Boys songs from my childhood playing on a mental loop in my head, we flew to the West Coast.

In the end there were no road trips or gambling in the desert. We had all grown up in grey concrete towns, so we fell in love with San Diego, with a gorgeous little spot on Pacific Beach. Seduced by the Californian sunshine and the people we met, we scored temporary jobs for pocket money. Ate at all-you-can-eat salad bars day after day, and hung out at busy beach bars at night. My skin tanned darker and my hair bleached blonder, and I began to blend in seamlessly with others on the beach. At twenty-one, we could drink legally, others couldn't, so one evening we headed over the Mexican border to Tijuana where the drinking age was eighteen. Loud, buzzing music pumped from rammed bars all along the street. We drank tequila in sweaty clubs and ate takeaway tacos on a busy street corner. The guy who drove us couldn't remember where he left the car. Bizarrely, another guy had purchased a large model of a Disney character from a roadside vendor, one of the dwarfs from *Snow White*. In a surreal end to an evening, we wandered in circles, around and around a parking lot. Tired, confused, and aimless, we searched for the car, while a drunk guy in a cheap sombrero carried a large ceramic dwarf.

Memory after memory formed in those unforgettable weeks. Beach life. Day after day. Night after night. Even more people came into our temporary world, some local, others travelling through. Guys from the navy on their days off. A guy who insisted on driving us to Los Angeles for the day, so we could stand on the stars on the Hollywood Walk of Fame. When our funds dwindled, two brothers let us sleep on their couches, in a little flat near the beach. That trip was my first example of the kindness of strangers.

Soon we were heading to the airport in their huge pick up. Once more I was not ready, but it was time to leave. Bouncing around the back of the pickup, drinking beers in the sultry evening sun. Nadia and Cara were about ready for home, but I was heartbroken it was over.

A summer full of adventure. Of sunshine, laughter, and freedom. Nights in bars and parties on beaches. Music, dancing, and campfires. Aussies, Americans, Canadians, and Kiwis. Friends who would last a lifetime. Memories that would endure forever. Uninhibited, reckless, carefree. A summer where souls collided, and life blazed in vivid splashes of colour.

I wished I could stay forever. After all, three days earlier, I had met you.

January 9th, 2021

The Layered Rocks

'I'm fine,' I insist, as Alanna helps me to the shower. 'Honestly. There's no need to wrap me in cotton wool.'

But still, half an hour later she brings me a bowl of soup with crusty bread, stokes the fire, tucks me up in a blanket. She gets me another pillow and asks if I need any painkillers. It's not painful, just uncomfortable. So again, I insist I am fine.

'Just shout if you need more tea. Or some biscuits, or anything. I'm just on the laptop in the kitchen. I don't have a Zoom call for an hour.'

I smile, squeeze her hand. Tell her not to worry. California dreaming has helped these last few days, getting me through the surgery, lessening my worries and aiding recovery.

I took a gentle walk around the garden earlier, but I long to walk along the cliff path. To feel the strong winds and gaze at the rocks. Formed in layers over time, one on top of the other, from the oldest layers at the bottom to the youngest layers at the top. A bit like life. Our experiences build up gradually, each one learning from the one before. Building on the strength of those below. The rocks get younger as the layers build, but we go in the opposite direction. Our years of experience make us wiser, but inevitably they age us.

As the experiences of that first American summer built up one by one, layer by layer, the number of days before we had to leave were dwindling at the same pace. Our return date was fast approaching, so I crossed the border into Arizona to see the layered rocks of the Grand Canyon. Experience the breathtaking vista of deep reds and earthy browns, the sheer depth, the vastness. There was so much to do, so many options – long hikes, rafting, camping at the bottom – but I was travelling alone, and I didn't have time for those things. I only had one day. Was it good timing? Or serendipity? I'm not sure, but I heard a man talking knowledgeably about hiking, so I asked him how I could make the most of seeing the canyon in just a few hours.

And he gave me a smile. An American smile, a smile with unfeasibly perfect teeth, and replied, 'Well, I guess I could fly you over it in my plane.'

It meant missing my train back, but he said I could stay at his flat and he'd find a cheap flight for me in the morning. He told me, with that dazzling smile, that he had travelled around Europe.

'A lotta nice people helped me out. Real kind people. So, I figured … if I do something nice for you, I kinda get to thank them.'

Something about the way he said it made me trust him. As my friend Bernie likes to say, 'Axe murderers don't pay it forwards.' So, I trusted Josh, the pilot with the perfect smile and we flew across the canyon in a four-seater plane that felt as if it weighed nothing at all. It rocked and bounced in the wind. Collecting a passenger on the other side, we flew back in a haze of red as the sun disappeared and set the sky alight. The canyon's contours changed colour and blended into each other. Again, I'm not sure if it was luck or fate, but it turned out to be a private flight with a spare seat up front. The lady who'd paid for the flight sat in the back and spent the entire time with her head in a paper bag, being as sick as a dog.

And that was it, where my love of tiny planes began.

True to his word, the pilot bought me dinner, gave me his room, and slept on the sofa. Thoughtful, generous, the kind of guy I should have fallen for. But back then I didn't like the sweet, gentle guys. Apart from Peter, he was the exception. I preferred the ones with an edge. Men with a sense of danger about them.

In the morning, he made me a special breakfast, with a cup of tea.

'This is so sweet of you,' I told him.

'Well,' he said, flashing that smile again, 'I called a friend who'd spent some time in England to ask her what you guys eat for breakfast.'

Instead of an American-style breakfast, he had cooked me a boiled egg with 'toasted soldiers'. The kindness of strangers.

After that, I had just five glorious days left before I had to leave California and I had no idea I was about run headlong into you.

PAY IT FORWARD

Many years later, sometime in my early thirties, I was on another plane, holding on for dear life as we hurtled into the most terrifying landing I have ever experienced.

Lukla Airport in Nepal. My first trek, heading to Everest base camp. Runways can be dangerous places to land if they are short, or they are mountainous, or they are prone to wind and fog. Lukla is all these things: one end a sheer drop, the other a large brick wall. We were on a Yeti Airlines flight, a ten-seater plane. An air hostess, impeccably dressed with a small flower in her glossy, pinned-up hair, walked the short distance from one end of the aisle to the other, gave each of us a boiled sweet and sat down, her job completed. We approached Lukla, weaving through the mountains, with no sign of the runway until we'd almost touched down on it. A violent slam of the brakes and I thought we were about to smash headlong into that wall. Instead, the plane screeched abruptly to the right to avoid it. The crisp coldness of the fresh air brushed our faces as we faced a panorama of soaring, snow-covered mountains.

On narrow winding streets, children stared up at us, some shy and reticent, others waving happily. A little boy passed by, pushing a hoop along with a stick like a child in Victorian times. These high mountain villages have a harsh and unforgiving winter climate, so as charming as it was, these were people who worked relentlessly. People whose livelihoods relied on tough, backbreaking work.

Carrying packs up the trails and working the land. People whose determination and hard labour could be read across the weathered lines of their faces. Faces that were always ready with a smile for the tourists.

So much happened on that trip. Long days of walking, where we passed through villages full of small children with red cheeks and woolly hats. The altitude hit us. Palpitations, headaches, insomnia. Then our first glimpse of Everest, rising in the distance, magnificent. The signature plume of snow floating above it, blowing in our direction by winds from the summit.

Everest has many names. In Nepal it is Sagarmatha, meaning 'Peak of Heaven' or 'Goddess of the Skies'. In Tibet it is Chomolungma, 'The Goddess Mother of the World'. Humans are powerless against the might of these mountains, and the people that live there treat them with reverence. Some days the peace of the crisp, clean air was broken only by the sound of yak bells tinkling and the noise of prayer wheels turning. One day I paid for a hot shower instead of washing in a bowl of freezing water. Standing in the steam, feeling my cold hands and toes thaw, was blissful. The further we trekked, the more profound the sense of peace became.

Until a far less peaceful day. A commotion behind me; I rushed back the way I'd just come. A yak had hurtled around the corner at a great speed and knocked Heather, one of my trekking companions, off the edge of the trail. She tumbled into a section of trees that broke her fall. It could so easily have been fatal; a few feet further on was a sheer drop. She was in a great deal of pain, with a suspected broken ankle. I didn't want to leave her on her own. The family at the nearest teahouse found us a couple of wooden beds in a modest room. The rest of our group carried on to Base Camp, promising to loop back and meet us in a few days. Hardly able to put weight on her foot, she struggled to make it outside to the long-drop toilet, and had to pee in a bucket in our room as if we were prison inmates, only going outside when necessary. Heather was a tough Aussie, so despite being in pain, she saw the funny side.

Communication with the family was hard, but we managed by smiling, pointing, and waving our hands. When it was time to leave, the mother placed a white prayer scarf around each of our necks. A gift to bless us and keep us safe.

The kindness of strangers once more.

Humans are inventive, showing such ingenuity under pressure. In Kenya, the children made shoes out of discarded car tyres to sell on the streets. Our guide Norbu was equally ingenious, fashioning a chair out of one of the porter's baskets to transport her: a contraption we nicknamed 'The Ambulance'. He carried Heather down to the nearest village with a hospital for her foot to be X-rayed and strapped up. With phenomenal strength for his small stature, he carried her for two days. I have a photo of Norbu, still smiling, as he carried her down those steep, rough mountain pathways.

Reunited as a group at lower altitude, we headed to a famous bar in Kathmandu – The Rum Doodle Bar. Paper messages covered the walls and hung from the ceiling. It was hot and loud. Packed with climbers, trekkers, and backpackers. A place where people who have summited Everest write their names behind the bar. Compared to the teahouses, it was expensive. One of the guys was trying to make his money last for a year, travelling around the world.

So, I paid it forward, bought a few beers and some dinner for him, and told him about a guy called Josh, with a plane and a fabulous smile who once did something generous for me when I was young.

January 10th, 2021

Free Bird

Peter had encouraged me to spread my wings. Even though it hurt him to let me go, he hoped and assumed I would come back. But it wasn't that simple. The world had been cleaved in half and was irreparable. A time before you and a time after you. A chasm as big as the Grand Canyon itself.

I found I couldn't cross it.

I wasn't fair to Peter when I returned home. My mind and heart were with you, even though geographically we were oceans apart. But I didn't explain. I didn't tell him. I just distanced myself, stopped taking his calls. I didn't know what to say. It was cowardly and he didn't deserve that. It hurt us both. Even when something is my choice it can still shatter my heart.

After a summer of drifting, I needed to work. I liked the idea of publishing and I fell on my feet. A temp job at Condé Nast in London, on their *World of Interiors* magazine. They liked me and kept me on. The plan was to stay a short while, save up for a plane ticket, and visit you. I hoped I might get to write articles or learn editing, but they gave me tedious admin tasks most of the time: photocopying, stationery orders, answering the phone. Occasionally, I helped select photos and assist with page layouts. I was taking photos constantly at that time. I'd become obsessed with it.

Aside from writing letters to you, going out with my camera was one of the only things that kept me feeling balanced and calm.

London was busy, my life hectic. Brett, Mick, and Phil, three friends from summer camp, rented a big rundown house in Earls Court. A constant stream of parties. People sleeping everywhere – on sofas, in corridors. Eventually they would all travel somewhere new.

There's a song I love from my seventies childhood: 'Free Bird'. A song about someone who always knows they must leave, that they need to move on to the next place. A song that reminds me there is no cage, that I am free to fly away at any time. It was there in the background at their farewell party. They had brought laughter and a touch of the wild into my world, but they were off again. We were a group of free birds and it was time for some of us to move on. Too many places to see.

Undertaking an epic journey, they planned to ride motorbikes from London to Cape Town through the sands of the Sahara Desert. It was 1990, by this time Cara was already in Nairobi, but I followed their motorbike journey from afar, having no idea I would soon be living in Kenya myself. Battered postcards arrived from time to time, news filtered back to us. Suspected Malaria, endless hours in dusty garages fixing bike parts, stolen belongings. A hair-raising story of a road accident, one of them ended up in hospital with a badly smashed leg. Then, eventually, the parting of the ways. Each moved on to their separate futures and their individual destinies: one on a farm, one on a boat, and one in a city.

If I ever hear that song, I remember those days when we all met. When it felt like anything was possible. It makes me smile until I realise that perhaps we will never all be in the same place again. A few of us have met up here and there, but not all of us together. But who knows, perhaps we can make it happen? Perhaps we could all fly in the same direction, even for a short time. The Free Birds, congregating once more.

I hope there's still time for that.

January 11th, 2021

Love in a Time Before Texting

Lighting the fire and warming the room on these freezing mornings takes a while. I wear furry ankle slippers and sit wrapped in a huge blanket. Writing these diary entries to you by hand has brought back that feeling of joy at the sight of a hand-written envelope.

There were only four months in the end, between the holiday romance in Kenya and moving there permanently. I kept a photo of Rhys and me folded up in my purse. The two of us standing on the beach. Snuggling against one another and laughing. I would show it to people on nights out.

'Ugh, honestly, that beach. That tan,' one of my workmates said. 'And Rhys is so cute.'

'Yeah, he is, and the tan makes his eyes look even greener,' I replied. As I smoothed the photo crease with my finger, I could feel the softness of the back of his hair, the part where it was shaved short, the top where it was thick and floppy. I could feel the stubbly skin on his face, smell his aftershave, and see his crooked grin.

It began gently: a letter once a week, the occasional phone call. Then the realisation we didn't want to exist on different continents. The distance between us was too far, our desire to be together too strong. Weeks passed and a fax each morning, waiting for me on the machine when I got to work at the magazine. So much faster than letters. More immediate.

I continued to write letters during the years I lived in Kenya. Page after page of scrawling detailed news or quick catch-up messages, scribbled untidily onto those blue airmail envelopes that folded into three. A brief snapshot or a feature-length film. Never something in between, no middle ground, no gentle compromise. Even my letter-writing habits seemed to mirror the person I am.

I wonder if people still use those blue airmail notes now that we have email? I have so many of them in the loft. Living so far from family and friends, a letter arriving in the post was such a comfort. A special gift in an era when there were no faces appearing on screens from the other side of the world. No clever software that could collapse distance and time zones. The internet when it came was so easy – instant messaging, spontaneity – but it wasn't the same, somehow.

No anticipation of the postman arriving. Letters marked with airmail stamps, the treasures of people's lives travelling across the sea.

It has been six weeks since my husband moved out and today another email arrived. Asking if I'd received the first one. Asking if I would like to talk.

'What's that, is it bad news?' Alanna asks. 'You look worried.'

'Nothing.' I slam the laptop shut before she can look. 'Just an online troll.'

'What's wrong with these people? Honestly. Anyway, I suppose I need to get organised. Start to pack.'

She is leaving in the morning. I can manage now; I just need to be careful not to overdo it, not lift anything heavy, just take gentle walks. But I will miss her.

'You've been amazing. It's made such a difference having you here. But you must be excited to see the boys.'

She's stayed longer than planned, but now she needs to get home to Jack and Harry and to Paul.

Alanna wipes down all the counters. Unloads the dishwasher,

folds the laundry. She dusts round every object in the lounge, dust that may have existed for months if not years. I wait impatiently while she folds the blankets and straightens all the cushions. I will miss the tidying too. The cottage has never looked so perfect.

Finally, she goes off to pack and I can't stop myself from opening the laptop again. I click on the email. This time there are no scanned photos attached. There's just a short paragraph:

I hope you got the photos. I'm real sorry I sent them out of the blue like that with no explanation. I guess it must have been a shock.

I wasn't sure what to say to you. I found you through your website.

Anyway, it was all a long time ago, but I thought you deserved to hear the truth.

PART TWO

WEATHERING THE STORM

January 13th, 2021

Part of the Breeze

Today is one of those days when the storm clouds gather overhead, when the sea feels vengeful. The fishing boats look fragile and jittery, making sudden, violent movements on the rough, rolling waves.

It feels so different to the calm days when the same boats do a gentle, rhythmic dance on the surface of the water. I observe the changing light patterns and the undulations of the waves. They move hypnotically, taking over my mind and leading my memories in different directions.

I am taking slow walks now, but on harsh, stormy days I stay away from the ocean. I don't go down to the water's edge or sit on the sand. The sea seems unforgiving and perilous. Foreboding fills the air. The water takes on a life of its own, swirling and moulding into threatening shapes. Liquid sculptures of immense beasts and serpents rise through the waves, towering over the sea like furious monsters ready to attack the land. Normally, I love to stand on the cliff path, in the full force of the wind, letting it whip my hair about my face as I hold my clothing tightly around me. I ground my feet firmly to the earth and respect the might of the elements. But until I am stronger, it's best to shelter by the wall of the harbour.

I read the message over and over, sent a reply to say I need some time. I am still waiting for my results; it makes me feel blocked from moving forwards. I want to know what the future holds before I can take on any more potential heartache.

It feels as if time is of the essence, and yet as I stand here, time feels meaningless. I could be any age now; I could hail from any century. The rocks and cliffs and the water remain unchanged, no matter how much time passes. There is nothing here that can visibly date where the world is right now. Which year, which century, which lifetime. The strangeness of the past year is not obvious here by the coast. I could be anywhere, in the same way that this land could be anywhere. We could both be existing at any point in the past or at any stage in the future.

Sooner or later, I will disappear, yet this wild and rugged piece of land will endure. Life, as always, goes on without us. The land and the sea will continue without us.

INTERNATIONAL ARRIVALS

It was November 1991 when my plane touched down at Jomo Kenyatta Airport. I freshened up, applied makeup with a shaky hand right before we landed. Jaded from lack of sleep, eyes puffy from the tears on departure. Too nervous to settle, slightly sick with anticipation. We were about to have that first moment of seeing one another again. Not a holiday this time, but here for good.

Out of the cabin, down the steps and into the fresh air … like walking into the blast of a hairdryer. Total sensory overload; I had forgotten the madness of it all. The hot oppressive breeze, the claustrophobia. The shouting. The overwhelming chaos of the airport. People everywhere.

'*Jambo, jambo.* Lady? Here, lady. *Karibu.* Taxi.'

I was surrounded by crushing bodies, people holding name signs in the air. Voices clamouring for attention, people trying to drag my bags out of my hands and take them to a taxi.

'Lady, I help you lady.'

Head feeling fuzzy, I fought through crowds of touts. 'No, thank you. *Jambo.* Okay. No. *Asante sana.* No taxi. *Asante.* I'm fine.'

I got to the other side. Then there he was …

Waiting for me, relaxed and smiling. Scruffy shorts and a Tusker

T-shirt. Suntanned skin and sunkissed hair. Neither of us were sure what to do, so there was no over-the-top movie-style kiss. Instead, I remember an awkward hug. Then Rhys took over, put his hand up, shook his head at the touts.

'*Hapana*, no taxis today.' He shielded me from the huge busy throng of men who were crushing into us. 'No thank you, my friend. *Sawa, sawa.*' Arm around me, guiding me safely to the relative quiet of his car.

I had forgotten the noise on the roads, the dust, the heat of the day. I had forgotten that cars swerved manically, that the streets reverberated to the sound of horns blaring from the brightly coloured matatu buses. Touts hanging off the back shouting, as the buses weaved across the lanes.

Then we were back at the house I'd loved so much when I was here on holiday. It felt cool inside, away from the heat. The garden looked lush and the pool inviting. He put my cases in the bedroom in our wing of the house.

'I need to take a shower,' I told him, 'wake myself up a bit.'

After about ten minutes, he joined me in the shower. Things became a little more like the movie reunion I'd pictured. We fell into bed and had champagne to celebrate. It must have come from duty free or from the NAAFI, and would have been expensive at the time. We could only get local beers in the shops, Tusker or Whitecap, and local spirits. Sometimes there was wine from Naivasha. Pretty grim and mostly drunk by tourists at the safari lodges. Champagne was a romantic touch, but I felt lost and overwhelmed. Then I must have crashed out.

'Kerensa, Kerensa. Where are you?' Cara's voice filtered through a heavy haze. She rushed into the bedroom, threw herself on the bed and crushed me in a hug. 'You're here. I can't believe it. How was the flight? Is it weird? It must feel weird. Oh my god.' Another hug. 'You are actually here. Do you feel okay? How long were you asleep? Anyway, listen I have news, we are all going out drinking this afternoon, there's someone you have to meet.' Her eyes sparkled. 'I can't wait for you to meet him.'

She talked so fast, but then she always did. Completely animated. We all headed to The Norfolk Hotel for the afternoon. I met her new boyfriend, Richard; I could see why she was smitten.

Too many faces, too many names to remember. All so welcoming. A long afternoon in the blazing sunshine, where I drank too much beer and vodka and got badly burnt.

Later, exhausted from the drinking and the sunburn, the jet lag and the emotion of the journey, I locked myself in the bathroom where I cried and cried. It was real now. I was there in Kenya. But despite our endless letters and faxes to one another, despite the intensity of all our feelings, we were just two naive young strangers.

January 15th, 2021

I feel wiped out today. Everything has caught up with me. I realise how much Alanna was doing to help. Only a couple of days have passed, and the cottage looks as if a bomb has hit it.

He has not moved back in yet, but he has promised to drive to the supermarket. To cook occasionally. He's helping with dog walks too; Honey pulls too hard on the lead at times, and I don't want to strain my stomach. Accepting his help is the most I can handle, for now. I just want to get through the next couple of months. I can't face the long talks, the analysis of the things each of us has done to upset the other. None of that was intentional on either side, I know that. I also know I've hurt him more. I've hurt him by retreating into myself. Living in the past too much. Not trusting him with the whole story. Not telling him the truth.

I never imagined you or expected you.

I never anticipated the sheer force of my feelings for you. Yet it happened. And there we were – you and I. Then it was over so fast. It was too soon, but there was no choice. I had to go home. We both knew it. You wanted an airport goodbye, but I couldn't bear that. I didn't want to drag out the pain. So, we spent the last hours at the beach – as we had so many of the hours before that. We watched the sun drench the waves in colour, and the birds swoop into the surf. We made plans and promises. Our reflections merged together, then fragmented, and eventually dissolved into the glistening shoreline.

Finally, I had to let go of your hand. I had to separate from you and walk away. We both had to walk in different directions up the beach, trying not to look back. Only looking ahead to the next time. To the future. To the reunion we were already picturing in our minds.

January 19th, 2021

LEARNING TO FLY

R ising early once again, listening to the birdsong in the garden. So often now, my mind is too troubled to sleep. It's bitterly cold but still, I find I want to be outside. A thick blanket wrapped around me; beneath it, my warmest coat and my woolly hat. I have made tea in a metal camping mug so I can feel the comfort of its heat through my gloves. I don't have much appetite, but tea is always a comfort.

I close my eyes, leaning back in the wooden garden chair. The dawn chorus and distant sound of the waves help to settle my mind.

You know, I nursed a baby bird once when I was a child. A bird that had left the nest and damaged its wing. I dug up a few worms from the garden and fed them to the baby bird, placed drops of water into its mouth with a syringe, and kept it in a little box indoors, safe, not too hot, protected. But still I couldn't save it. I couldn't replace its mother and keep it alive. But I always thought it was brave to leave the nest in the first place.

My early memories are filled with birds. The geese on the farm we stayed at in Devon one year. I was convinced they were going to bite me, and my mum had to carry me screaming from the car. A school trip to Wales, aged about ten, a B&B by the beach, a room with bunk beds. Lots must have happened on those few days, but I only remember the seagull that sat on the ledge outside our window, and the cormorants and puffins nesting in the rocks. I bought my brother a stick of rock and my mum some sweet pebbles. Browns and greys and beiges. All wrapped up in a big scallop shell, exactly like the real stones from the beach that I collected and took home from our trips to Wales.

And later memories. In Australia there were rainbow lorikeets, adorned in swathes of green, yellow, blue, and orange. I worked on a boat for a while. I would wake early, sit alone, watching them perched contentedly along the boom. In Kenya, hordes of elegant pink flamingos, radiant sunbirds, and lilac-breasted rollers. Grey-crowned cranes and shining kingfishers. And the less attractive birds – vultures skulking around waiting for food in the game parks. Black kites that would occasionally come out of nowhere, swooping into a garden at a BBQ, scaring children and stealing food from people's plates. Secretary birds. Tall birds that looked stylish – almost as if they were wearing white tights – but cruel hunters. Known as 'serpent killers', they stomp fatally on their prey with their large feet. And there were the marabou storks, nicknamed 'the undertakers'. Huge birds with pale legs, bald heads, and a body shape resembling an evil cloaked figure.

A campsite early in the morning, but already baking hot. Breakfast cooking on the campfire. The spot where we pitched our tents faced a clearing in the trees, a river winding behind. Rhys had a slingshot. Marabou storks kept walking through the clearing. Every now and again one would march through looking thoroughly miserable and someone would fling something at it, like one of those old-fashioned fairground shooting galleries. It was cruel looking back, but funny at the time. The storks would look even more miserable and then disappear.

And the condors. Distinctive white collars and full wingspan visible as they soared across the South American sky. I watched them in wonder gliding through the Chonta Canyon. A week later, I reached the famous Sun Gate, the entrance to Machu Picchu. I had been walking since 4 am, and it had been raining solidly for hours. Water dripped from my jacket, my body drenched through and my bones tired, I was finally there, the magical end of the Inca Trail.

The point where the whole ancient city would be laid before us ... except there was nothing. Everything was shrouded in a veil of thick fog. But gradually, the sun filtered through the misty air and the fog began to lift, forming into a lighter, almost mystical haze. Little by little Machu Picchu revealed itself through the mist.

It seems almost impossible to fathom that these huge stones were transported by hand. It is believed when the Incas abandoned the city, they burned the trails behind them to hide the pathways and protect it from discovery. I walked the pathways around the ancient interlocking stones, past the Sun Temple and Moon Temple, drawn for some reason to the Temple of the Condor. Wings are carved into the rock and the head and neck carved into the floor, forming an altar. A place the Incas would have made sacrifices to the Sun God. Condors were considered immortal. Revered as sacred birds, because of their size and their ability to travel such large distances. In Andean mythology, the condor represents Hanan Pacha (the heavenly world). The world of the sky and the future. At this point in my life, I was in my mid-thirties, at a crossroads of crushed expectations and confusion. Lacking direction and unsure how the future might look. So, in the slowly increasing heat of the day, I sat silently in the Temple of The Condor. In a place where the power of the ancient gods felt tangible. I thought of my Irish grandad and imagined mighty condors soaring through the air above.

I will always be distracted by the sight of birds in flight. I am fascinated by murmurations, birds dancing in formation across the sky. Twirling into shapes. Sometimes gliding, like choreographed clouds, at other times accelerating and shapeshifting into twisty tornadoes. Almost as one they perform mesmerising swirls, then travel onwards, leaving trails of their dance across the sky. I am captivated by birds heading to another destination, not content to stay where they are. Like the condor, they make me think of travel and of the future. It is the same when a plane flies overhead – I always wonder where the people onboard are heading. Are they off on some exciting adventure somewhere, or are they travelling home? Heading for that first moment of reconnection. That first hug. When whatever else has happened, everything is forgiven in that moment of homecoming.

NEW KID IN TOWN

Those early weeks in Kenya were a rollercoaster of emotions – highs and lows. Being white and English, I had never experienced the feeling of being part of a minority, of looking and feeling different to the people who surrounded me. It was unfamiliar, humbling, and unsettling at turns, and it shone a light on how privileged my life had been. Homesick for ordinary familiar things and curious about my new home, I was faced with constant challenges I did not expect.

That first week was bliss, a surprise trip. Rhys whisked us away to a rustic beach cottage in Mombasa, an idyllic week of romance by the Indian Ocean. Gentle, slow days baking on the beach and warm, relaxing nights. A cosy terrace, drinks, fresh fruit, fresh fish, and gorgeous views across the ocean. A magnificent mosquito-netted bed. Long, lazy, sensuous mornings tangled up in the sheets, laughter, contentment. A glorious little bubble, protected from reality.

But that perfect week flew by and soon we were driving back up the Mombasa Road to real life. The bubble burst as he returned to work, leaving me home all day. With no job or transport, the days dragged on. Moving there had seemed romantic on paper, the build-up, the anticipation. The reality was rather different.

My evenings were busy and varied – meals out, drinks at friends' houses, dancing in nightclubs – but so many of my days felt long and without purpose. Days where I sat alone in the seclusion of the garden, hours spent lying in the sun, the sound of cicadas filling the air. Days where I swam in the pool. I had always dreamed of living in a home with my own pool, so it was a novelty at first. I tried to fill my time with reading and sunbathing, but the novelty soon wore off when it was the only thing I had to do.

Bored, frustrated, and lonely, each day blended into the next. Modern-day Nairobi would be such a different prospect I imagine – Wi-Fi, Netflix, mobiles, Uber – but in the early nineties there were constant power cuts and no TV to distract me. I was living in Lavington, a small suburb some distance from the centre of town. I didn't have a car, Rhys was at work, Cara was teaching full time and nearly all the people I knew had jobs. On the days I felt lonely, I wanted to call home, speak to my family, but so often the phone lines were down. We had a small generator when we needed to fix the power, but with the phone there was no quick fix.

I had the freedom of a spacious, sprawling house, and enormous garden, and yet I felt hemmed in. Trapped. Surrounded by windows with bars on them. I was like a fifties housewife waiting for her husband to return home from the office each day. But I wasn't even a housewife. We had staff for that. Grace, our housekeeper, and various cooks who seemed to come and go in quick succession. I knew from my holiday that there would be full-time staff, but it felt so uncomfortable. I could cook, I could clean, I could iron. It seemed so wrong for someone to do all this for me. But that is how things were. Having house staff was normal. My discomfort was irrelevant. And it didn't take long for me to enjoy it, to appreciate someone else doing the tedious chores I disliked. Funny how our convictions change so quickly. How our discomfort rapidly dissipates when life is made easy.

The best days from those early weeks were the ones when Faith swung by unannounced. Her husband, Dario, was a friend of Rhys's: a loud, enthusiastic Italian. Faith would speed into the compound, a whirlwind of gossip and fun. My heart lifted whenever I heard car doors slamming, laughter and loud Swahili chatter – I would see Grace sweep up Faith's toddler Benito in her arms, making him giggle. Sometimes we would chat in the garden while Benito played nearby. Sometimes Faith would say, 'Let's go and find some lunch, come on,' and she would drive us into town. We would occasionally come back via the supermarket, butchers, or the small shopping mall, having stocked up on things for dinner. Sometimes Benito came with us, but often Grace offered to watch him.

Faith knew instinctively that I needed to be rescued. That I craved company and needed to be cheered up and entertained. She was guessing in the beginning, but as time went on, I confided in her constantly. Poured out my heart when things got difficult. At the start, I wouldn't ring people, or ask for help. I worried I might be imposing or being too needy, but she just turned up sometimes. A ray of sunshine. A port in a storm.

One day, after I'd been in Nairobi for about a year, Faith announced she wanted to be called by her tribal name, Makena, from now on.

'I like it. Does it have a special meaning?'

'Ahh, Kerensa,' she said with a smile and a shake of the head. No one pronounced my name like Makena. She drew out each syllable, almost turning it into a caress: Kaaa-ren-saaar. 'You are always searching for some deep meaning in life. Sometimes things are just things.' She shrugged. 'However,' she continued with a broad smile, 'my grandmother always told me this name means "happiness", so perhaps I should have used it sooner. It is perfect for me, don't you think? Faith was always a little too serious after all.'

Makena was my lifeline in those early days, but like my other friends, she had a busy life with a toddler. I needed to find work; I was going crazy stuck at home. There were restrictions, work permit issues. Understandably, there were not that many jobs for non-Kenyans. I was fortunate, my British passport had its uses and I got an administrative job at the High Commission. My start date was not far off, but for a while my days continued with no real direction. I watched the staff going about their day. The cook making lunch, Grace changing the beds, the distant sound of singing floating down the stairs. Unable to face sunbathing for yet another day, I decided to take Rocky the dog for a walk to the local shop.

Rocky belonged to our housemate, a wonderful man who threw endless parties and could pour a perfect gin and tonic. He travelled a great deal so I thought I was being helpful. It was lunchtime. Baking hot. Under the shade of a large tree at the front of the house, all three staff were chattering amongst themselves. As Rocky and I headed towards the gate, the askari jumped up quickly, leaving his food. He let me out, shouting something I couldn't understand back to the other two. They burst into laughter. As I set off, Grace wiped tears from her eyes.

Walking along in a daydream, I gradually became aware of people staring at me and crossing the road to avoid my path. One man hurled himself into a ditch in his rush to get away from me. Bewildered, I tied Rocky up outside the shop. All the little children, who usually hung around giggling at me and asking for spare change, ran away, their bare feet sending clouds of dust flying into the air. I picked up a few bits, untied Rocky, and walked home.

When I returned, both Rhys's car and Makena's were parked

outside the house. I heard their laughter from the patio, where they'd just opened a couple of cold Tuskers.

'Hey, where were you?' Makena called. 'Grace told me you were walking the dog. I can't believe that is true.'

'No, she's right, I was.'

They both laughed.

'What were you thinking?' Rhys chuckled, incredulous.

'Ahh, Kerensa.' Makena shook her head, giggling loudly. 'When do you start work? I think it needs to be soon. Being at home is not good for you.'

No one had told me that in most home compounds, dogs were there as guard dogs, to protect the property from intruders. Perhaps they are more popular as pets now, but at the time they were there purely to do a job. The only other dogs were strays wandering around town. Some even carried rabies. For this reason, people were scared of dogs. To me, Rocky was a soppy German Shepherd, but now I realise to others he looked like a menacing guard dog.

An innocent mistake. One that terrified some people, but certainly amused others.

January 20th, 2021

Numb

S ome days I am numb. Others I am furious. Frustrated that I can't go running or take Honey out for miles along the coast path. I knew taking it easy would be tough and I am struggling. I am not taking photos now, my idea for a project with stone circles long forgotten. Nothing inspires me; the world feels lacklustre and colourless.

Keeping my promise to my husband, and to Alanna who agreed with him, I book an online appointment with a therapist. I don't hold out much hope, but I want to try. I owe them that. I choose a woman; she looks approachable and is around my age. I trust she will understand me better than the male counsellors I have tried in the past.

'My mind is never quiet,' I tell her. 'It's always moving, buzzing, firing on all cylinders. Draining me, exhausting me.'

'You're probably depressed. It's common in women your age. Lockdown hasn't helped. You could ask your GP to prescribe some antidepressants?'

Another doctor, another suggestion of antidepressants. I've been here before. A circle of repetition. I don't believe I am depressed; I have too much capacity to be thrilled by life, to be animated and excited by the world. But I get burnt out, exhausted. I am emotionally hollowed out, but not depressed. I think this is different.

I try to explain. 'It's as if my feelings are so overwhelming, I need to rest. As if my soul is tired.'

She's serious. Pragmatic. She bristles slightly at this statement, but I continue.

'Almost as if the noise of the world and the noise in my head are competing. I need a volume switch for each of them that I can just turn down. Does that make any sense?'

'We could try something more holistic,' she says with a note of hope in her voice. 'That suits a lot of people.'

I try not to sigh audibly. I'm convinced my irritation is evident through the screen. 'Honestly, I feel as if I've tried it all. Talk therapy, cognitive behavioural therapy, meditation, mindfulness classes, reiki, tapping, yoga, crystals, you name it. My bank account is poorer for it, but my mind is no clearer or calmer. Is there something wrong with me? I have a great life, why isn't that enough?'

'To be honest, it does sound a lot like depression.' She pauses. 'Or menopause. They can feel very similar. Haven't you just had a hysterectomy? It's probably that.'

I explain to her that I was already on HRT before the operation. That the doctors think that's probably why the fibroids were still growing, since the opposite usually happens in menopause. I also tell her this has been going on for years. This is not new. Having exhausted the menopause option, I can see she's at a loss.

'Could be anxiety.' She suggests in an inappropriately jolly tone. 'I have a colleague that may be able to help. That's not really my speciality.'

I wonder what her speciality is, but I thank her for her time and say I'll think about the antidepressants.

LEARNING TO DRIVE

We took a drive today. A trade-off for me having the therapy session. I usually take so many short trips to different parts of the coast. Often on a whim, when the mood takes me. Especially at this time of year. Off-season, the coast path is quieter, the tucked-away beaches almost deserted. But we are in the third national lockdown, technically confined to necessary travel only, but it's half-hearted to be honest. Not like the first one – the roads are busier, the definition of 'essential work' has become much broader. So my husband swings by the cottage and asks if I fancy a change of scenery. A road trip down the coast. Stopping for takeaway coffee in a village on the way out. A little walk around somewhere we've never been before on the way back.

As he drove, we reminisced about other road trips. Easy ones: good roads, memorable scenery, fast cars, and music turned up loud. Tearing across the miles. And some of the tougher ones. The ones where we got completely lost. The ones when I had to dig the car out of the mud or a group of us had to winch the overland truck out of the sand. Trips on terrifying roads in local buses. Journeys in places like Asia, Africa, and South America. Roads where the width seemed impossibly narrow and yet vehicles drove past one another without slowing down at all. Roads where the cliffs were crumbling and there were sheer drops. Heart-in-your-mouth journeys where I feared for my life. Roads with shrines on the roadside to lost travellers or sections with tyre tracks going over the edge.

We had a family holiday in Greece when I was small, a long time before Gareth and Alanna were born. I remember being on a coach travelling up steep hillsides and swinging round sharp bends to get wherever we were going. Mostly I remember that my dad was scared: he doesn't like heights; thin, winding roads; and sheer drops. I remember thinking it was a bit strange when I was young, because dads aren't supposed to be scared.

———————

Nairobi was such a city of opposites. A strange mixture of modern and antiquated. Of luxury and poverty. Past and present. Sophistication and simplicity. Some things felt the same as they did at home – the boring day-to-day of shopping and planning, the entertaining of visitors. Celebrating someone's new job, a hen weekend in a lodge up country, yet another farewell party for someone moving on to their next posting or next chapter of life. But other things felt entirely different.

Driving should have felt similar; it's the same side of the road as the UK, at least in theory. But, driving there was a baptism of fire. Insane traffic, no real rules, few speed limits, and seemingly no drink-driving laws. The roads were a hot cacophonous mass of cars and buses. Matatus with blaring music, disco lights, and ticket sellers hanging off the sides. Air thick with exhaust fumes, horns blaring, and in some parts of town, the stench of refuse rotting in the heat. Anything could happen. Someone might slam their brakes on to stop to talk to a friend in the middle of a busy highway. Cars and lorries abandoned in ditches. Vehicles driven into the wooden poles of power lines or broken down on the sides of roads. Sometimes, while travelling up country, car parts and wheel hubs or spark plugs would be stolen while you were in a shop and sold back to you when you came to a stop a little further up the road. You would often pass a lorry in a ditch, facing the wrong direction, on the wrong side of the road, and spend your journey trying to work out how it got there.

Rhys found an ancient, rattling, bright yellow Suzuki jeep for me. I loved that car even though there were only seat belts in the front seats, and it always sounded as if it was about to break down. It didn't have a back seat, so if I wanted to carry passengers, they had to yank open a heavy door at the back and sit on two hard wooden benches facing one another. It looked exactly like the sort of car a child would draw, like a box on wheels. The day we collected it was my first attempt at driving alone on those unpredictable streets. I had to follow Rhys home in the car. We crossed a roundabout, and he took the first exit, but it was busy, and I was in the wrong lane. I had to cut right across to follow him. A man wanting to go all the way around the roundabout was also in the wrong lane. As I put my foot down, cut up the vehicle behind me, and managed to make the exit, I glanced into the mirror. In my wake, a matatu had smashed headlong into the back of a pristine Mercedes.

Much like the differing personalities of the city itself, here the old and traditional was crashing into the sleek and modern. Rhys was waiting further up the road. He had taken the exit to allow me to catch up. Now we needed to go back again, past the scene of the accident.

'Should we stop?' I ask, 'You know, get insurance details and everything.'

Rhys laughs. 'Not a good idea. I suggest we get the hell out of here.'

When I drove back past, the driver of the Mercedes was screaming abuse and strangling the driver of the matatu.

January 25th, 2021

Adjusting My Speed

I am being forced to slow down now. Develop patience. We are no longer any good at handling inconvenience in our privileged lives. The art of patience has been lost. Instant gratification; the answer to any question right at our fingertips. Next-day delivery. Bingeing an entire series in a box set. Running on adrenaline. Burning ourselves out.

I am staying positive as always, but there are moments when I find myself dancing between courage and fear, between hope and despair. Surely it must be normal, don't you think, to look back on your life when you are concerned for your health? On the days when you fear the worst? Or perhaps reaching midlife always makes people face the reality of time slipping away. We all die eventually; it's simply a question of how soon it takes place. How far we are along the pathway when it happens. To be honest, I never saw myself as someone who might check out early. I always planned to be like the Queen Mother, fortifying my immune system with copious amounts of gin and tonic and living out an entire century.

I have lived on this section of coast for a few years now, and I think you would love the wildness of the scenery here. People cling to their traditions, try not to let the ways of the past be forgotten. Fight to preserve the beauty of this land from the ugly side of modern life. I never pictured myself living in such a small place, but strangely I find it suits me. I too do not want the ways of the past to be forgotten.

I used to crave the anonymity of a city, somewhere I could disappear, go unnoticed. But now, I find I like the comfort of familiar faces. Knowing that some things can be relied upon to remain the same, day after day. Towns and cities feel soulless these days, even though I know they are not.

Since moving to Cornwall I have travelled back to London occasionally, trying to conjure the feeling of when I worked there in my twenties and thirties: the frenetic pace of life, the last train out of town filled with inebriated workers, the cheap cocktails at 'happy hour', meeting friends in Soho clubs in the early hours. The night buses to a friend's house, having once again missed the last train home. A regular occurrence, needing a rushed trip to the shops the next morning to grab new tights and underwear to wear to work. Boozy lunches where the bosses put their credit cards behind the bar, and no one returned to the office that afternoon. The hungover bacon sandwich run in the morning. But now London feels too fast for me, too faceless and cold. All the new buildings make it harder to recognise my old haunts. It's a long way these days, of course. But I still like to go for a weekend now and again to meet friends for dinner, take in a West End show, drink cocktails in stylish bars. Visit Columbia Road Flower Market on a Sunday for brunch or take in the skyline from a rooftop restaurant.

In normal times, when everything is busy, the Tube depresses me. People working such long hours, crushed into the train carriages barely speaking to one another, avoiding eye contact. Rows of zombies staring at phones. A hamster wheel, day after day. Public transport in other countries always seems friendlier, no matter how packed or uncomfortable. A strange kind of camaraderie; an amusing sense that we were all going through something together. Over the years I have travelled on local buses and trains all over the world. I never hired cars on my travels. Kenya was different though; I didn't use the Kenyan buses because I had my own transport.

Until one day my car broke down and I boarded a matatu. People kept piling in, despite it being full to bursting. I stood at the bus stop, determined to wait for the next one. A man in the doorway laughed and kept insisting I get on board despite the lack of space. Eventually, ignoring my protests, he grabbed me by the hand and hauled me onboard, so I was wedged right in, almost at a right angle.

'You *mzungus*,' he announced with an amused shake of the head, 'you do not know how to crush,' and the whole of the bus laughed.

CAMPFIRES AND SUNDOWNERS

A night-time campfire. Seductive flames. Heat. The scorching embers of possibility.

I think I am at my most content sitting and watching a fire. In Kenya we cooked food over the flames and told stories. There is something about the light disappearing, the stars coming out, and the mesmerising nature of the roaring fire that makes people loosen up. Makes us remember certain moments in our lives. Encourages us to reveal our secrets. And when the stories have all been told, no one is uncomfortable with the silence, and we are content to sit staring into the flames.

Later there were fires far less comforting. When the passionate flames of our early attraction to one another had transformed into slowly cooling ash. The smouldering heat that tried so desperately to reignite the flames, mimicked the lingering sense of hope that hung in the air between us.

But nights like that one, camping in the early years, were glorious. We would drive to the Mara for the weekend, pitch our tents in the wild, drink beer and vodka around the campfire, and head out on game drives. Sometimes we pulled up and sat on top of our Land Rovers and jeeps, where we drank sundowners and watched the sky change colour over the acacia trees and thorn bushes dotted across the landscape. I adored the distinctive shape of these trees and the simple thrill of watching the wildlife running free.

On one trip we pitched our tents by the Mara River and were almost finished setting up when a ranger arrived and told us to move on. There were no signs, but the pitch was reserved for a private safari company. We dismantled our tents, but two of our group couldn't be bothered, and undid the guy ropes and put the whole tent on top of the Land Rover in one piece. One drove, while the other stood on the back, holding on to the vehicle with one hand and the tent with the other. We followed their vehicle in trepidation, hoping the guy hanging onto the tent arrived in one piece. We had soon caught the attention of a nearby elephant who was pursuing our convoy up the track.

A pot of beef stew cooked slowly on the campfire for hours in a huge aluminium sufuria, replacing the usual BBQ burgers, and sausages. It felt wonderfully filling and indulgent. We played drinking games with vodka shots at night and washed ourselves in the river in the mornings. We witnessed a warthog ripped apart by two lions. We listened to the sounds of the natural world surrounded by stars, while the wood crackled, and the flames danced. When it was time to sleep, we stoked the fire, hoping it would burn all night and protect us from wild animals. I was always scared to leave the tent at night, but sometimes it couldn't be avoided. Rhys would often get up with me, to make sure I was safe. Scanning the dark, listening for sounds nearby, searching for glinting eyes, my heartbeat sounded deafening, as I stayed as close as possible to the tent. In the dark of the night the sense of the wild was palpable, and the threat of nature seemed almost overpowering.

Nothing could beat camping in the game parks, in the middle of nowhere. We always returned home tired and covered in dust, but utterly rejuvenated by our encounters in the wild.

I have not returned to Nairobi for many, many years now. We are, after all, encouraged to live in the present. Some memories are like the silt in a river: we must keep them at a distance, tread gently, and try not to churn them up, all while knowing they have the power to destroy the pristine, calm waters of the now. Even if part of us would like to make sense of them, they cannot be altered or done over. We must believe they are there to teach us, to forge us into stronger material. To sculpt us into kinder, more empathetic people.

But the pull of Kenya is strong, so I hope in my heart that I will find my way back one day.

THE JACARANDA TREES

Eight months into my time in Kenya, the honeymoon period was over. Back in England the autumn colours were in full swing, but in Kenya, October and November were filled with completely different shades. Springtime was heading for summer then, and the Jacaranda trees flowered. Roads lined with lilac beauty; trees boasting vivid purple blossoms; pathways covered with petals that looked like violet-coloured snow.

Adjusting to living together took time. We were both fiery and often clashed. We argued frequently and I was experiencing pangs of homesickness. My untidiness drove Rhys crazy at first. We laughed it off in the in beginning.

'It's lucky we have staff,' he would joke, but after a while it became something that angered him.

He wasn't a good communicator and didn't like to discuss his emotions, preferring to turn everything into a bit of fun. I know now that was immaturity, but it made me insecure and clingy. I wanted him to spend more time with me. I'd try and force a conversation and he'd always walk away.

'What do you want from me, Kerensa? We live together, how much more time can we spend with each other?'

'I mean private time. We always go out with other people. I don't know … meals, weekends away. Just us would be nice sometimes.'

'What are you talking about? We eat out all the time, and we went to Mount Kenya Safari Club for your birthday a couple of months ago.'

'I just feel like I'm not enough for you. Like you need other people there or you'll be bored. Am I enough for you?'

'Seriously? I can't do this right now. I'm going to the club for some beers. Go out with the girls. Give Cara a ring. Or Joy. Have some fun … chill out a bit.'

Joy was my newest friend. We worked together at the High Commission offices, where she worked on the Kenyan Projects, and I worked on the Tanzanian ones. We shared a little office and a similar sense of humour. She was always keen to go out dancing.

So it went, back and forwards. Highs and lows. Passionate rows and intense make up sex.

Things would improve for a time, then we'd have the same argument again. I would feel lost and unhappy deep down. But in between life was unpredictable. It suited my need for constant stimulation, for spontaneity.

Whatever else was difficult Rhys always encouraged my photography. In fact, he was the one who suggested I send photos from time to time to my old boss at Condé Nast. My boss had moved from *World of Interiors* to *Traveller* magazine. Gradually, the odd photo made the cut and was printed in the magazine. Sometimes they'd ask for some accompanying text or on rare occasions pay me to visit and photograph a new luxury camp in a game park or a hotel at the coast. It didn't replace my main job, but it gave me a boost. A creative sideline.

Did you know the Jacaranda tree is a symbol of good luck? As it turns out, the photo of the dancing child, the one that made my name in the photographic world, was entirely the result of luck. A serendipitous click of the shutter at exactly the right moment.

January 26th, 2021

Universal Languages

Attempts to improve my dreadful Swahili had fizzled out. English was so widely spoken, it made me lazy. Like so many of my countrymen, we let other people do the heavy lifting when it came to languages. My social circle was a melting pot of Kenyan and English friends, with some Irish, Canadian, and the occasional Scandinavian thrown in – I could order drinks and cover the basic niceties in Swahili, but that was about it. But there are always universal languages, things that bond people and work anywhere in the world regardless of your ability to understand one another. Laughter, music, dancing. Showing a child a photograph of themselves. And football – the strongest universal language of all.

I suppose because it can be played anywhere. Purpose-built stadiums, sports clubs, muddy, potholed roads. A patch of grass at the side of a highway, a rough area of concrete. Anywhere you can mark out a pitch or draw some lines in the dust. Driving around the country we would often pass children playing football in the dirt.

Rhys played for an amateur expat football team that didn't take itself too seriously and was usually beaten by the far more talented local teams. I dislike the term 'expat' intensely. It is so typical of British exceptionalism: thinking of other people as immigrants, but ourselves as somehow superior. Somehow deserving of a different title. But the world was the way it was then, so that is what we called ourselves.

As soon as I got off that plane, I fell into a ready-made social life. I almost didn't need to try. In time I developed other friendships, met people through work and exercise classes, but in the beginning when it was all so new, it was easy to settle into the life he had created before I arrived. A group of friends ready and waiting, bonded through a shared love of kicking a ball around a field.

And so it was that I found myself within the expat circles and the affluent Kenyan circles. I found myself surrounded by people who were much like myself, with similar life experience to my own. Looking back, I regret that a little, a missed opportunity in many ways. But I was young, so I stayed in my lane.

I found my closest girlfriends at the football club – Kenyan, English, Canadian. Teachers, lawyers, UN staff. Fellow girlfriends and wives, friends of friends who came to parties and to watch the matches. Friendships that endure to this day. The team would go 'on tour', playing other teams from tiny villages upcountry and staff from the huge hotels in Mombasa. Great trips away. One weekend we headed to Kericho, to the middle of the tea plantations. A small hamlet, surrounded by tea fields on all sides, with a pitch in the middle. People turned out from miles around to witness our team being humiliated in the match, the crowd was the biggest we'd ever had. The pitch was on a slope, so the teams took turns to play downhill. A group of children surrounded me. Fascinated by the camera, faces eager, hands over mouths trying to stem the squeals of laughter. Eyes shining, they pointed and giggled as I clicked the shutter.

The World Cup 1994. Away with friends in a lodge near Lake Naivasha. The rangers in charge of the night drive shot around the park so fast that night getting back in plenty of time for the start of the game. These days I imagine we'd watch a huge flat screen TV in the bar of the lodge, but not then. Instead, one of the waiters gave us a room number for the staff quarters and four of us joined twenty or more people crammed into an 8 ft square room. A bulky old TV was balanced on a stool in one corner. People sat on the floor or stood wedged side by side. The picture kept sticking and occasionally revolving on the screen, so every now and again someone got up and walloped the top of the TV until it restarted. I don't even remember who we watched. Brazil? Argentina, maybe. It didn't matter. I only remember us all squashed in that room, animated and enthusiastic over the exact same thing.

I have never cared about football itself, but I love the way it brings people together.

January 27th, 2021

Some days I feel as if I am in freefall. I am scared to respond to the email. I'm not sure I want to hear the truth. Perhaps I can live in blissful ignorance a little longer. I always thought of being in freefall as a negative – a sense of panic, a feeling of spiralling ever downwards into a pit of despair.

But one New Year's Eve I experienced actual freefall, it was bliss. Alanna, her best friend Ellie and I jumped out of a plane, over a huge lake in New Zealand.

I crossed paths with them a few times that year, we all overlapped on different routes across the globe. We were in Taupo, in the North Island, looking at options for the next couple of days.

'There's a big hike people do.' Alanna was reading from a leaflet. 'The Tongariro Alpine Crossing. Sounds tough and it takes hours. We'd have to be up at the crack of dawn.'

I flicked through my *Rough Guide*. 'Yeah, it says about eight hours, walking across three active volcanoes.'

'Active?' Ellie looked concerned. 'I'm not sure I like the sound of that. And three of them? One seems stupid enough.'

'Says here one of them was Mount Doom in the *Lord of the Rings* films.' I continued reading out the names. 'Ruapehu, Tongariro and

Ngauruhoe. Don't you just love all these names? All the Māori legends?'

'Oh yeah,' Ellie replied. 'That's your thing, I remember.'

The first time Alanna introduced us, on her first Christmas home from university, Ellie grabbed me in a rib-crushing hug and said, 'I'm Elinor. The Jane Austen spelling, not the usual one. You know, from *Sense and Sensibility*. My mother's a writer, you see.'

'Wow, brilliant. Would I have heard of her?'

'Oh god, no. I hope not. Well, not if you read decent books, anyway. I prefer Ellie. My boyfriend's mother is the only person who calls me Elinor and she's a bloody awful woman.'

I liked her instantly and could see why Alanna hadn't stopped talking about her.

'What about the tandem skydive?' I suggested. 'It's better than hiking for eight hours. Tomorrow is New Year's Eve. We don't want to start the night exhausted. Come on, it'll be incredible.'

'Oh my god, you'll want to bungee jump next.' Alanna gave me one of her exasperated smiles.

'Brilliant. Can we?'

'Forget it – you must be insane. Just book the skydive, that sounds perfect,' Ellie said, relaxing back on her hostel bunk.

'Okay, so walking on active volcanoes is stupid, but throwing ourselves out of a perfectly good plane isn't?' Alanna shook her head.

'It'll be fine,' Ellie replied. 'Anyway, the pair of you are single. You'll be strapped onto some fit, handsome Kiwi with any luck, just make the most of it.'

The skydive was the ultimate adrenaline rush. An exhilarating way to watch one year turn into the next. I can see why these things become addictions, why humans are drawn to such extreme highs in life. It felt like pure freedom. A sense of being unstoppable. Limitless. It's odd that I loved it so much, because I'm not great with heights ... but falling out of a plane, well, I suppose it's almost too high up to matter anymore. That doesn't make logical sense, of course, but our deepest fears rarely do.

THUNDER OVER ULURU

My earliest memory – around three years old – is leaving a Greek beach in the middle of a thunderstorm. My dad scooped me up from the sand and sprinted, Mum and Finn running ahead of us, while huge raindrops pelted our skin. Then I remember a sandy path, with hundreds and hundreds of ants crossing from one side to the other. I crouched down and watched them, mesmerised. They were all carrying things on their backs, little bits of mud or wood. I asked my mum if they were moving house that day.

I don't remember the thunder or lightning; I only remember leaving the beach. Later a man smashed an octopus against a rock, over and over until the octopus was dead. Someone cooked it and my parents ate it in a small taverna at the water's edge. I remember I cried. My mum told me not to be silly, and to eat it all up.

Many, many years later – 1999, heading to the end of the century – I watched a phenomenal thunderstorm over Uluru, in the Red Centre of Australia. I was irresistibly drawn there, a place so deeply infused with the magic of storytelling. Stories passed down through generations, oral traditions embedded in the hot burnished earth. So many cultures have their own myths. Those things that cement their identity and create their history. The Aboriginal story-telling is centred around The Songlines – dreaming tracks that cross the land. There are paintings, songs, and dances about this time of creation – the dreamtime. Ayers Rock is its modern name, but the indigenous Anangu tribe always called it Uluru. A spiritual place, a sacred site. A resting place for ancient spirits. We were asked not to take photographs in certain places, sections of the rock that the Anangu believe possess spiritual significance. I took a picture of a small cave without realising; my shutter clicked just before the guide pointed out that the spot was sacred. I felt dreadful, but it was too late. Strangely, when I had my film developed, that picture was missing …

The journey of the sun changes the rock to many different colours. Grey to rusty orange, becoming bright red as the sun gets higher, then a golden colour as the day continues. Then at sunset, as darkness falls, it is often dark pink. Purple, even. A whole range of spectacular colours, completely altering the look of its surface as it rises out of the landscape. I hoped to see this array of colour changes, but instead the thunder raged. A storm swept in, and lightning patterns illuminated the skies above Uluru. Rain poured all night long. Waterfalls ran down the surface of the rock the next day; a rare sight, I was told. Later that afternoon, I walked through Kata Tjuta, the Olga mountains. As the orangey-red domed rocks surrounded me on all sides, I understood why the Aboriginal word for this place means 'many heads'. The crystal-clear desert air made the full brilliance of the constellations visible. While our dinner cooked and the fire burned, we listened to the ancient wisdom of the dreamtime. I pictured other worlds, as the stars formed a sparkling canopy overhead, stretching from our small dusty spot in the Northern Territory out towards infinity.

That night, with a head full of star formations, I dreamt you and I were back on that beach.

January 28th, 2021

LESSONS FROM THE RIVER

We have dinner delivered from a local restaurant. Fresh crab linguine. He suggested we have a meal together, catch up. Neither of us have much news, but it's a relaxed evening by the fire. The pasta is gorgeous, and he brings a lovely bottle of red with him.

'Remember that incredible pasta we had when we went to Florence to see Makena?' he asks. 'So simple, but so delicious.'

'I remember,' I say with a smile. 'That was a great trip. You had to keep having espresso shots in cafés so I could use the toilets.'

'Yeah. I couldn't get to sleep for hours. Too much limoncello as well.' He grins in that way I have always loved. It feels comforting to reminisce.

We finish our food and move to the sofa, he pours more wine, and we sit close together, almost cuddling. A playlist hums away in the background. One of his, a chillout mix from a beach club we once visited in Bali. A mellow, acoustic cover of 'My Way' comes on and I smile to myself. The fire is baking hot, I feel safe, it all feels familiar and reassuring. I lean right into him on the sofa and close my eyes.

A balmy, sunny day in my thirties and I was attempting to hold a tune while floating along the Mekong River. The driver had insisted that each of us perform some impromptu karaoke. Someone has just finished belting out an awkward rendition of 'My Way', and as we admired the passing scenery and day-to-day life along the river-banks, I was handed the microphone. I don't recall what I sang, but I imagine I did it badly. Singing is not one of my talents. Later that day, sporting conical hats, we switched to wooden dugouts and navigated smaller sections of water, like narrow canals. There was a gentle, peaceful pace of life there on the water.

We wound our way along the river, passing wooden houses built right on the banks, with slatted porches jutting out over the water. Women prepared food in bowls as they chatted and laughed – sometimes calling to one another in the distance, their feet dangling in the water, clothes drying on lines of rope above their heads. Children played nearby; babies sat on the porch next to them, content in the sunshine. People waved and smiled as we floated by, children danced and giggled and pointed at us. Ladies held items in the air in case we wanted to pull the boat to the side and buy something.

Our journey down the river took us past small restaurants, places where building work was taking place, people tending vegetable patches, people selling produce at floating markets. We sampled wine made from bananas, rice, and honey. We bought fruit and coconut candy –a bit like toffee – from food stalls on the banks of the river. Later that night a friend on the trip woke to loud rustling in his dorm room, only to find a massive rat sitting on his backpack, helping itself to the candy.

There, where things moved at a much slower pace, revolving around the river, around transportation, life appeared to be about appreciating simple blessings. Similar to the life I have now. A life that is slowed by the motion of water.

JANUARY 29TH, 2021

FEAR OF FALLING

I remember dozing off on the sofa. I remember him bringing me water and tucking me into bed. Then, morning light and he wasn't there. He must have left last night. I'd slept deeply for a change. My head felt heavy. Our relaxed evening felt hazy, was it real? Or had I only seen it in my mind? I have such vivid visions at times; the line with reality can blur.

Did I ever tell you that I have a vision of myself riding a horse down a beach at sunset? I have never done it. I could, of course, at any time. I could ride along the stunning Cornish beaches and gallop around the headlands, as if in a scene from a bygone era. But I haven't yet.

There was a time I thought I might work with horses, but that is a story for another day. The first time I went riding was on an Argentinian estancia: glorious sunshine, rolling grasslands, and handsome gauchos. A trip where I rode all day and then spent the evening eating steak and drinking red wine by a roaring campfire.

Well, strictly speaking it wasn't the first time. Visiting Peru, on a short ride to an old Inca site above Cusco, I was thrown off a horse. I hit the ground with great force, just minutes after mounting. Returning to my guest house battered and muddy, the owner insisted on taking me to see his wife at a pharmacy around the corner. She checked me over and cleaned up the cuts. He made sure I drank lots of coca leaf tea. As ever, I benefited from the kindness of strangers. And I had grown fond of coca tea in my short time in Peru. In Nepal I had suffered with bad altitude sickness, but the Peruvians tell you to drink plenty of coca leaf tea and you will be fine. They were right.

Struggling with a painful, bruised hip, I swapped my four-day Inca Trail trek for a two-day version. By coincidence, Ellie and her boyfriend were in Cusco, so this change of plan gave us the chance to meet up. Her boyfriend wasn't feeling well, so he went to bed early, leaving Ellie and me to have pizza and beer in a quaint little place overlooking the central square. It was full of hawkers, street stalls, and Spanish-style architecture. People were walking their alpacas across the road below the restaurant. We finished the evening in a busy backpacker's bar, drinking pisco sours until the early hours.

'How's the hip now?' Ellie asked. 'The alcohol's probably helping.'

'There's less pain than yesterday. Not sure I'll go horse riding again anytime soon, though. You should have seen the state of me afterwards. For some reason, earlier on, random people kept asking to have their photo taken with me. No idea why. But limping back to the bus covered in dung, absolutely no one asked for a photo.'

Ellie laughed. 'How funny. Maybe you look like a famous American celebrity? Or it might be the blonde hair. Alanna had that all the time in Thailand.'

The noise in the bar was deafening; we had to shout at one another.

'I bet you got tons of attention in Thailand as well,' I yelled. 'You are gorgeous. And so tall.'

'No chance – I looked like a bloody giant over there. Women shouted things like "No big sizes" at me if I walked anywhere near the clothes shops. The women are tiny, about 4 ft tall. You'd be okay, you'd blend right in.' She patted me on the head and laughed again. 'So where to next?'

'Well, thanks to this injury, I have a shorter trek now, so I think I have time to fly to the Nazca Lines. Cuts it a bit fine getting to Bolivia but that's okay. I'll just wing it,' I yell.

'Slow down, take a breath, you are wearing me out. You are so impulsive, I need a nice, organised itinerary.'

'That's why you get on so well with Alanna. She thinks I'm a nightmare. Come on down that drink. I'm getting another round in. And how about some Tequila shots?'

By the time I reached Argentina, I was ready to give horse riding another try. Conquer the fear.

I still try to face my fears, but I no longer have that wild fearlessness I had when I was young. I'm not sure any of us do. With age we begin to understand the preciousness of life. We want to protect ourselves as best we can.

Endure for as many years as possible. Not risk cutting our lives short …

January 30th, 2021

Weaving a Web

I have always looked for signs … symbols … messages to guide my way. It's always fascinated me. As a child I loved to read *Charlotte's Web*, where the spider weaves messages into the web. A lovely tale of friendship and probably the reason I have never feared spiders. All I see is the incredible way they spin their works of art, creating masterpieces from silvery gossamer thread.

I thought of that book the other day. I passed a circular shadow at the base of a tree. A shadow resembling a web. That same morning at dawn, when I walked around the garden barefoot, I spent ages staring at a perfect dew-covered spider's web. It stretched between a branch and the edge of the gate, completely intact. The morning light caught the icy dew drops and made it sparkle.

Much like people, the fragile strands of a web are far tougher than they appear. Tough enough to withstand a struggle. I don't regret the parts of life that turned out to be a struggle, because I no longer believe in regrets. I think all the things that happen have something important to teach us. I don't believe in coincidences either. I believe there are always signs if we are open to seeing them.

There are always messages written in the silk threads of life.

YOU CAN ALWAYS COME HOME

He isn't ready to come home yet. He hasn't said as much, but I know. If he was ready, he would already be home. I have no idea what I want this time. I don't think he does either. But for now, he pops round for a visit. He picks up shopping and drives me to places even though I am more than capable of driving myself. We have dinner together sometimes, which makes my days in the cottage feel complete again. But still I'm torn. Should we just carry on as we have always done, or do I want something else?

Perhaps he wants something else too?

<hr>

I always buy a return ticket when I travel. Just in case. Sometimes we need reassurance that we can always come home. Heading to Kenya that first time, despite being head over heels in love, I bought a return ticket. It never crossed my mind not to have a solid fallback position. In case I had jumped in too fast. In case it turned out to be a mistake. The big romance, the heightened emotions, the exciting story. The fact we had only spent two weeks together in total before I went. The wild safaris at the weekend, the lifestyle that was so different to other people's lives. All of it was so thrilling, but I am a pragmatic soul at heart. Part of me always wonders if I will be content enough, fulfilled enough. Part of me always thinks I might need to run at any time …

At the start things with Rhys were perfect, I didn't need the ticket. However, knowing I could always go home and pick up where I left off was a comfort. I knew that I wasn't missing anything – I don't mean that in a bad way. The lives of others were no less fulfilling or their weekends less exciting. It is just that I have discovered the definition of true friendships: they are comfortable, familiar, and enduring, and even after a long time away, things remain exactly as they were. You can pull them back around you like a favourite warm blanket and you can feel as if you never left in the first place.

Much later in life I realised that this is also how love should feel. You should not feel insecure and fragile. You should not wobble dangerously on the edge of an emotional precipice, not need to second guess another person's emotions. Not feeling nervous deep down inside, worrying that you might make someone angry, worrying the things you say and do are wrong. You should not feel unseen, unsupported, taken for granted. Even in the easiest relationships there will be arguments, petty fighting, or even blazing rows – after all, there's no harm in a bit of fire – but they should only be a small part of the whole. Quickly forgotten.

I realised eventually that love should feel like home. It should feel like being curled up in front of a blazing fire in winter or watching the moonlight sparkle across the water on a warm summer's night.

But too often I loved the wrong people.

January 31st, 2021

When Hurricanes Collide

Some people are like hurricanes, and some are like sunshine. You were a mixture of both.

When it comes to attraction, I am always drawn to the excitement of the hurricane force. To the promise of danger. Loves like this appear like fireworks. They arrive all guns blazing, powerful, dangerous, and seductive. But there are still the sunshine people. The ones who gently break through the storm clouds, brightening your world, covering you with warmth and making you smile. For too many years I preferred the excitement of risk and destruction. Sunshine was safe and predictable, hurricanes were not. The wildness of the storm would usually win. So too often there were hurricanes, some more forceful than others.

Hurricanes are not all bad. They keep you guessing, they keep things unpredictable, and there are wonderful times amidst the chaos. There is calm before the storm and calm after the storm. But there is also calm in the eye of the storm and, if you are careful, you can play by its rules, you can protect yourself. It is possible to find the calm to balance out the times that are stormy.

Years ago, I knew someone who wanted to walk down the aisle to the Neil Young song, 'Like A Hurricane'. As a couple they were opposites, it likely lasted because of that.

When two hurricanes collide, it has a name. It's called the Fuji-whara effect. You would think it makes the storm more dangerous, but it doesn't. What happens is the two hurricanes dance around one another, resulting in one storm making the other storm much weaker.

Over time, with Rhys, I became the weaker one.

THE WINDSWEPT TREES

Sometimes my insides feel strange; I suppose there is more space there now. After all those years when I was desperate for a child, it seems strange I no longer have a womb at all. On the positive side, I am getting stronger with each day that passes, my walks are longer now.

Today, needing space and solitude and not caring about rules and restrictions, I walked across Bodmin for over an hour. The moor is a place that can still feel deeply lonely even when it's filled with people. A landscape peppered with trees that have become bent over permanently from the wind. They look as if they fought for years to remain upright, but then they finally had to give in. They had to bend to the greater strength of nature and stay forever swept to one side.

You were strong. I always admired that – you followed your path regardless of what others wanted from you. But no matter how strong we are, there are still times we bend to the will of someone stronger.

I drove home along winding one-track roads. Moss-covered banks that will be covered with bluebells in a few months' time. On the side closest to the sea, the wind has made all the trees bend over time. Exactly as they do on the moors. The branches curve and twist and they stretch out over the road. They reach across until they meet the branches of the trees opposite, they clasp onto one another, much like people in need of comfort or support, and they create canopied tunnels overhead.

Later I sat near the water, as the fading sunlight began to illuminate the waves. Sunset approached, slanting across the cliffs, and the white foam on top of the waves mixed seamlessly with the golden light. I listened to the crescendo of the sea and the howl of the wind. To the seagulls as they circled above. Their cries carried away on the scented breeze, reverberating out over the ocean. Constantly circling. Round and round.

I returned home with dinner: plump mussels and fat chips from a local restaurant, the mussels swimming in a green sauce, like a pond full of algae, all piled up, drenched in garlic, parsley, and wine. We sat in the kitchen where the warmth of the old Aga filled the room. Crunchy green sticks of samphire were sprinkled over the top of the mussels and tasted of the ocean.

I was bitten earlier, sitting near the water at dusk, and my mind drifted back to the Indian ocean coast. To Mombasa. To the high-pitched sound of mosquitos in my ears at night. I remember killing the horrid creatures, clapping them between my hands, their bodies bursting and creating splatters of my own blood across my skin. I remember trails of old-fashioned, sticky fly paper, covered in black spots, hanging in the hot immovable air. Or those machines that made a hissing, zapping sound as the insect fried. I remember struggling to sleep, knowing there was a whining mozzie some-where in the room. Constant buzzing around my head. Tossing and turning endlessly. The circular motion of the ceiling fan throwing shadows across the room, each clunking turn repeating monoto-nously in my ears.

For a time, Rhys made me forget everything … even you. But intensity of that nature cannot be sustained. It didn't last. He trav-elled all over Africa with his work, so I was often home alone. The longer I stayed, the more I found myself trying to create a life that was independent from his, while still clinging to the things we shared together. It started with different weekends away – him to Kilimanjaro with friends from football, me up country to a lodge with Cara, Makena, and Joy. Then we began to take separate trips back to the UK. We had both retreated from the place where we began.

I am doing it again now. Retreating from those who love me most. Becoming insular and existing apart. Perhaps I am beginning the process of leaving … in whatever form that takes?

In Kenya, Rhys became distant first, I think. Physically and then emotionally. Now, it's the opposite. I am the one who has moved away first. Reversing the pattern. Back then, I tried to convince myself that I could manage without the affection I so desperately craved. I wanted to believe I was enough for him. I veered between pushing him for reassurance and acting as if I didn't need anything from him at all. I tried to tell myself I was tough, that I could manage without love. Without affection. Without reassurance. Without the promise of commitment to a future together.

I told Makena things were up and down with us, but I could handle it. That I would be fine alone if need be. But I didn't convince her. I didn't convince myself.

'Ah, my dear,' she said. 'You spend so much time pretending you do not need anyone. We all need people. None of us can thrive without one another. Humans are like the earth and the water in the rainy season. We can manage okay without each other, but when the rains come, well, then we are soaked in goodness. Filled with nourishment. We are truly given life.'

She took a big swig of beer, draining the bottle.

'You can act however you want, Kerensa, but I know you too well. You are a thirsty little plant.'

I laughed at the fact she had me figured out and at the image of myself as a greedy plant in the rain. 'For goodness sake,' I said, 'how do you always do that? Give me a free therapy session and make it sound like a line from a book?'

'Perhaps I should become a therapist,' she replied with a grin. 'Or maybe a poet? What do you think?' Then she laughed that deep, soothing laugh of hers. 'Of course, you do realise that you are not that complicated, right?'

And I laughed too.

'Now, enough serious talk. Kindly pass me another beer.'

Those days seem so long ago and yet some things feel the same. On nights like this when sleep feels impossible, I stand outside for a while to hear the waves at a distance. But not for long, as it is still too cold. So, I try to recreate the sound. Sometimes I find a sound-track of the sea, and if I close my eyes, I find myself back on our beach. I can see the waves coming in and out and I imagine the sound. The waves come in and the waves go out. The waves come in and the waves go out. It is like a hypnotic meditation in my head. In. Out. In. Out.

And like the trees on the moors, I bend to the sound of the sea. I move in the direction of the waves and sleep inevitably follows.

THE ROAD ALONG THE WATER'S EDGE

I am driving to work along the edge of the Indian Ocean in an old High Commission Land Rover. Seven am and blazing hot already, there's no air conditioning so all the windows are wound down and I can feel the wind in my hair and tiny splashes of salt water in the atmosphere as I head to the office in the centre of Dar Es Salaam. My last two weeks covering for a colleague in Tanzania – soon I will leave and return to Nairobi.

Some mornings I get a lump in my throat looking out at the beauty of it all, knowing no other drive to work will ever look like this again. I don't know then that in about seven years' time my office window will be the Whitsunday Islands in Australia, that I will be looking after backpackers on an 85 ft racing yacht. I also don't know that, after even more years pass, I will walk daily along the coast of Cornwall, surrounded by the beauty of the wild seas. This just goes to show, we don't know the things we think we know. We can't see what might lie ahead in our lives – for good or for bad.

But on this day, I savoured the beauty, believing that this scene would not come again. And that much is true: I have yet to return to Dar es Salaam and drive down that ocean road. That morning the water looked shimmery and calm, as if it was barely moving. The view was broken up in places by the distinctive shape of the dhows and their sails. At other times of day there was a golden band of sunlight across the water, sailing boats visible in the far distance. Some days the water looked grey and reflected the clouds above. Other days the water was pure blue, with a mix of purple, yellow, and gold across the sky. I drove under a shady avenue of trees. People were jogging along the oceanfront, silhouetted against the sun. Every single day it looked different, and I never tired of it.

On the way home that evening, I stopped to buy fruit at a road-side duka. Children played barefoot in the dust, food was cooking, the stalls lit up by hurricane lamps. Woodsmoke, gasoline, and salt water filled the air. A little boy, only a child himself, carried a baby on his back, tied on with a brightly coloured cloth kikoi. He smiled at me and said 'brother' when he saw me looking at the baby. His mother was busy serving food and taking payments. Laughing aloud, she clapped her hands together at something funny someone had just said, then shook her head and continued to chuckle as she stirred the pot of food. An old man sat on a stool to one side of the duka, smoking a cigarette and looking out to sea, laughing occasionally at the chatter on the stall. The waves were black and quiet, with only a few distant lights on the horizon, lights belonging to ships far, far away.

I wanted to stay for longer, standing in the sea breeze close to that family and their customers. It felt peaceful, gave me a sense of restfulness deep down inside. But I didn't have a place there and so I thanked them with a smile, and headed home alone to my quiet flat. Being alone there was not lonely at all. Different from being alone in Nairobi. Regenerating, somehow. It was the beginning of me remembering who I wanted to be. Realising I deserved something more. That I could move on to pastures new.

In the end I didn't, I forgot this feeling of possibility and confidence. But it was a start. In the future, when this feeling returned, I remembered it and was reassured by it. In the evenings I would read and go to sleep early. There were no big parties like in Nairobi, because I was just passing through, I didn't have a big friendship group here. But I had a couple of good friends, so sometimes we had drinks at the sailing club together. Occasionally on the weekends, we would take their boat out to a little island. An island with turquoise water, white sand, and baobab trees, where we relaxed in the sea and drank sundowners at dusk.

The boat was called 'Amani'. In Swahili this meant peace and tranquillity.

Adrift

People look at my life and assume I have it all figured out. They see me here, in this chocolate-box cottage by the sea, living my artistic dreams, taking my photographs. So many of us imagine other people are fulfilled and content because they don't tell us otherwise. They don't reveal the truth. They allow us to form misplaced beliefs about their perfect jigsaw of a life.

In Kenya we had the big house, swimming pool, riotous parties, endless sunshine. Romantic trips to paradise beaches and magical safaris whenever the mood took us ... it was such an amazing existence, so of course I was supposed to be having the time of my life. But beneath the surface the joy was fading, all the things I wanted began to look unattainable, and my desired future seemed to be slipping away.

The truth was I relied on Rhys for too much. I relied on him for love, for safety, for friendship, for desire. Comfort, intellectual sparring, silliness, and even for peace. I expected so much from him. I expected him to provide everything, to instinctively know everything. To *be* everything.

Whenever I felt insecure, I would pressure him. Sometimes he would walk away. Or tell me, 'I don't want to do this right now,' or 'I can't handle this anymore.' He never wanted to talk things through.

It was unfair of me to expect so much. One person cannot give us all the things we need; they cannot be our everything. But I was only in my late twenties, so I didn't know that yet. I learned later those different friendships and relationships all salved different wounds in our lives. That I needed a whole diverse range of people to fulfil the conflicting desires within me. That our complex souls need more than one mate.

Kenya was such a transient place. Of those friends born there, some would never leave, but others were keen to explore the world. The same with my European or Australian friends. Some stayed permanently, but many did not. I found myself constantly getting close to people who left. People were posted elsewhere, offered jobs in another country, or simply missed the comforts of home and decided to go back.

At the worst possible time for me, a time when things were terrible between myself and Rhys, Makena called round with big news. Wonderful for her, not so much for me. She was leaving. Her husband's five-year contract at the UN was finished. They were going to live in Italy. He wanted Makena and their son to experience

Italian culture as well as Kenyan culture. For Benito to understand both sides of who he was.

She knew I would be devastated. She knew she was one of my beacons in the dark.

'Don't cry now. This will be good for us as a family. It is important for Beni to experience the European way of life. This has not been an easy choice, but you understand.'

'I'm so sorry,' I told her through my tears. 'I'm a mess, but you knew I'd cry. I'm happy for you. Honestly. It will be amazing.' I hugged her again. 'But I will miss you so much. I can't imagine this place without you.'

'We will visit all the time, I promise you. For holidays and to see my family. And you must come to Italy. We will have spare rooms for visitors. There is always a bed for you in my home. You know that.'

I nodded, trying to smile.

'Ah, my dear,' she said, hugging me back. 'Come on now, think of the pasta and the ice cream.'

A couple of weeks later they were gone. Life was quieter. My world became smaller.

———

The long rains that year felt relentless. Lasting forever and mirroring my tears behind closed doors. But as Makena always told me, the rains brought new life. This new life should have been a celebration. In so many ways it was, but it came alongside pain that I couldn't speak aloud.

My friend, my fellow free bird, Cara, had just given birth. A boy. Jacob. All chubby cheeks and pale wisps of hair. I was delighted for her and envious in equal parts.

Two weeks later Joy had a baby girl. She called her Nyambura.

'In Kikuyu this means "born of the rains", she told me with a wink. 'I knew you would like that. Here, do you want to hold her?'

Feeling the warmth of her little body, my throat tight, staring into her liquid brown eyes and marvelling at her delicate curly eyelashes, I swallowed hard. It didn't work. The tears came.

'No, no. Come on.' Joy laughed. 'I am supposed to be the one with crazy hormones right now, not you.'

I held Nyambura's tiny baby hand, with its perfectly formed nails, and it hurt. It hurt in a visceral way. Yet another gorgeous baby to mix in with the babies who already surrounded me. I tried to plaster a smile on my face and act delighted, but beneath the facade the ache was real and the longing acute.

Like the continuous abundant rains, the baby announcements and births seemed to have no end in sight. My world filled up with baby after baby – Kikuyu babies, English babies. Canadian, Irish, Luo, Kalenjin. Black babies, white babies, biracial babies. Babies I fell in love with at parties. Toddlers and young children I played with at BBQs. As time went on there were fewer single people, fewer childless couples. The weddings too became more frequent. Cara and Richard married in their back garden, there was a makeshift bar and we played volleyball in the afternoon. Religious weddings, traditional church weddings. Weddings with customs brought over from Europe and those that followed age-old Kenyan customs. Ever-growing families that joined the safaris, the beach trips, and the football club outings. So many emotions were beginning to stir within me. Pulling at both my heartstrings and my ovaries.

Of course, you would not have known this or guessed at it. Only one or two people knew. I kept up a pretence. I talked generally about wanting children one day but did not reveal the depths of my unhappiness publicly. I wanted to convince the world my life was perfect. All my letters home were filled with enthusiasm, accompanied by joyful photographs. A photo of a painting I'd just bought, pictures of my colleagues on work trips, me attending fancy diplomatic balls. Images of smiling people in the wilds around campfires or huddled in a line, laughing at a party. Lazy afternoons in the sunshine drinking gin and tonics and lying in a bikini on paradise beaches. Long nights at the Carnivore nightclub drinking honey-filled dawa cocktails and dancing until the sun came up. The nineties equivalent of the images that spill across today's Instagram feeds, a printed version of those modern posts entitled 'living my best life'.

In some ways it was still amazing, but when something is

wrong, our hearts know before our heads figure it out. I watched the dance of death and the circle of life. I saw the predators observing the prey from afar. I sensed it. I sensed unease in the very air I was breathing, I knew that danger was circling me, waiting to pounce. I knew deep down things were not as they should be, that the spark had waned, and the fairy tale was not going to follow the age-old happy ending. I knew that this life was not enough to sustain me. But we don't leave people when we should. Too often we lie to ourselves. I was lying to myself.

My life was full of adventure and sunshine, but I knew deep down I could find these things somewhere else. Somewhere I could easily go if only I was brave enough. I knew I had a dying relationship on my doorstep and the promise of exciting new ones across the sea. The paperwork for a working visa to Australia was lying on my desk at work.

I had a choice to make.

But I had been weakened inside, changed from the strong, independent girl I used to be and turned into an insecure, dependent girlfriend. My innate sense of bravery slowly and insidiously lessened by my surroundings. Somewhere along the way I had stopped being myself and become someone I didn't recognise. Emotionally worn down, tired of the way things were, drained by my cravings for constant reassurance. I wanted to believe that part of what we had was still worth clinging onto ... even if it felt like the wreckage of our former happiness.

'Stop packing. You aren't going anywhere.' His voice was full of vitriol.

'I'm going to Cara's,' I replied.

'Don't be stupid, she's got a young baby.' He sighed, not meeting my gaze. 'Look, I know things have been crap, but we can fix it.'

I stopped packing my things and slumped onto the bed.

He sat next to me, looking straight ahead. 'Listen, I know you want us to move forwards. Talk about marriage, kids, all that ... stuff.' He ran his hand through his hair, the way he always did when he was stressed. 'We'll do that ... at some point. I promise. Just not right now. This is enough for now, isn't it? Living together?'

I didn't respond.

'Look, I can't get into it now, I have to go. I'll be back in a couple of days; we can talk then.' As he walked out of the room he shouted over his shoulder. 'And for Christ's sake get rid of that visa application.'

He convinced me to stay. So, I stayed.

I stayed for the echoes of the good, knowing deep down they were just that: echoes of something we had already lost.

And I allowed whatever future lifetime I had ahead of me slip away on the tides.

February 1st, 2021

Objects in the Rear-View Mirror

'What exactly is it that you want?' my husband asks me, again. 'I don't get you sometimes. I thought this was it. Here. This life we've got now? That's what you said.'

'I did. I mean, I *do*. I do want this.' I stumble over the words. 'I can't explain it. Everything feels so hard right now, almost as though nothing will ever make me happy.'

'Well, that's not new,' he snaps. 'Sorry. I don't mean that ... But come on. We all feel like that at the moment. What do you want me to do? Me moving out hasn't made much difference.'

And for once I was the one to say, 'I'm sorry, but I can't do this right now.'

I wonder how the world would look if you and I had been together this whole time? Do you ever think about that? I revisit so many things I see in the rear-view mirror. Things that might have been. You, of course, but other loves too. Crossed paths and stars that never aligned. Different destinations, different continents, miscommunications, and mistiming. Life decisions that never managed to coincide. Plot twists along the way.

Sometimes people are trains heading to the same station, but forever moving at different speeds and travelling on separate tracks. He and I are like that now, I think. But then we always were.

SOLITAIRE

I am alone in the house today. Completely alone. There were so many times I felt alone in lockdown, yet someone else was actually there. A strange feeling, but one that isn't new to me.

People always tell you that to be alone is one of the hardest things to handle in life. Humans are social creatures after all – craving connection above all else. But to feel alone when you are still with someone is a far worse place to be. I have always searched for reassurance that I was safe and loved. If those things are absent, when the person able to provide them is present, that is the greatest loneliness. In Kenya I knew they were absent. I was still lying to myself.

I used to play a lot of Solitaire. Hours looking at exotic plants, in a sunny garden, feeling an infinite emptiness. Times of tears and times of hollowed-out nothingness, which is far worse. And at those times I played Solitaire on a stunning set made of precious stones. Now you can play this game on a phone, but there was something so calming about holding the smooth stones in my hands, one by one, as the sun went down. Perhaps they reminded me of my childhood marbles, those precious spheres of multi-coloured light? I played repeatedly, hour after hour of Solitaire. Sometimes Solitaire and vodka, Solitaire and gin, sometimes just Solitaire. But always loneliness. Loneliness, sadness, and Solitaire. The irony was never lost on me. Beauty and sunshine make up for a lot of things, but they are never enough to fill a heart that is longing to be appreciated. You need more. I needed more. We all need more.

I played Solitaire again today, on my own precious stone set, brought home from Kenya many years ago. For a long time, it brought no joy, but now it makes me smile. As I moved the stones, reducing the number in play, the years rolled back with each stone and the memories took shape ... only more positive ones these days. My older self looks back differently. Objectively. I was expecting too much then. Expecting someone else to make it right, to fix my longing for something more. Meet emotional needs he couldn't even begin to try and understand and I doubt I explained at the time.

We were so young. Life should have been carefree, but I was insecure, and I didn't understand that people can't always give you the things you seek. It was never his fault. It wasn't anyone's fault.

Do I still expect too much? I'm no longer sure. Part of me has always felt broken.

These days I realise the best partner is one who balances and supports you, not one who saves or completes you. I try to believe we are not incomplete beings needing to be made whole, that we do not need anyone to save us. I tell myself that none of us need 'fixing'. None of us are broken, despite what the world wants us to believe.

February 3rd, 2021

Tears in the Water

Tears came from nowhere today. I felt so unsettled. I had a long chat with Finn this morning. He moved to America years ago and he often wakes early; he sometimes calls while his family sleep. Talking to my siblings makes me emotional. Some days it feels as though all my tears have congregated over time, blended seamlessly into the water, and returned to the earth.

They have fallen on an ordinary day, on a day when the world has lost its colour. Beginning as drizzles in the wind and gradually forming into droplets of rain, streaking down windowpanes, landing on leaves, settling on the path in jagged, messy puddles.

They have fallen in endless streams down mountainsides, forming vast, rushing waterfalls. They have tumbled to the base of the rocks, into pools of sunshine. Into sparkling rivers and winding streams.

They have dropped unexpectedly into the stillness of a lake, on a quiet day, disrupting the glasslike surface. Creating ripples that begin as small circles, then grow and grow.

They have burst in angrily, violently. Rushing up from the depths, filling the river with bitterness and vitriol. They have travelled fast, with force, bursting the banks and crashing through the land, destruction in their wake.

They have crashed into the waves, sometimes joyfully, sometimes not. Joining the peaks and the troughs, riding on the highs of the surf, then gliding calmly into the bay, caressing the softness of the sand. Or they have smashed into the rocks, hammering the shore. Finally losing their momentum and bubbling through the pebbles, soaking deep into the mud.

They have fallen softly through the air; the cold has frozen them into snowflakes and so the weight of them has changed over time. Edges and patterns form and if you look closely, they resemble pieces of lace. They are works of art. They make no sound as they float silently to the ground.

The tears fall to relieve the pain
   The tears fall as a part of nature
   The tears fall …
   And the world carries on.

February 4th, 2021

Circles of Life

Living in rich Western countries, we were sold such one-dimensional pictures of places like Kenya growing up. Poverty and misery. Starving children with fly-infested eyes and downtrodden women working in fields. Alternatively, athletes winning Olympic medals, awe-inspiring long-distance runners. Nothing in the middle. No images of ordinary life. No images of families celebrating birthdays, children going to school, office blocks full of accountants and lawyers. University campuses. Writers, artists, and chefs. Lives that are just the same as ours. We didn't see stories of day-to-day existence, with all its drudgery, boredom and its endless, utter ordinariness. And we didn't see any images of joy ... yet I was surrounded by joy.

Living there I saw all aspects of life, the joyful and the devastating. Beauty alongside pain. But all countries are the same when it comes down to it. Humans are the same wherever you go. There is always good and bad. There is always a divide between the rich and the poor; it's just less obvious in some places. In Kenya poverty was visible, right there on the surface. Disease, suffering, lack of clean water, lack of medicine – all these things existed. Some people can ignore these realities, keep them at a distance from all their Instaperfect travel stories. But I am not that person. I cannot ignore poverty and carry on as if the world treats its citizens equally.

While that side of the country was heartbreaking to me, it was a small part of the complex beauty of the whole place. But that was the side broadcast to the world. The Kenya my mother saw on the news never felt like the place I called home.

She would phone in a panic now and again.

'Are you okay? The BBC says it's terrible there. Riots, tribal clashes, fighting ... it sounds dangerous, Kerensa.'

I always reassured her these things existed on the outer periphery of my world. That I was somewhat cushioned. Privileged. I would joke that the only tribal clash I'd seen recently was a row between our Kikuyu office manager and one of the Luo drivers. Colleagues who irritated one another.

Sometimes though, the harshness of life did come too close. My job exposed me to positivity on one hand, despondency on the other. One minute, I could be waving at a group of teenagers playing football or being chased by giggling children through a village. The next, I would be knocked sideways by the reality of how much suffering exists in the world. A mother bringing a lifeless child to a clinic or the sound of wailing grief piercing the air in a village. I would always carry my camera on these trips, capturing both sides of life.

Once again, the mask of comedy and the mask of tragedy existed side by side as the play went on.

My job also allowed me to indulge my love of small planes. Working on High Commission projects meant there were frequent work trips and then the three-month transfer to Tanzania. There were planes that were broken. Planes that couldn't land because a giraffe was sauntering across the runway. Planes we couldn't board because of 'technical concerns'. Hours spent sitting in scorching hot airport lounges with no air circulating, drinking bottles of warm fizzy drinks and awaiting updates. Further hours in Land Rovers on dusty roads and in meetings, drinking gallons and gallons of coffee.

Heart-warming education projects and heart-wrenching health projects. Clinics in small towns that were completely overrun, deaths caused by entirely preventable medical conditions like malaria, diarrhoea, or dehydration. And deaths caused by more complex illnesses. Aids was taking its toll. As a fearful student in the late eighties I had seen the beginnings in the UK, the frightening government ad campaigns, the occasional high-profile death. People like Freddie Mercury, who died the same year I came to live in Kenya. Before I left England, HIV and Aids were kept somewhat hidden; they still seemed to exist at a distance. But here these diseases were so visible. Work colleagues died, staff at friends' schools, extended family members. Here, this disease was not confined to one section of the community. Here the disease had begun to spread through all sectors of the population, as it would do everywhere else in time.

Many years later, I travelled to Zanzibar with my husband, and we walked past the house where Freddie Mercury was born. The Old Stone Town where he spent his childhood is a magical place. It feels as if you have returned to biblical times. Donkeys carry their loads down winding cobbled streets, past intricately carved wooden doors. All of your senses are assailed at once: air scented with exotic, pungent spices; the evocative sound of the call to prayer; the rough pastel textures on the old walls of the buildings; the sight of children playing in narrow alleyways and women dressed in brightly coloured hijabs. Looking through my old photos, I see people on bikes at the harbour's edge. Clear silhouettes of dhows against the shimmering, silver surface of the water. I can smell the wafting fragrances of street food and taste the sweetness of plates filled with mango and passionfruit, served for breakfast on a sunny rooftop.

The last song Freddie Mercury ever recorded was called 'Mother Love'. Well, part recorded. The song was unfinished, its last verse added by Brian May after Freddie died. A song about losing hope, wanting peace, and returning to the safety of the mother's womb. Ultimately, a song about the cycle of life and death. A cycle that, at least to me, seems so much more tangible in African countries than it does in any other part of the world.

TRUSTING YOUR GUT

I have always had strong intuition, a sixth sense, a radar for danger. I often travelled alone, sometimes visiting dangerous places, but I followed my gut, worked out who to trust. Relied on my instincts and kept safe. I could usually see danger approaching and mostly avoided it.

But still, I was mugged once. In the middle of Nairobi. In the middle of the day.

A man came from nowhere, ripped my necklace off my neck, leaving nasty scratches across my skin, and disappeared through a hedge as if he'd never been there. I shouldn't have worn the necklace, not in the centre of town. I wore no other jewellery or a watch. The necklace was an eighteenth birthday present from my mum and dad, so I had always worn it. Nothing ostentatious, a thin sliver of gold, but the sun was shining, so perhaps it caught the light.

That day, I took a new route from my office to my partner's office. Usually, I walked a different way, the same walk I had done for months, up through Uhuru Park in the middle of town. I would see the same people day after day. Newspaper sellers, groups of friends sitting on the grass. Everyone was friendly, they recognised me each day, they smiled, I smiled. I would say something in my limited Swahili. A *sijambo* here, a *habari za leo* there.

Familiar territory. I never felt unsafe. But then someone at the office told me I shouldn't walk through the park. Said it was dangerous if you were white. So I listened. Still a newcomer, I assumed they knew best. That day I walked a different route, along the main road, past a big hotel. That day a man came from nowhere. I sensed him seconds before, saw him out of the corner of my eye. I suppose I expected him to grab my bag, so his hand at my throat was a shock. I made no sound.

I think we always wonder what we would do if something like that happens. How we might react.

I always thought I would shout, but when it came to it, my voice didn't work.

The following day I went back to walking through the park again. Back to the faces I knew. Back to listening to my own intuition about what was safe.

The next time I flew home to the UK, I replaced the necklace with one that looked exactly the same so my mum wouldn't notice and worry about me. But I never wore it in Kenya again, and I realised later that she worried about me anyway.

Every single day.

February 6th, 2021

A Place to Shelter

Being strong is exhausting. Holding it together. Making others think you can handle anything. Any day now I expect my results. It's dragging, the wait more uncomfortable than the aftermath of the operation. As you know, I have had to allow others to help me these last months. I have had to share the load. It's not easy – being strong is my default – a persona developed over time. Always tough enough to cope, brush myself down after each knockback. Go back out and fight through the storm.

When I was younger, whenever I lost someone, in love or death, I would use it as fuel for the fire. I would move at one hundred miles an hour. I wouldn't stop and assess the damage; I would don more armour and return to the centre of the hurricane. But it takes its toll. There came a time I needed to batten down the hatches. Slow down and just breathe.

Facing illness is like facing loss. I have been doing the same thing again, trying to move too fast, to feel normal again. These last couple of days I feel exhausted, almost like a relapse.

In my thirties I worked on racing yachts in Australia. Making food, looking after backpackers, helping on deck. You'd have loved it. I know how much you adored sailing. It would have been your dream job I imagine, it was certainly mine for a time. On one trip, the weather looked perfect as we left the port, but the winds raged, and a storm was brewing. We couldn't risk putting our passengers in danger. Our usual moorings were too open, too vulnerable to the elements. So we found a little cove, a place to shelter and ride out the storm. That afternoon we should have been miles out to sea, boat tipped on its side, racing through the waves at full sail. Getting soaked by salt water as we crashed onwards. Instead, we motored along slowly.

We surrendered to what was, instead of fighting for what should have been.

I expected complaints, people moaning that they'd missed out on the sailing. But they were all totally relaxed. They swam, went snorkelling, and lay on the deck in the sunshine. When the storm rolled in that night, instead of being out in the middle of it, blinded by the rain, we were protected. Hatches in place. Warm and dry, with the worst of the weather raging at a distance. The next morning dawned calm and peaceful; all was serene in our little cove.

Surrender has always been sold to us as a form of giving up, showing weakness, letting the enemy win, and waving the white flag. But it is just about trusting. Following a gentler course, staying more in tune with the whims of nature.

I am learning that fighting the raging storm is futile after all.

FEBRUARY 7TH, 2021

CALL OF THE WILD

A memory. A trip to Tanzania with my husband. Dawn in the camp, facing the snow caps of Kilimanjaro. Water for tea being heated on the fire. Even though we are right on the equator, there is always snow on the peaks due to the altitude.

A slingshot sits by the fire in case of visiting monkeys; it prevents them coming close to the tents and stealing all our food. It isn't safe to leave anything in the tents. Monkeys can steal large objects, so when we set off to go game watching, we pack all the food into the jeeps just in case. Right now he is sitting next to me. We exchange no words. An elephant ambles past in the distance, two more follow along. Out here in the wild, that sense of pure wonder never lessens.

My memory goes further. Back to the Kenya of the nineties once more. Wild male hunters and nurturing female gatherers. Roles that have existed since the beginning of time. Men facing danger hunting in the savanna, women gathering food and looking after the children back in the camp. I knew I was tough and independent. I knew that I could stand my ground. But in a society where the threat of danger was sometimes palpable, those primal roles seemed to reassert themselves. The world around me contained tropical disease, unrest, and political insurgency, unsettling in the extreme. My bravery diminished. Over time, I became less tough and independent. More submissive. More reliant on others for my security and my wellbeing. I began to see men in the role of protector. This happened slowly. Insidiously. Almost without me noticing.

A group of us were sunbathing by a pool in Mombasa in April 1994 when we heard the Rwandan president's plane had been shot down over Kigali airport. An ominous foreboding filled the air. That same foreboding filled the newspaper headlines … there was a sense that things could get violent. But even so, no one foresaw the sheer horror, speed and extent of the massacre that followed.

During the Rwandan Genocide, the High Commissions in the surrounding regions helped to organise repatriation flights. People arrived at our building in Nairobi, eyes filled with images of unimaginable violence. People who had seen friends and neighbours murdered in front of them, people who could barely speak, people who had managed to get out alive, but who would never recover. Refugees poured into camps on the borders of neighbouring Tanzania and Zaire. There were joint initiatives with the UNHCR, with various charities: World Vision, Save the Children, *Médecins Sans Frontières*. Around that time, I travelled home for a visit. Every image on the news reinforced the horrors while bringing back all the stereotypes of the continent. As the Ethiopian famine images had done in the eighties, the genocide images in the nineties turned Africa from a distinct group of nations into one homogenous whole in the eyes of the average person in the West. Portraying only the dark side of a continent. Focusing only on violence and hate. An entire population stripped of joy and shown devoid of dignity.

So I tried to look for the light and find normal day-to-day happiness. Then one afternoon, outside a small village clinic, there was a queue of new mothers; some taking a nap, others standing and talking with one another. An old radio sat in the dust; an upbeat song drifted through the hot air. Two friends sat on the floor breastfeeding and laughing with one another. Nearby, a dainty girl, maybe three years old, began to dance. She wore a T-shirt so big it resembled a dress and had a look of pure bliss on her face. As she twirled around, the mothers began to gather in a circle, to clap along, others swayed and began to join in. Her arms were outstretched, her eyes shining as she spun, and I clicked the shutter. By then my old boss had some great contacts so the photo made it into a National Geographic spread and won a couple of press awards.

But despite these moments of lightness the shadow still existed. In Kenya, unrest bubbled beneath the surface. Riots, political differences, instability, robberies that ended in tragedy, fatal machete attacks – all of them trembled beneath the joys of daily life. Someone I knew was shot in a carjacking. Anxiety and insecurity affected even the strongest of people.

But equally life was exciting. Raw, wild, and filled with adventure. Danger existed in the background, but we tried not to think about it too closely. It sat alongside such incredible natural beauty, a paradise coastline, majestic creatures running free across the plains as they were born to do. It sat alongside a fabulous life filled with parties, good friends, camping in the wild, safaris, incredible opportunities to take photographs and work which felt fulfilling. Danger was a minor part of living in this special place, surrounded by gentle people. People who tried to see the good in life. People who described most days as 'fine days'. I loved when people asked, 'How are you on this fine day?' or said, 'One of these fine days we will go to the coast.'

The sun nearly always cleared away the shadows. And, as ever, I was okay. I was lucky that danger never came too close.

Later, Rhys's job took him back to his hometown and I wanted to be nearby. I returned to studying, signing up for a journalism course. I needed time to decide what I wanted next in life. His flat was too far from the university, so I rented a house. It was in a rough neighbourhood, by local standards. The week before I moved, there was a murder two roads away. My mother predictably went into 'doom mode'. Said it sounded too dangerous, that I shouldn't move there. I told her I had survived five years in East Africa, so Manchester would be fine. Another tough life transition.

And so, I left a busy shared house in a country full of sunshine, a place where every day was a fine day, to come and live alone in a town where it seemed to rain all the time.

February 8th, 2021

On Separate Continents

February already. Hard to believe it's been seven months since I last saw my parents or Gareth and Alanna's families in person. We talk on the phone or FaceTime. We make the best of it. We last drove up there in August, when the rules had eased. When everyone felt safe enough. Those first hugs were more emotional than I could ever have imagined.

Being forced apart feels like living abroad. Only that was a choice. This is not.

Wanting to be somewhere else was never, ever simple. I think people thought I found it easy to leave. To get on a plane and go once again. I was further from some friends and family, nearer to others. Wherever I was in life, someone was always too far away, painfully distant. My loved ones were spread all around the world. Separate continents, inconvenient time zones, different hemispheres. Light years away, or so it felt.

It is impossible to have all those you love close by and still be where you want to be. It is impossible to spend enough time with people. It is impossible to know when it will be the last time you see someone, hug someone, speak to someone.

My grandfather died while I was overseas. The funeral was only small, so my mother told me it was too far to fly home, that everyone understood. Rhys did his best to comfort me. We were in one of our phases where life was strained. The cacophony in my head, the voices, thoughts, confusion were making me more and more insecure. I felt like a burden to him. I lived in constant fear of rejection, and he became even more distant.

My grandfather wrote to me every couple of weeks, telling me things about his world. A world he found lonely after my grandmother died. So many of the envelopes up in the loft were written by him, sent from that little terraced house in the Welsh valleys. The house I visited so often as a child.

Airmail could be erratic. Letters often went astray or took a long time to arrive. Sometimes they travelled by surface mail in error. So, three weeks after my grandfather died, a letter came from Wales.

It was the strangest thing. Words from beyond the grave. It took me days to open the letter. I wanted so badly to hear his voice and yet a huge part of me couldn't face it. In the end I poured a gin and tonic, something my grandmother would most certainly have approved of, and I sat in the garden in the sunshine. I expect he wrote other words near the end, but these were the last ones he wrote with me in his mind. The letter, as always, ended with 'God Bless'.

I don't think an email would ever have had the poignancy of that final letter.

THE TRAIN AT THE END OF THE WORLD

It's the mid-1970s and we have moved to a new home, backing onto an enormous woodland, next to a park. The park has a little wooden train with a real engine and it goes around a short track. A journey that feels so exciting when I am small. A train that feels enormous and a track that seems to go on for ages, until I grow up.

It is now 1995 and I am sitting on the grass in that same park. I watch the excitement on the children's faces as they board the train, and it starts to move. I remember that when I was young, like all children, I just enjoyed life. I didn't wish things were different, that the train was bigger, or the track was longer. I simply enjoyed the thrill of sitting on the little train. This morning I came home from Kenya on an overnight flight. I have only been back in the house for an hour, but my family were being so kind and attentive, I had to get out. I needed air. I needed to go for a walk. I had to get away from Nairobi for a while too, for the same reason ... I needed air. So, I am back here. Back home with my family for a few weeks. A few weeks to decide what I want to do next. Whether I want to return to Kenya at all.

One week earlier I went to bed early with terrible stomach cramps. Food poisoning or something similar. Catching various forms of dysentery was not unusual and I always suffered excruciating cramps. But this pain felt different. A deeper sort of pain. I woke up hours later, on a sheet soaked through with blood. I reached into it instinctively. Looking down at my wet hand, it dawned on me that I was losing a baby. A baby I had no idea I was carrying. A baby I would never have the chance to love.

A night drive to the hospital. Fast, panicked. Neither of us said a word. Then ... bright lights, raised voices, beeping machines. I don't know how long we were there; it felt like hours. Then I realised it was the next day. Uncomfortable examinations, all the necessary procedures. I stared at the ceiling, wishing I could be anywhere else. Anywhere else at all.

There were no tears – only numbness. There were no explanations – only statements of fact. I didn't cry when they scraped away 'the remains' (their words) of the baby that would never be. I didn't cry when they talked about the foetus being around eleven weeks old and telling me the probable due date. I felt myself almost observing the conversation from afar, wondering vaguely why they would even provide this information, given the due date was no longer relevant. I was given no reason why this had happened. I was given almost no comfort. My partner held my hand, but he was oddly cold and detached. He showed almost no emotion. The fact there would be no baby did not upset him. He sat with me because part of him still loved me and because the rest of him was still my friend. Mostly, he sat with me because it was the right thing to do.

As I recall, the doctor was brusque and matter of fact. The two of them made a good pair. Their words seemed to exist somewhere outside of me. Muffled. Almost as if the sound was turned down.

I sat silently, not inhabiting my own body. These two men

discussed me as if I was not even there ... and I suppose wasn't there. Not really.

Words and phrases floated into my consciousness.

'Failure.' 'Common.' 'Not viable.' There were statistics and percentages.

'Nothing to worry about,' the doctor informed me. 'You are young and healthy. There's no reason you won't conceive again quickly. Try again soon, that's my advice.'

A sentence that hung painfully in the air; a statement that filled the entire room with discomfort.

We had not been trying. If anything, we had been doing the opposite, as much as I wished that were not true.

An intensely awkward journey home where neither of us spoke. I rested my head on the window of the car, trying to cool down in the heat of the day. A solitary, silent tear ran down my cheek. But still, I didn't cry. I remained empty and numb for the entire journey. We were both still shocked. In disbelief. Neither of us had known I was even pregnant. I always assumed we would plan a baby when the time was right. Life was so busy, my mind was all over the place, I had been so unhappy and stressed about the struggles of our relationship. What with travelling with work, my cycle had been erratic. Despite wanting children in my future so badly, the possibility of getting pregnant never crossed my mind. I never paid much attention to the calendar.

As we walked through the door in silence, the house felt cold and somehow less like home. He attempted to murmur the odd word of reassurance, but it wasn't convincing. He was relieved. He didn't say so, but he didn't need to. I knew. He knew that I knew. Nonetheless, he tried his best to be kind, even though he had no idea what to do or say. Later, he ran a bubble bath for me, brought me tea and a hot water bottle.

'I'll be fine,' I told him. 'It's Thursday, go to the football club.'

'No, I shouldn't ... it's not fair to ...'

'It's okay. You can't do anything anyway. And I want to be alone.'

I still hadn't managed to cry, but I know that I must have seemed small and fragile sitting there in the bed. He looked worried as he left, but he left anyway.

I booked a flight home the next day and soon I was sitting in the park where I played as a child. Watching the smiling faces of tiny strangers on a little wooden train, wondering how it is that you can miss something you didn't know existed until it didn't anymore.

Later that night, I was lying in bed in my old bedroom, in the house I grew up in. There was a gentle knock at the door. My dad, with a cup of hot chocolate. He put it on the bedside table, something he used to do every night when I was a child, and that was the thing that finally broke me. My throat closed, my breath choked. Finally, the tears came. Dad wasn't sure what to do, said it wasn't 'his department,' and sent my mum up instead.

I cried loudly and painfully. Sobbing that completely exhausted me and continued until the whole of my body felt as empty as my womb. My mum held me for a long, long time. Until all the tears had nowhere left to go. Until they seemed to have dried up. Until I fell asleep.

Two weeks later I went back to Kenya. So many people told me not to return, but despite it all I was not ready to leave. There were only a few months left on Rhys's contract at that point. I wanted one last trip to the Mara. One more night sitting round the camp-fire listening to the animals; one more morning watching the dawn light up the sky, covered in the red dust of the savanna. I wanted a few more nights staring at the sun setting over the Indian Ocean. Walking on white sand beaches, dancing under the stars and swimming in turquoise water. But something fundamental had changed between us. We had left one another in spirit. Or perhaps I had left him. We both knew it, but we tried to continue as if things were the same. As if life was exactly the way it had been before our manic dash to the hospital in the middle of the night.

And shortly after the due date passed – a date I never wanted to know, but which was seared into my brain anyway – I finally walked away.

I have romantic notions about train travel. I like to imagine I am on one of those old steam trains from Agatha Christie films. As the years passed, my lost baby would occasionally float into my mind when I travelled by train. On a train in Peru where women dressed in colourful clothing held trays of grilled corn cobs up to the windows for people to buy. In Vietnam, on an overnight train, where we slept in tiny bunks. Waking in the morning to a radio blaring out communist propaganda and a breakfast trolley containing chicken foetuses. In Bolivia, there was a train that travelled up to an altitude of 4,700 ft before coming back down again and arriving at the Salt Flats of Uyuni. A train with one small carriage, but full silver service from a waiter dressed in a tuxedo. He looked the part and did the job perfectly, but he only had a handful of people to serve. It reminded me of the stylish air hostess on the tiny plane in Nepal. Uyuni is surreal. When it rains, the entire sky is reflected in the water across the flats and forms a mirror image. The blinding white landscape is transformed into a piece of living art.

I thought of my baby again at the end of a four-month long overland trip, after travelling with a group of fellow nomads through Peru, Bolivia, Chile, and Argentina. After we had camped in the wilds of Patagonia, we finally arrived in Ushuaia, the last town before you reach Antarctica. And there, in a park full of beaver dams, we went on a train called 'The Train at the End of the World.' An impressive name, but an unimpressive train. We were only on board for around ten minutes, for the slowest, most uneventful of journeys. But once again, after many years, I thought of the baby.

A baby who was never able to take a ride on the little wooden train in the park next to my childhood home.

FEBRUARY 10TH, 2021

DOES THE DESERT MISS THE RAIN?

I don't know if you know it, but there's a song called 'Missing' by Everything But The Girl, a band I used to love. 'Missing' was a huge hit in the mid-nineties. There's a line about missing someone in the way that the desert misses the rain. A few weeks after our baby would have been born, the night I finally drove away from Rhys, the man I still loved despite all that had gone before, that song was on the radio. In the years that followed, I would hear it and it would make me cry ... for the lost baby, for the life I thought I might end up living. For so many things.

But not anymore. Now, if I listen to it, it makes me pensive ... the wisdom of age. Of time passing. I close my eyes, turn up the volume, and I feel the lyrics almost physically. In the song it's crystal clear. One person had left completely, while the other wasn't willing to believe it. One had moved on, yet the other was returning to their old house, passing their old door. I had wanted to believe for so long that we were still in the same place, that the desert really did miss the rain. I wanted to believe I was enough for him. That we still needed each other.

We didn't.

As it happened, distance meant I never had to walk past his old

179

door. Not that I would have done; we were well and truly over at that point in time.

Such a basic sentence signalled the finale. Ironically, we'd been to see a house. Something with a new door. A house for both of us, I assumed. But I was wrong. And there it was. A conversation about a future that would never happen. The same conversation I'd been trying to have for years. One he always avoided or tried to postpone for another day. It never progressed, never changed, never went away.

It was our personal Groundhog Day and it had been going on forever.

There were no tears, no recriminations. No temporary breakups, no packing of bags, no staying with friends for a few weeks – our standard pattern. This relationship had taken up almost the whole of my twenties, so I thought I needed to cling on to it for dear life, instead of giving up and moving on. I kept fighting to save it. But this time was different. Empty inevitability, simple clarity. No real grieving. The end had happened a long time before, covered over with the day-to-day muddling through and my refusal to admit the truth. I suppose it felt like an anti-climactic end to such whirlwind romance, such a grand passion, a crazy story of running away to an exotic continent in a moment of wild impulse.

I didn't make a statement about wanting to break up. I didn't say we were over. I didn't even say goodbye. Instead, I stood up and said, 'I'd better get going, I have a couple of hours' driving ahead of me.' And I walked out of the door.

A song on the radio filled the silence as I drove away into the rainy night, and I heard Makena's voice in my head: 'Ah, Kerensa, you are a thirsty plant.'

And I realised. I was the rain. I wanted to nourish, to enrich, to give life.

I had always been the rain. And he was the desert.

As it turns out, the desert doesn't need the rain at all. It might miss the rain, but the desert is designed to carry on without it, and so are all the things that manage to grow there.

SHIPWRECKED

I didn't expect to mourn anything. I expected to walk away relieved. Finally realising I had stayed much too long. Knowing the future I thought I wanted would have made me smaller. The sacrifices would always have been on my side. I would have followed his chosen path around the world, instead of carving out mine. Supported his dreams, not created my own.

Nevertheless, sometimes life breaks you. It cracks you open, painfully, or it shatters you into a million pieces. Cruelly. Mercilessly. It can feel as if shards of your heart are scattered all over the place and you have to watch them being trodden into the dust.

It took him weeks to realise that I wasn't coming back, that I hadn't rung him or officially ended things. The fact he barely noticed I'd gone wasn't something I'd seen coming. So, I suffered an aftershock, an unexpected emotional storm. The build-up from years of pent-up feelings came pouring out.

Turbulent, violent gales, torrents of water smashing the sides of the boat. Huge waves beating against the rocks, driving rain, cutting wind. Smashing through the swell, helpless in the face of nature's wrath. Stormy seas, rough weather, chaos, and devastation.

Sometimes we run aground in shallow waters, or we hit dangerous rocks. Sometimes it's the iceberg we don't see coming, and even when the damage is done, the band keeps playing on deck while the boat sinks, slowly but inevitably.

Sometimes we've held it together for too long and something snaps. And sometimes, we may already have sunk to the depths of the ocean bed, where all hope of finding anyone alive decreases as the days pass by.

But there are always survivors. People that managed to reach the lifeboats, people hoisted from the wreckage, people washed up safely ashore, and even people that decided not to get on board at the last minute. In a crisis, at the scene of a tragedy, people will always tell you to look for the helpers. They are always there. There are always helpers.

My helpers rallied around me then in the same way they are rallying now. Helpers back in Kenya and here in England. In Italy, Australia, and America. All the people who loved me then and those who love me now. The people who lift me up. My family, my friends. Alanna and Ellie. Makena, Cara, and Joy. Bernie, Nadia. Even the Free Birds.

Shipwrecks can hold such a fascination for people, for those looking on. Around the world there are famous shipwrecks that act as diving sites, tourist attractions, or points of interest on a beach. Perhaps it's the sense of the macabre that draws observers towards the eerie remains of other people's damaged lives. Their dreams dashed to pieces on the rocks. Or perhaps it's a form of therapy ... a relief that this was not their own fate.

But still. Look for the helpers.

FIGHTING THE TIDES

1997 and I was single once more.

I was still young, there was no need to rush into the next stage of my life, but I thought there was. It is emotionally complex for women. Men don't have to fit the constraints of time in the same way. Society allows them to age differently, to have a much longer window to achieve their goals.

But I was short on time. I felt this before we split up. Felt the constant societal pressure. Now I was 'officially' single, it got worse. No husband and no children. I was made to feel as if my life was over. I had missed the boat. Myths. Nonsense. But it was there, nonetheless. In the attitudes of my own generation as well as the older ones. In advertising, magazines, and films. Conversations I overheard in cafés, bars, or at exercise classes. Pervasive. Insidious. I'd love to tell thirty-year-old women now that they still have so much time. That they don't have to rush. But then, as a single woman in my thirties, I had fallen for it myself. I had fallen into the trap of believing I was doomed to spend my life alone.

Now, of course, I am glad we split up at that point in our lives. That I was able to continue to explore the world. I realise how different a person I would be if those intervening years of adventure had never happened.

February 12th, 2021

Life Rafts

Onboard the racing yachts, as part of the passenger briefing, we used to tell the passengers that in the unlikely event someone fell overboard, they should try not to panic. We would throw out a life raft and then we would circle back and pick them up.

Sometimes people are life rafts. They notice that you are being pulled beneath the surface, struggling to tread water. They become something to hold on to and they help pull you to safety.

Leaving Rhys in 1997 was the right decision, but still fragile from the miscarriage, I was lost. Stuck in a city I had chosen for him. I had rented a new flat that I had no desire to live in and accepted a job that I didn't want. I had done it all to be near him and now I felt trapped once more. By responsibility, by the expectations of others. I thought I needed to stay where I was, despite the emotional turmoil I felt. It seemed like the right thing to do. But I hated Manchester. Hated how unhappy I had been there. How devoid I was of joy, how lacking in sparkle.

Fortunately, someone noticed me fall overboard and threw the life raft as quickly as they could. An old friend who reminded me that we always have choices. That I had a haven elsewhere, friends who would pull me up out of the water. A reminder that life should be fun and carefree. That I could return to the places where I had friends. People who had known me forever. I didn't need to start afresh with new ones.

So I walked away. From Manchester, from the uninspiring magazine job I'd taken in desperation, and from the final connection to Rhys.

Returning to London, more life rafts appeared. A fantastic job opportunity in London via my old boss at Condé Nast, I became a picture editor at *Traveller* magazine. A chance to begin something new. And a new flatmate. Someone who would jump aboard a plane with me anytime I asked: Bernadette, or Bernie as she preferred to be called. Recently divorced, she became my single sidekick, my travel buddy. My partner in crime.

BROWN EYED GIRL

Then there was Janelle.

It was a random Monday morning and a new temp appeared in the office, all sunshine and wild curly hair. She crashed into my life like a meteor. A fiery ball of energy and fun. Part way through her world travels, she brightened my life just as I had come alive again and left part of the past behind me.

London, Paris, Amsterdam, Palma, Oxford … weekends away and long lunches in backstreet pubs. Nights which began at 5 pm in Oxford Street and finished at a bar in Soho in the early hours. In Paris it rained all weekend, the outdoor café tables were all empty, so we could not emulate the chic women I so admired in my youth. We ran drenched from place to place, finding bars along the way. Notre Dame, Saint-Germain, Châtelet. I resembled a drowned rat, but she looked like a wild ocean creature. Hair dripping, eyes full of mischief.

That night we were included in an all-night lock-in at an Irish bar, dancing to Van Morrison until the early hours. In Amsterdam, the last people still dancing at the end of a friend's wedding, we hitched a ride back to our hotel in the back of the van that belonged to the wedding band. The following day we admired Van Gogh paintings in the morning and were hopelessly stoned on little cakes in a café in the afternoon. Sitting by a canal, tears running down our cheeks, laughing until our stomachs ached. Palma was all tapas, paella, jugs of sangria, and sun-soaked heart-to-hearts.

From the Dreaming Spires of Oxford to the Parisian City of Lights, there was story after story.

February 13th, 2021

The Walls We Build

Sometimes, with each new heartbreak, us humans build an invisible barrier to protect ourselves, or perhaps not so invisible. A wall around the heart. After I left Kenya, something changed within me at a deep level. I chose not to be vulnerable; I chose not to show any cracks in my tough exterior. I let people believe I could handle whatever life wanted to throw at me. I donned my armour, and I hardened my heart.

My personal wall took years to build. Not everyone will allow their walls to be smashed down. Some won't even allow them to be dismantled gently, piece by piece. Walls keep out all the heartbreaks and the hurts, but they also keep out all the love. You can't have it both ways.

In time I would come to see that. I would come to realise it was time to remove my armour.

Between the occasional work assignments in an exotic locale and trips away with Janelle or Bernie, I began to collect tales from around the globe once more. All of this turned my thirties into an extraordinary decade. A decade where my feelings of hopelessness and despondency at the start were replaced by unforeseen blessings by the end.

February 14th, 2021

Marriage Material

Tossing. Turning. Pulling the pillow into different shapes. The thin trail of light from a streetlamp sneaks through the shutter and across the ceiling. I realise I've been looking at it for ages. Trying not to think of overhead strip lights in hospital rooms and possible visits to oncologist's offices. I tell myself if I have cancer they'd have been in touch by now, that no news is good news. Finally, I give in and get up. Take the dog out in the semi-darkness of the early morning, stroll through the chilly morning mist.

Early spring flowers are starting to break through the earth now. But the morning air is still filled with cold dew before the sun comes up. I pass an old stone wall covered with tiny succulent plants. Hardy little rosettes. No water or soil, just plants surviving amidst the inhospitable cracks in the rock. Strong and healthy with no real support system, with nothing there to nourish them. Thriving despite their surroundings. People do this too. I think it shows the immense resilience of the human spirit.

Especially when it comes to love. Despite the conditions, we still cling onto our belief in love. We keep going. Our minds can torture us with the memories, only giving us flashbacks of those perfect romcom moments, making us feel as if we cannot survive without that person. But we do, of course we do. We carry on without them. We continue to hope for better days, we hope to love again … even if it feels impossible.

Today is Valentine's Day. Normally we don't bother, I can't bear forced commercial holidays, but after this last year celebrations have become so magical, time together so meaningful. So I extend an olive branch, invite him over. I light scented candles and cook a fancy dinner. We both get dressed up and have champagne by the fire. We seem to be finding our way back to one another. Slowly but surely.

There is such comfort in returning to people and places that are familiar.

I imagine you'll be surprised that I didn't get married until I was much older, given my desperation in my late twenties to settle down. I was almost fifty. By that stage I wasn't too bothered, and he was the one who was keen. A complete reversal.

When I was single in my thirties, I was desperate to find someone. Dreaded the inevitable questions from relatives about settling down, the implications of 'getting past my sell-by date'. With people my own age it wasn't an issue. Many envied my freedom, and married friends lived vicariously through me, always wanting to hear about dating disasters, exciting encounters, or travelling adventures. Wanting entertainment on nights out. But after a while it became painful to make light of my disastrous personal life for the enjoyment of others.

I assumed I would meet someone in London. Someone at the office, or a friend's office. After all, I was in a busy, bustling, thriving city, full of people my age.

But a busy city can be the loneliest place in the world.

FEBRUARY 15TH, 2021

THE PATH ALONG THE CLIFFS

Today I drove across to Rock and took a long walk through the sand dunes. Twisting paths edged with rough grass and empty tangled blackberry bushes. The rocky outcrops at the base of the dunes are covered in seaweed. Over time it has been softened and smoothed by the water, as if swathes of green velvety material have been draped across the rough surfaces.

The beach runs along the side of the Camel estuary, a place where the river meets the sea. The famous Doom Bar sandbank is here, with its legend of a mermaid curse. Stories of shipwrecks and a wailing cry that can be heard across the bay, a cry bemoaning the sailors who died because of her curse. Some days I come to the dunes for a change of view, to walk along a lower path. Put my feet into softer sand, watch the dog chase a ball into the water. But most days I will walk along the high cliff paths nearest to my home. There are days I need to be alone with my thoughts. To process the things that are happening right now. Days I can't cope with distraction. I need to go inward and be solitary.

Today is much calmer after the storms of yesterday, as is always the way. Yesterday the wind smashed against the windows of the cottage, while we drank our champagne and watched a light-hearted film. Hailstones pelted the roof during the night, despite spring hovering around the corner. There is a strangeness to our seasons now. Earlier in the day, I walked up the path that rises above the harbour and sat on a bench overlooking the village.

I can spend hours walking those paths, listening to the song of the sea, and watching the ever-changing dance of the waves.

You Just Have to Get to the Next Teahouse

Sometimes life feels like trudging uphill, day after day. Impossible to catch a break. Aching legs and seemingly no end in sight. But hard times do not go on forever; the sun always comes out from behind the clouds.

I recall trekking through the Annapurna mountain range in Nepal in 2012. Over the years my husband had been on many tough hikes and even climbed huge mountains, so he found it far easier than I did. Some sections felt as if we were walking straight up a flight of stairs for hours and hours and hours. Thousands and thousands of steps. Surrounded by rhododendron forests and snow-capped mountain ranges, there were ruddy-faced, smiling children playing in the crisp, clean air. It was a breathtaking sight, but we still had some distance to travel before we'd be able to rest.

Midway through the longest, toughest stretch of our trek, we were struggling with the high altitude, the heat of the sun, nagging headaches, tired legs, and sore feet. Our guide smiled patiently. Guides and porters can run up these trails, barely getting out of breath. We call them mountains; the Nepalese call them hills. So many things in life are relative. Used to seeing trekkers struggle, they always know the right things to say.

This one said we didn't need to worry about the whole journey. 'Is okay,' he told me. 'You just get to next teahouse. Then rest. Have tea.'

Leaning on my walking pole and looking up at the huge slope in front of us, I asked, 'Where is it?'

'Is up there.' He pointed up the trail, to several buildings visible on the high mountainside.

'Which one?'

'The blue one.' A big smile.

'But they are all blue.' I laughed.

192

He laughed too. 'Is that blue one,' he said, pointing to the one furthest away.

We were heading for the last blue teahouse in a long row of blue teahouses.

Soon, with the luminous sun beating down, we were resting our weary legs and clutching hot drinks. We sat peacefully, listening to the distant sound of the yak bells jingling as they ran up the trails carrying essential supplies to distant villages. We relaxed and refuelled amid a calm mountain vista, while coloured prayer flags blew gently in the wind above us.

Finally, our destination for the night: a village called Ghorepani. I felt such relief as we passed under the village sign. The weather was beginning to turn, and the cold was settling in for the night. A little girl wandered past alone, waving and grinning, holding an apple. She must only have been three or four years old. All grubby cheeks and wonky teeth. I waved back and I was about to ask if I could take her picture, when she spotted a couple of backpackers carrying a tube of Pringles and shot after them like a hungry dog chasing a bone.

I looked around at the buildings.

'So, we are here,' I said to the guide. 'Which teahouse are we staying in tonight?' Though I thought I'd already guessed the answer.

He laughed and pointed. 'This one at the top.'

The guide explained that this was 'lower' Ghorepani, and we are staying in 'upper' Ghorepani. So we needed to keep on walking up. He assured us this was a good thing, that in the morning we would get up early and go up to the peak of Poon Hill to watch the sunrise. If we stayed at the top teahouse, the journey tomorrow would be shorter, and we would be grateful in the morning.

Sometimes, even when you know the end is in sight, the last few steps are the hardest. While the others went on ahead, I took my time trudging upwards. But sometimes, we can't do things alone. Sometimes, we need a helping hand. My helping hand appeared out of nowhere.

My little beaming friend with the apple reappeared, seemingly knowing I needed encouragement. She held onto her apple with one dusty hand and took my hand with the other. Her legs were only just long enough to manage the height of each step, and yet this smiley Nepalese child literally dragged me, one knackered, dirty westerner, up the last few steps to the teahouse at the top of upper Ghorepani. Then she ran off, her laughter ringing out in the cold air, as I found a nice hot fire to sit in front of and a place to toast my tired feet.

The next morning, we walked uphill to see the sunrise over the Annapurna mountain range, freezing cold, in the pitch dark. At around 4 am we followed the line of head torches moving steadily up the trail. Someone was vomiting into the bushes, others were swearing and complaining.

Getting to the viewpoint was tough, but we were rewarded with a perfect sunrise. An enterprising person had set up a stall making tea and coffee. Savouring a cup of hot tea, I read a commemorative plaque. Meaningful words about the life of a stranger who loved those mountains and asked to have their ashes scattered there.

I often think of my little friend with the apple. Another person from my travels who will now be an adult, but who exists forever as a child in my heart and in my photo albums.

February 16th, 2021

Landslide

I wake up on the sofa in the early hours as I often do – cold and stiff – normally he would have covered me with a blanket. That's when I remember he is not back permanently. Normally, he's up early to go to the farm and brings me tea before he leaves, or if I've dozed off, he makes sure I am warm enough.

My insomnia is worse. I should get my results in the next day or so, they said. There's been a delay, the system is overstretched. I know everyone is doing their best, but the waiting is stressful. Dread, nausea, the occasional panic attack.

Hollywood blockbusters always give the impression that something sensational needs to happen to cause a landslide. We anticipate a long tense build-up, full of drama, before the crash comes. But that isn't how it goes most of the time. An earthquake or a volcano can set off a landslide, but it can also be caused by the slow, persistent weathering of the rocks. Disappearing under the surface. Steady, but unnoticed.

The older I get, the more people will be lost. Life and death are part of the cycle, but still, the deaths when they come can paralyse us. We seek answers, we battle against the unfairness of it all. Some deaths in recent years have shaken my foundations. Challenged my search for meaning, shattered my belief in a kind universe. It

195

should be older people – lives well lived – deaths that follow the natural order of things. But some were children and babies. Tragedies that will never make sense. Then there are the women – all too soon, all too young. Strong, vibrant, one-of-a-kind women.

So even when the rocks beneath have weathered slowly, the falling debris shocks us as it smashes to the ground. The end is traumatic no matter how prepared we think we are. When the landslide brings everything down in its wake, people somehow muster the energy to keep going. They show up. One foot in front of the other.

How this world can be filled with such breathtaking beauty and such arbitrary cruelty at the same time remains the deepest mystery.

February 18th, 2021

FOLLOWING THE SUN

S unflowers. A surprise gift.
  Yesterday I finally heard. My results are clear, everything is benign. Relief has sunk in overnight. The flowers arrived this morning from Nadia, making a miserable grey day brighter.

Did you know that sunflowers are among my favourite flowers? They remind me of France, where we have a family home in a rural village, surrounded by fields belonging to local farmers. Driving towards the house in summer, you feel almost as if you are crossing a sea made entirely from sunflowers.

Yesterday, almost immediately after I got the results, I received some heartbreaking news. A small landslide in my world, but a tragic one in someone else's. Kathyrn, an old work colleague from *Interiors*, put an update on social media. October last year she had the same operation I've just had. Unlike me, her results weren't clear. Stage 3 ovarian cancer. She's been having aggressive treatment, but today she shared the news it has spread to her liver.

We could so easily have been in the same position. Battling the same storm. I am lucky.

Life, in its simplest form, really is a lottery.

Then there it was – an unexpected gift of sunshine in my kitchen, while the rain tumbled down outside. Reminding me that some things in the world are still miraculous. I love the fact that sunflowers follow the path of the sun all day and they are always looking for the light. They make staying away from the shadows look effortless.

Trying to find the light is a good way to live.

I notice patterns of light, I always have done, even before I began to take photographs. Moonlight on the water, sun glinting on the snow, pretty shapes and shadows stretching across buildings and pavements. I notice how the colour and the intensity of the light changes in the same way that the seasons themselves change.

I placed the sunflowers in a vase on the table. I focussed on their sun-shaped heads, and I tried to find the light.

FEBRUARY 19TH, 2021

PIECES OF THE PAST

I must have been out walking the dog for ages. My post-op check is next week; I want to be assured that everything is healed before attempting a gentle run. When I got back, his car was there. I wasn't expecting that. He hadn't said he was coming over. He does that now, checks if it's convenient. Whether his visit interferes with anything else that is happening. But there is no sign of him in the cottage when I walk in.

'Where are you?' I call into the garden. No answer. 'Hello? Are you here?' Perhaps he's just left the car here and walked to town.

'Up here,' he yells down the stairs.

When I go up, I see the loft hatch is open, the stairs pulled down.

'What on earth are you doing up there?' I stand on the ladder, look up into the loft and see him sitting amongst all the boxes.

'Christ, it's a mess up here. I can't find anything.' He's pushing his hand through his hair in agitation. Shoving boxes to the side and piling them on top of one another. Rifling through piles of stuff.

'Why the rush?' I ask, laughing. 'It can't possibly be urgent if it's been left up here since, well, goodness knows when?'

'I'm looking for my old climbing photos. Which boxes have got my stuff in?' He carries on rooting through. 'I found some prayer flags and some camping stuff.'

'Hmm?' I say, not taking much notice of him. I'm checking the boxes, checking none have an 'R' on the outside.

'This looks like one of mine.' He grabs a box and starts to rip the packaging tape off when I see the letter written on in marker pen. Given I have just been laughing with him, he's unprepared for my reaction.

'No!' I say sharply. 'Don't touch that one.' From nowhere tears pour down my cheeks. 'Put it down,' I say more softly. 'Please. Just don't touch it.'

'Sorry. I wasn't trying to upset—'

'That's fine. It's just some personal stuff. Letters. Things like that. I'll help you. I know which ones are your boxes.'

He doesn't press me for explanations, and we start to sort through together. Soon we both become distracted. Old trips, old memories, reminiscing. There are boxes of journals, and letters. I have such clear flashbacks of individual journeys, of people's faces. Deep yet fleeting connections. Crystal-clear images of unforgettable scenery. Powerful, evocative scents that drift back to me across the years. The smell of pad thai from a street food vendor in Thailand; fresh bread baking in earthenware ovens in Peruvian markets; huge pans of paella, the contents stirred round and round as the scented steam rises into the air; the smell of charred pieces of fish being barbecued outdoors. Then a little gem of a detail ... a forgotten moment ... a treasure that I thought to include as I scribbled my rambling feelings onto the page.

Pieces of the past.

As well as the journals, there are so many photos. Children on the floating islands of Lake Titicaca; in the dusty villages of Cambodia; playing football in the tea plantations of Kenya. Photos that transport me back instantly, causing an internal warmth.

A sudden flash of inspiration hits. I begin to separate out certain images and put them onto a pile.

An ancient old lady selling lottery tickets on the Vietnamese border, her face an exquisite canvas of thousands of lines, thousands of stories. Another lady, as old if not older, sitting on a high mountain pathway in Nepal, smoking a cigarette and grinning with a wide toothless smile.

I pick up a picture of two Vietnamese schoolgirls. Dressed in colourful uniforms they are squatting on their haunches, giggling together. I remember that day so clearly. As the sun rose, we took a trip on motorbikes out into the countryside and through the demilitarised zone. Passed the village where the famous photograph was taken of the little girl running naked from the napalm attack. A picture once seen that is impossible to forget.

I add another photo to the pile. A picture of a girl, her back to me as she walks barefoot through lush grass. A photo taken in the killing fields of Cambodia. A place where there is a central exhibit filled with skulls, but there is also the sound of children's giggles as they play. Their voices float across the same land where the atrocities took place. Innocent laughter that is so at odds with the reality of what happened there, and yet, as they run and play, their presence fills the place with a perplexing comfort.

Children are one of my favourite photographic subjects. On that visit to Vietnam and Cambodia I photographed as many as possible, willing them, with their mischievous faces, to replace the more painful images of horror I had seen elsewhere.

A theme begins to form in my mind as I select certain images and leave others behind. A collection starts to take shape.

February 20th, 2021

The Safety of the Harbour

Sitting by the harbour is something I do so frequently these days. A place to think. To contemplate those early days. Those days I first set out into the world. When I left the safety of the harbour, heading for the open seas. I realise I was looking for the thrill of the unexpected, to brave the unknown ... to walk into uncharted territory and see what might happen. To leave behind the familiar.

To leap out of the plane.

I have always loved the sight of a harbour. Here in my peaceful haven, my quaint village on the coast, the harbour has only a few local fishing boats. The cobbled stone slopes down to meet the tide, lobster pots are piled by the wall near the water. Further up the coast are tiny, deserted coves, coves I picture as they were in days gone by, not packed with tourists, but filled with rogues and smugglers, sneaking ashore under cover of darkness. Not far from here is a place known as the 'village that died'. There is no longer a working harbour, no longer any fishermen; instead children go to play in the rock pools, and locals walk their dogs. Legend has it a huge storm came in and took away all the men, drowned them all, the entire village widowed. In time the women all moved away, and the cove was abandoned. Now there are only a handful of houses.

Even with these signs of habitation, on dark and stormy days, when the sea is at its most fierce, this is a place that really does feel as if the world has deserted it.

Here on the harbour, as the tumbling waves and high winds batter the shoreline, my mind returns to a magnificent marina in the sunshine, a marina where impressive racing yachts and the occasional tall ship basked in the relentless semi-tropical North Queensland heat. Here in Cornwall, if they've had good luck, fishermen will unload their daily haul of crab and lobster directly onto the cobbles. Hardy, weathered fishermen, in yellow waterproofs and strong boots.

Over there we loaded up the boat with crates full of beer and groups of suntanned backpackers. There were smiling boat crews with sunglasses, shorts, and bare, deck-toughened feet.

Two such different landscapes, such different harbours. Two places of happiness, safety, and peace. Two places to sit and watch the water, to feel the breeze on my face. To feel alive.

Two different lifetimes.

Navigating the Traffic

I apologised to him for my outburst the other day. Told him he deserves an explanation for my tears and my frustration. And he does. After all these years he deserves to hear all of it. I told him I'm not ready, but soon. It will be soon. I am going to reply to the email. Ask the questions I have waited so many years to ask, and even though I'm fearful of the response I will finally have closure.

I drive to my post-op check. They are happy with my recovery. Everything is healing nicely.

The traffic is getting busier again, I notice. Visitors starting to return to the coastal areas as the rules are easing. I never liked rules, so I naturally adored countries that seemed to have none. Where the traffic was chaos. Combinations of bicycles, cars, motorbikes, vans, and buses, all battling on the roads. In some places tuk-tuks, cows, rickshaws, horses, dogs, and llamas.

My first taste of Vietnam was arriving in Hanoi. The air was full of fumes from hundreds of motorbikes. The place buzzing with the deafening sound of horns. A little like busy parts of Italy, only with far less swearing and gesticulating. The safest way to get around town was on the back of a motorbike-taxi, weaving effortlessly through the traffic. Being a pedestrian was far more daunting, watching the madness unfold from the safety of the pavement, but wanting to cross the road. We were told to stroll confidently through the mayhem, making no sudden movements. In that way, apparently, the traffic would flow right past us. To my amazement, this worked.

It is true of life when you think about it – we dodge decisions, making false starts. We stop and start, not trusting our instincts. We second-guess ourselves and we navigate badly most of the time. Perhaps if we moved forward with absolute confidence, with smooth steps, trouble would simply flow around us, and we would cross safely to the other side.

FEBRUARY 22ND, 2021

THE SINGLE LIFE

Back in my early thirties, when marriage and kids looked unlikely, I embraced adventure instead. I had a bucket list, before they had a name. A dream board as clear as day inside my head before Pinterest and Instagram came along. I promised myself I would travel as much as possible, and do all the things it would be so much harder to do if I became a parent. And so, when friends lived abroad or moved temporarily for work, I would make sure to visit them. Italy, Holland, New Zealand, and Geneva.

And of course, Australia where the Free Birds were based. Bernie and I, both resolutely single and not wanting to celebrate the millennium surrounded by couples, booked tickets to Sydney on the spur of the moment. To spend our New Year watching the fireworks fill the skies above the Sydney Opera House. We found a fabulous vantage point and camped out from early in the morning. Eskies full of beer and wine, and enough supplies to last all day and all night. The atmosphere was electric: there were so many people, superb music, stunning fireworks – a massive, massive party.

Afterwards, when the music and fireworks were over, thousands of people left the area en masse. Crossing the Harbour Bridge, Bernie went the wrong way, and we were separated. At some point, a guy found her looking confused and lost. He rescued her and offered her a bed for the night.

The phone lines were jammed, and Bernie couldn't get through to any of us on her mobile to reassure us she was in one piece. But she returned safe and sound the next morning.

The kindness of strangers.

'Darling, it was fine,' she told me. 'I could tell he wasn't an axe murderer. We took the bus, for goodness' sake. Axe-murderers don't take the bus.'

'Was he handsome? Did he try it on?' We were all keen to hear some gossip.

'Yes – extremely handsome. And sadly no – he didn't try anything on. The perfect gent. Gay probably, based on the stunning art all round his flat.

It is fitting that New York, the city that first gave me the travel bug, is one I have visited in all the seasons. Seasons of the year and seasons of my life. I have seen the sunshine of spring, summer, autumn, and winter hit my favourite building, the Chrysler Building. Watched the Art Deco arched terraces turn to blinding silver, the curves and triangular shapes sparkle in the daytime and light up at night. Sleek and stylish, nestled like a jewelled tiara in the middle of the skyline.

So many memories: Christmas lights on the houses on the drive in from JFK; cocktails in Grand Central Station; a strong rum in the warmth of a scruffy little bar in Little Italy; a wobbly rickshaw ride after too many glasses of fizz at brunch near Central Park. There are walks through the park to Strawberry Fields. Lunch at the Algonquin Hotel, where one of my literary idols, the legendary wit, Dorothy Parker, once sat. A lost afternoon of wine and cheese in the spring sunshine at the Lake House in Central Park. Walking in the snow past the Flatiron Building; crossing the Brooklyn Bridge on a crisp sunny winter's afternoon.

Bernie and I had booked a trip to New York City for the year 2001 going into 2002, with a couple of other girlfriends. Shopping, fancy cocktails, seeing the sites, boozy brunches near Central Park, and welcoming in a brand-new year in the 'City That Never Sleeps.' Then, three months before our trip, two planes crashed into the Twin Towers of the World Trade Center.

One of my favourite things to do in New York is the Brooklyn Bridge walk back towards Manhattan. I love its iconic shape. But this time we weren't keen to walk across, worried we might take a wrong turn and pass the site where the towers used to be. Bodies were still being excavated from the rubble; posters of the missing were still displayed across the city. It was so recent. So raw. The shock of that day still hung in the air. You could feel it on your skin.

Many years later, I visited the 9/11 memorial, a moving and powerful design. So sensitively done. The sheer size of the footprint of each tower, the cascades of water, the seemingly endless names of those lost carved into the metal, sun glinting across the surface, flowers laid next to names. Somehow the constantly flowing water and the relative silence in the middle of a usually chaotic city has created an eerie sense of enormity and peace.

February 24th, 2021

A Lonely Road

Break-ups are complex. Even when you are over someone, it can still be painful to see them settled years later. It can hurt to realise that someone else is able to give them something you were unable to give them. Happiness you could not provide.

Rhys got married. He always said he never would. It was a perfect storm, coinciding with my own string of dating disasters, more baby announcements and yet another wedding invite. Everything converged and my world imploded. At least, that is how it felt at the time. Someone so opposed to marriage changing their mind convinced me that it was never about marriage, it was about me.

It had to be.

When having a baby drifted ever further from my reality, I tried to fast forward even the most casual new relationships. Desperation seeped from me, sending unsuspecting men running for the hills. I started to feel quite unlike my normal self. I began to feel a special kind of inadequate. A particular blend of 'not good enough'.

The end of some of those nights out around that time stayed with me. Nights that began with fun and anticipation. Catching up with girlfriends, new outfit, big smile. Flirtations, numbers swapped, a liaison regretted the next day. Then sometimes, back home alone, a depressing song on the CD player, and tears.

Or nights in with single girlfriends, grown-up sleepovers. The early hours of the morning, surrounded by the debris of a wine-fuelled evening, the laughter a distant memory. All the fun replaced by maudlin conversations and the ill-advised opening of another bottle. Perhaps some dancing. Or more likely crying. Mascara-streaked cheeks. Lonely roads. Broken dreams.

It feels like a lifetime ago and seems over-dramatic now looking back. I picture it like a compilation of scenes from late-nineties romcoms, ending with Bridget Jones singing 'All By Myself,' alone in her flat on New Year's Day. Now I do so with a wry smile, but it was so painful at the time.

February 25th, 2021

Seasons in the Sun

The birds are singing a morning greeting: a comforting, reassuring blend of sounds that floats upwards from the garden, pulling me into consciousness. It doesn't take much these days, my mind is too busy, so I sleep fitfully. Another chilly dawn, hands clasped around my tea, as the light brightens, and the dewy mist lifts.

There was another online update from my old work colleague, Kathyrn. A prognosis of a few weeks at most. It throws my positive mood off track and lines from an old song form in my head. I haven't thought about it in years, yet is poignant today. That song played when I was a child, the sound of the radio drifting through the house. A haunting song. 'Seasons in the Sun.' I always assumed it was written by someone who was dying, that's how it sounds, but it turns out the singer lived to a good age, the lyrics inspired by someone else who didn't, someone who had to say goodbye too soon. A song that reflects on past days of joy. Days of fun.

Seasons in the Sun.

Hard seasons appear without warning. Life can be fine on the surface, but then events clash together and leave you in pieces. Feelings you thought were long buried, lying deep on the ocean bed, become disturbed, dislodged. They bubble their way up to the surface until they are floating in full view, spoiling the calm of the day, and leaving chaos in their wake.

I had hit such a rough period as a single thirtysomething and I needed to find some joy again. To let go of all the expectations I had put upon myself to find someone and settle down. I needed to meet new people and feel warmth on my face once more.

I needed a season in the sun.

THE TICKING CLOCK

Mine is a big family, so I thought I would have a big family of my own. My dad had ten cousins. My parents have seven grandchildren. I knew one of my great-grandmothers when I was very young. Her name was Matilda. She read me stories and held me when I was a few hours old. Another, I never met, but my mother tells me she had twenty-six pregnancies. Some were miscarriages, twins, possibly even triplets. Thirteen of them made it to adulthood. She named three babies named John, but each of them died. After the third one, she stopped calling babies John.

When my great-grandmothers had their children, there was so little choice. They did what was expected of women: married, produced children, looked after the house, and looked after the family. Men worked and provided for the family. But these days, motherhood is such an emotionally loaded subject. So many women cannot conceive, cannot keep a child safe inside them. Women who feel their bodies are failing them at the one fundamental thing they are designed to do. The agonies of multiple miscarriages, or round after round of IVF. Women who have starved themselves to fit in with the world's glorification of 'skinny' only to realise, much too late, the devastating harm they've inflicted on their reproductive systems, the damage to their life-sustaining organs.

I wanted to be a mother; I always did. You knew that. To tell you the truth, I just always blithely assumed that I would be one. Perhaps it was arrogant of me, but I remember thinking it wouldn't be a problem. Assumed it would happen naturally and with ease. I have always had that pull towards babies, towards children. I never pictured my life without them.

I think back to the days after I lost the baby. Since I was in the

UK anyway, I sought a second opinion. I received similar informa-tion to before. 'One of those things.' An unexplained occurrence. The doctor made statements much like the ones I remember from Nairobi hospital. He used different words, but the language was no less accusatory. Apparently, I 'failed to support this foetus,' but it happened early, therefore my cervix should still be 'competent'. His conclusion was that I was a statistic.

My baby was also a statistic. There was nothing to prevent me from conceiving again in the future.

As it turns out, the future can come around faster than we imagine.

Time sped forward and I assumed my fertility was declining at a similar rate. Before I knew it, my window of opportunity was shrinking. Relationships were becoming harder and harder to find, and the perfect picture containing a husband and a child became more elusive with each month that passed. As I moved through my thirties the pressure increased – both from a place deep, deep inside me and from those around me. A pressure sometimes spoken aloud, blatantly. A pressure at other times inferred by pitying looks or awkward silences. The shaking of heads; the 'poor you, not having a plus-one to take to the wedding' look; the invites to week-ends away with settled couples, invites I needed to find a way to decline with kindness.

Years and years earlier, aged thirteen, I remember sprinting up the stairs at the hospital to see my brand-new baby sister, Alanna. I almost knocked Finn out of the way as I went, determined to be the first one to see her. It was a point of principle to me. When Gareth was born fifteen months earlier, I was stuck in Wales when my grandad's car broke down. I didn't see him until he was ten days old. By then everyone else had already met him, which really upset me. My grandmother tried to cheer me up by plying me with gin and tonics, even though I was only eleven years old.

Fast forward to 1999 and my first little niece, Raven, had just been born. I held this delicate bundle in pure wonder, not wanting to let her go. I remember the deep ache and longing I felt after Gareth took her home. I surprised myself by bursting into tears, ferociously missing a tiny little person I had only just met.

Fast forward again to 2001, and I was meeting my second niece,

Alice, for the first time. She was Finn's first born. At ten months old, she had travelled from America to a family celebration. I was the only person who could always get her to sleep. She would snuggle into my shoulder, warm and cuddly, with the softest, finest blonde hair. Her chubby arms clung to me, night after night. I played with both of my nieces and sang to them. I watched them giggling together in a bath full of bubbles and felt a sense of total hollowness.

Soon after that, I booked another plane ticket and set off across the world once more.

Despite the march of time and the ticking of my biological clock, I put babies out of my mind and concentrated on satisfying my wanderlust. As the airmiles stacked up, the likelihood of my having even one baby dwindled year on year.

SOMEONE LIKE YOU

All these years I have hoped beyond hope we would be together again someday. It's foolish. After all, your letters stopped abruptly years ago. When I called the phone number I had for you, the line went dead. Someone began to return my letters one by one. Not known at this address. Return to sender.

It made no sense. The connection we had, the intensity of it all. Every word we said to one another, the promises we made. How could it all just stop?

I searched for you online once social media came along. People everywhere were reconnecting with long-lost friends. But it was no good. Nothing came of it. Perhaps your name was common? It always sounded unusual to me, I found several online, but none of them were you.

So, adventure continued to beckon, and I continued to follow. I visited so many places. Ticked things off that bucket list. Mountains, rivers, lakes, and dreamy sunsets. Beaches, rainforests, deserts, and moonlit skies.

February 26th, 2021

Lotus Flowers

Airport after airport. Departure lounge after departure lounge. Story after story. A time that turned into several years on the road. The years where I spread my wings once more. At first, short photo assignments, then month-long holidays; later, a sabbatical from the real world. The life I had long pictured for myself was dead. I was blossoming, coming out of the darkness and into the light. Re-imagining a new path, a new life, a new future. A butterfly burst from a cocoon.

One afternoon in Cambodia, I found myself in a silent garden, a place where just a few minutes earlier some Buddhist monks had been chanting, and I came upon some ponds filled with the most exquisite pink lotus flowers. The lotus is unique because its roots are fixed into the mud, and the flower submerges into the water at night, re-emerging to seek out the morning light. It can thrive in the most unlikely of places and will resurrect itself from the depths of the murky water looking clean and perfect, just as stunning as it was before it disappeared.

The monks began to file back into the central temple, the sounds of their trancelike chants filtering through the humid air. I realised I had been there for hours, sun beating down, incense burning, surrounded by peace and lotus flowers. Buddhists associate the lotus with purity, rebirth, and enlightenment. They believe that the mud where the flower grows represents suffering in the human world, and rising out of the mud shows strength and spiritual growth. Literal and figurative rebirth.

The day before I had seen evidence of the depths of suffering in our human world. Historical records and photographs of torture. Skulls of innocent people who'd been murdered. I had set out that day to fill my mind with ordinary life, to drink in the culture of this country and its gentle people. Strolling through street markets where smiling ladies in colourful clothing wearing floppy sun hats sold baskets of fruit. Stalls with unusual foodstuffs: bowls of frogs and eels, baskets piled high with fried snakes and cockroaches. Enormous lumps of meat hanging from metal hooks in the sunshine. Women sitting cross-legged, chopping up more meat on wooden chopping boards with huge knives that glinted in the sun. I bought postcards from cheeky, persuasive children on the side of the road. Then, hearing chanting, I stumbled across a pathway to an oasis of tranquillity in the middle of a busy city.

A secluded haven where the beauty of the present emerged shining from the murky waters of the past. Where a new version of me began to emerge and attract people who reminded me of you. Those irresistible dark-haired adventurers.

DIAMONDS ON THE INSIDE

Working on the racing yachts in Australia I met the Canadian snowboarder with the long ponytail. We drank Bundy Rum and Coke and danced to Ben Harper. Sat on the deck under the stars, having extraordinary conversations, deep into the night. Conversations about travel and adventure, love, and soulmates. We listened to musicians I had never heard of and had heart-to-hearts basking in the Whitsunday sunshine.

Now, on Instagram, I see photostreams of adrenaline-fuelled beauty, spread across the wilds of Canada. Photos taken around roaring fires at night on wild camping trips. GoPro footage flying along dangerous trails on a mountain bike and blazing through the Rockies, snowboarding. Images of that thick dark hair sparkling with droplets of snow, icy droplets that look like diamonds.

ROAD TRIPPIN'

Travelling through South America on a huge truck, I met the Kiwi farmer. Almost black eyes shone from under those thick black curls. Eyes full of 'devilment' as my grandad used to say. We drank whiskey made with ice that was hundreds of years old, from glaciers that will now be much smaller. Watched the sunrise from a tent, pitched at a wild campsite in the middle of the Torres Del Paine National Park in Chile. Nothing there, just wilderness. Breakfast cooking on the campfire. Someone handed me a cup of hot tea. The famous Torres Del Paine mountains were right in front of us, ice-topped peaks and three tall granite towers visible across a stretch of glistening emerald-green water. Yet more stunning scenery on a journey that had contained wonder after wonder. Shimmering salt flats. Volcanos. Orcas, penguins, seals. Extraordinary lakes of different colours, with lyrical Spanish names – Laguna Colorada, Laguna Verde. I thought back to a couple of days earlier when the two of us stood on a viewing platform at Perito Moreno Glacier. Enormous. Icy blue. After a deafening crack, a piece broke off and smashed into the freezing lake beneath – an ice wall so big the sound was thunderous.

At the end of the trip, we parted ways, keeping in touch online. But at that moment we sat silently, drinking it all in. Side by side. A picture I could not paint in words. The chatter and laughter and noises of the morning were still there, but I had zoned them out, noticing nothing apart from the crisp, clean air, the colours of the mountains. I was part way through three years of my life where I had no possessions aside from a backpack and a camera ... and I didn't need anything else.

REBEL REBEL

In Bali I met the Aussie poet. Adorned with tattoos of mandalas and powerful song lyrics, like a human canvas. Living art. Dark hair shaved short, torn T-shirts from rock tours. Unlike anyone I had ever met before, yet also a kindred spirit. A unique cocktail of fire, joy and passion with a laugh that could curl itself around my heart and a smile that lit up the room. We had profound conversations, funny conversations, conversations that went on forever. Took yoga classes by day and went night swimming under the stars, a Bowie playlist drifting from a nearby iPod.

Tough and fragile. A nurturer and a thrill-seeker. A fascinating blend of contradictions as all the best people are – after all, there is no depth to be found in something that is one-dimensional. We speak often. I see photos from places like Burning Man and poetry that explodes across my social media feeds, filled with fierce beauty and honest pain. Words that scream loudly and words that whisper to my soul.

Words that dance ... Words from the heart of a rebel.

February 28th, 2021

When Paths Cross

A nd then there was the American Climber. I have always believed that there are people we are supposed to meet – paths that we are supposed to walk down when the time is right. Like you and I, for example. Chance crossings that happen in life when you least expect them. Some of these are short-lived, they are great fun, they make marvellous stories to tell later. Others are so much deeper and more profound.

There are places I have only been once and there are others I have returned to again and again. New York, Australia, Bali, and Nepal are among those I go back to. So, a long, long time before visiting the blue teahouses with my husband, I was in Nepal on another trek. I was sitting on a section of rock in Namche Bazaar, in the heart of the Himalayas. It is known as the 'gateway to Everest': busy, friendly, and built around a central stupa with buddha eyes painted on each of its four sides. The skies were perfectly blue, I had been walking all day, and I was at peace, looking at the immensity of the mountains and writing in one of my travel notebooks.

A little ruddy-faced girl with black hair in two bunches and a cheeky smile stood staring at me, her head tilted to one side. Often the only thing children want from you is a smile, and sometimes pens to write with. I had lots in my bag just so I could hand them over when needed. As expected, she pointed at my pen. I handed it over with a smile, expecting her to laugh and run away, but instead she painstakingly wrote one word on the open page of my notebook, a word in elegant script that I could not understand. It was probably her name, but I like to think of it as a message of love.

I took her photos out of one of the boxes the other day. A photo of her writing, the corner of her tongue sticking out of her mouth in concentration. Another of her giggling, eyes shining, her skin looking freezing cold as she handed back the pen. The little piece of paper with her name on was still fixed to the back of the print.

After she disappeared and her giggles faded, a stillness and eerie silence descended on my peaceful spot on the mountainside. That unique, strange quiet that you get after it has snowed. When the world itself does not dare to breathe or whisper a sound. During the silence, clouds came from nowhere and rolled in over the mountains, completely obscuring them, as if they had never existed. It was time to let that magical moment go. It was time to go back to the warmth of the teahouse.

Another new teahouse that evening. They were all different, but some characteristics never changed: big fires, friendly chats, new people each time – people from all over the world – people all drawn to the irresistible magic of Nepal. As it turned out, meeting my little friend with the bunches, on the side of a chilly mountain, wasn't to be the deep and profound moment where two people's paths crossed in a distant land.

When I returned to the comfort of the raging fire with a drink of hot lemon to warm my cold hands, one of my trekking companions called over to me.

'Kerensa, come and meet these two gentlemen from America. They are going up Everest. Right to the top.'

A few days later, I sat peacefully at a ceremony at Tengboche, a Tibetan Buddhist monastery built for the Sherpa community, nestled high in the mountains on the way to Everest Base Camp. After listening to the hypnotic chanting, I relaxed in the sunshine, watching the children playing and the monks go about their day. A group of young Americans were setting off on their expedition to Everest. A lady blessed each of them in turn, placing a white prayer scarf around their necks. They all posed for a group photo outside of the monastery, a mixture of trepidation and excitement on their faces. I recalled a line from a climbing memoir. An observation on how easily a pre-expedition image can become someone's obituary photograph. Sunshine blazed down yet I shivered, eerily cold.

Later this felt like a premonition.

MARCH 5TH, 2021

THE SINGLE MAGPIE

I leave Cornwall for the first time in what feels like forever. I am staying with Mum for a few days while Dad visits his best friend. The same friend he played with on the Blitz-damaged parts of London. A friend who is now terminally ill.

Alanna and Gareth live close and help out all the time. But now it's my turn. Lockdown has increased my mother's anxiety. Once so strong, she now needs reassurance about the simplest things. It feels as though we have switched roles from when I was the help-less child. So I lift heavy things for her, remind her to take her pills. I try to get her to eat a bit more food. Take her tea in bed and cut her toast into squares. Tell her not to worry about things.

One afternoon she suffers from a huge panic attack. I hold her hand and I keep her talking to calm her.

'Thank you for looking after me,' she says softly.

'Don't be silly, after all the things you've done for me?' I reply, swallowing the lump in my throat.

'Oh, don't cry,' she says, 'don't cry.'

Just as she did when I lost my baby.

Just as she did after each heartbreak and every scuffed, bleeding knee.

Just as she did during our first long hug after lockdown. When I tried not to squeeze her much frailer shoulders too hard. When I hung on, in the same way I had as a child at bedtime, when I used to cuddle her goodnight and say, 'Gotcha, gotcha, never let you go.'

I've been going for a run each morning across the park. Past the little wooden train, down to the canal. In the evenings, missing Honey, I take a walk along the river, listening to podcasts or mellow playlists.

On this morning's run a single magpie sat on the bridge by the canal. Single magpies seem to be everywhere this week – each time I go for a run or a walk, drive to the shops or water the plants in the garden.

I remember the rhyme from when I was young.

One for sorrow, two for joy …

I keep searching for a second one. For a companion. For a sign. The magpies feel like an omen of sorts; a portent for times to come that can bring nothing but heartache.

MARCH 7TH, 2021

THE MAGIC OF THE HIMALAYAS

The truth is, I fall in love with people all the time. Especially people with passion, people who are fearless. People who go after the things that fascinate them in life. People who are following their dreams. So, at first, I thought perhaps it was just all in my mind. That the climber was just being friendly. That my overactive, romantic imagination was trying to create another story to tell my grandchildren one day.

But still … I remember sitting around the fire in the teahouse, listening to funny mountaineering stories. I remember us walking together along the trail, talking about so many things, putting the world to rights. Him asking me if I had a partner or husband (in a good way, in a 'I hope you don't' kind of way). I remember how easy it was to talk to him, to be honest about the past. I remember taking his photo as the sun beat down on us. We had stopped for tea, and he was leaning back in a chair, brushing a hand through his hair. Completely at ease with the world, at ease with his surroundings. He seemed so grounded and content, grinning across at me, never taking his eyes off mine, even through the lens. I remember him asking me to take a picture of him on one of those wobbly suspension bridges before he set off on his way, off up the trail, off to catch up with his teammates who were now further ahead.

Further ahead because he chose to stay and walk by my side. To keep me company for the entire day in the Himalayan sunshine.

My group was stopping for food and would carry on again shortly. We were all heading for the same teahouse that evening.

'Hopefully, I will see you later this afternoon?' I said as he took his camera back out of my hand.

He gave me that relaxed, self-assured smile again and said, 'You definitely will.'

Then he was off. I remember trying to ignore the nagging headache I had had all day, the band of gradually increasing pain across my forehead. As we sat waiting for food, I looked up to where the trail carried on. I could just see him, so tiny against the immense mountain backdrop. It reminded me how vulnerable we are in the face of nature's power; how small we are in comparison to all that will exist long after us. It reminded me that books about the Himalayas say that the mountains are in charge.

Altitude sickness meant I couldn't carry on any higher up that day. Our guide thought it best for me to stay where I was. Back in Kathmandu I sent the climber an email to explain. There were no mobiles, just internet cafés, but these disappeared further up the trail.

So, for a while I didn't expect to hear anything at all. It was possible I never would hear from him. But deep down, I know that something magical clicked on our long walk that day. A spark of something so unexpected that over the next days and weeks I daydreamed a little, and whenever he floated into my mind, I sensed the possibility of something new and adventurous in my future.

He reminded me of something I hadn't felt in a long time.

Hope.

March 8th, 2021

The Warmth of the Fireside

Arriving back in Cornwall, I felt exhausted. The long drive took it out of me. But those few days at home had made me treasure the people I love and the things I have. It felt special returning to my cottage. Returning to my little family.

Honey came bounding up to me as soon as I opened the door. My husband had offered to clear the loft whilst I was gone. All my boxes were placed to one side, untouched. He found so many of his old photos. Canada, Tanzania, Switzerland, Nepal. Places we had been together and separately.

We sat and cuddled by the fire, warming our toes. Reminiscing about days gone by.

Years after I first considered it, I finally filled in the Australian visa forms. A plan I'd been mulling over long before I knew I'd be trekking towards Everest. Janelle was heading home to New Zealand, via a long overland trip through Africa. It made me restless. It made me feel frustrated and unfulfilled, despite having a great job. I googled different routes and researched potential destinations. Now and again I would remember sitting by the fire in the teahouse with him. I would dream about handing in my notice and just taking off. I wondered if perhaps I might go to America. Or if he might come to the UK. At the time I didn't know if he'd received the email – the internet was so poor then in Nepal. I wasn't brave enough to send another in case I was making a fool of myself. I thought I would make contact later. Find him online somehow.

I worked out different itineraries. Heading to Australia via Vietnam and Cambodia, travelling overland through South America. Occasionally, I would look at the Everest news sites. See how the climbers were doing – looking for news of his American team. The weather window was open, and the climbers were going for the summit. I hadn't looked for a couple of weeks, my London life was busy …

And then, on that totally ordinary day in the office, there it was. The most dramatic reminder I could possibly have received that life, after all, is short.

Exposure, the report said. He'd suffered extreme exhaustion and just stopped walking. He sat down, unable to continue, and began to freeze. The Sherpas managed to get him to a lower camp. But he still died. Died before achieving his goal. Died before reaching the summit.

I wish it could have been different for him and I always will. That he, like so many others, could have lived to climb another mountain, another day. But that was not to be. Perhaps it was always going to happen, maybe in another place, on another continent? Because the truth is, the mountains will cast their spell, time and time again, upon those who love them. Those who are addicted to their power and their fatal beauty. Those who always return to the slopes and the summits, despite the deadly risks. Those who know all the dangers, but they go anyway. They follow their hearts and seek out their dreams.

But he was gone. And another door closed.

March 10th, 2021

The day after I heard that the climber had died, my Australian visa was approved. It is so strange to meet someone so full of life, someone so brave and inspiring, and then to discover that they no longer exist. Do you think it is permissible to grieve someone you barely know? To mourn the loss of a future that lived only in your imagination. A fragmented dream of a 'maybe'? There are no rules for that kind of grief.

I was reasonably hardened to tragedy by this time, and really, I hardly knew him, yet something seemed to break within me. There would be no visit to America now as I had conjured up in my mind, but equally I felt I had nothing to stay at home for either. In London there were many people that were important in my life, but at that point none of them could have convinced me to stay. And none of them tried. Sometimes you really do have to let people be free no matter how much you want to keep them close. My parents knew that. They'd been letting me go since I was seventeen.

So, I went. I travelled through country after country, collecting story after story.

I honestly feel that I am the most 'myself' when I am seeing and experiencing new places. When I am breathing different air. I somehow shed one of my outer skins. My connection to life is deeper; my soul feels as if it is where it is supposed to be.

One day, a long time later, I was wandering through the quirky shops of Byron Bay, when thoughts of the climber floated through my mind, as they occasionally did. And I met a psychic healer. She knew about him. She knew he was gone, that a door had closed. She said I had my own journey to follow and that I would find peace working with nature, being outside, work that was to do with the earth, perhaps with horses. That this was the path I should follow, the one always intended for me.

This won't sound insane to you, but it did to others. However, talking to random psychics, in a shop full of tarot cards and crystals, is the kind of thing a free spirit does in Byron Bay. It's a New Age paradise, like the Glastonbury of Australia, built next to a stunning beach rather than an ancient tor. A place watched over by a lighthouse on top of a rocky outcrop. I decided to follow her advice, as bizarre as it was. I put on my backpack once more.

Now, when I look back and piece things together, when I try to connect all those dots of mine, it seems as though thinking of him that day, in that shop, wasn't a coincidence after all. That chance conversation with a healer was the catalyst that made me abandon my plans to discuss a possible magazine job in Sydney and head north to Queensland instead. Deep down I knew returning to work in an office wasn't the right thing for me; it wasn't the reason I had journeyed to the other side of the world.

So I headed up the coast to a place where you could live and work with horses, right near the beach.

March 12th, 2021

T he two of us walk Honey along the cliff path hand in hand. The warmth of the sun on my face feels healing, removing any anxious thoughts from my mind. My husband spends most nights at the cottage now, only staying overnight at the farm occasionally. I still owe him the truth, but things are returning to a kind of normality.

———

My trip north to Queensland made me stumble across a job based in a different kind of nature – a different kind of wilderness.

The ocean.

I spent my time on the water. Working on racing yachts. Sailing around the Whitsunday Islands. Swimming and diving in the outer waters of the Great Barrier Reef. Existing in a paradise limbo of life.

So, in the end there were no horses or earth, but there were dolphins and sand, calm waters and raging storms. Laughter and friendship, crazy nights of parties and lazy days of peace. Rum and beer and heart-to-hearts with travelling nomads. Sundowners on the deck and perfect views of the Milky Way in the endless night. Weeks and months of freedom and lack of responsibility.

There were people who would brighten up our days and nights and then move on, just as suddenly as they'd arrived. The people in my life ebbed and flowed as surely as the tides. Some would end up staying forever, as dependable as seeing the Southern Cross on a clear night. I could return tomorrow, and they would still be there. Others are long gone – ticking off the next destination on the backpack trail or finding some roots and settling down somewhere else, somewhere out there in the world.

So, I never rode along the beach at sunset because when the coach I was on drove over the brow of a hill, the sea was laid out in front of me, boats moored up bobbing in the breeze, sun glistening over the water. I realised instantly that I had found somewhere I didn't want to leave. For two years this little slice of heaven was my endless summer. My break from reality. It was a time I was able to step off the world and not think of the future.

But the future had other plans because summer was over, a new dawn was glimmering on the horizon, and I had a reason to come home.

I had a new love to focus on.

And she hadn't been born yet.

FLYING THE NEST

My daughter catches up to us on the cliff path, hair flying, eyes sparkling. She had stopped to take a selfie. She is out of breath, laughing.

She is enjoying this gorgeous spring day, having spent most of the winter hibernating in her bedroom. Between typical teenage behaviour and endless Zoom classes it was almost as if she wasn't there. It made me feel lonely at times, but she needs her own space these days. Studying hard for GCSE exams, we still don't know if they will take place in the traditional way. Later, my husband takes Honey home and the two of us sit on the grass looking out to sea, she tells me fragments of gossip involving her school friends, sharing worries that are on her mind. We watch the birds swooping into the surf, then flying off into the distance.

You and I both flew so high, didn't we? We flew as soon as we possibly could, wasted no time finding our wings. This must be such a bittersweet moment for a parent. I am not sure it is possible to fully understand how our parents feel watching us fly the nest, until our own little birds find their wings. At least that is how I feel now.

When I was growing up, my siblings and I were surrounded by so much love. Love that was generous, supportive, dependable, and kind. Occasionally tough, but only when it needed to be. Love that was never in doubt, but there were four of us, so it was a big net to spread. Gareth and Alanna were still young, keeping my parents far busier than Finn and I ever kept them. I suppose I thought that if I left, it wouldn't matter too much, because there were still three other children. My parents still had some spares, although Finn left a couple of years later too.

But I didn't understand. I wasn't a parent yet, so I didn't understand that's not how parental love works. Of course, even when I was a parent much later, I only had my one, all-consuming love, for my one, all-consuming child.

I think I thought it would be easier, not having to split the love, but all it really means is that I don't have any spare children should she, like me, choose to spend her life running. Missing our children, or our parents, is the same as missing our friends ... there will always be a gap when one person goes, regardless of how many others there may be. The gaps where the people we love used to be are never filled. In time they simply become a little easier to walk around.

It's so ironic that my baby bird was the reason I stopped running in the end and I finally flew home.

PART THREE

FLOATING IN CALMER WATERS

March 14th, 2021

Ocean Dreaming

I still dream in blue. Aqua Blue. Blue like the ocean.

There are calm, dreamy waters, gently washing the shore. There is a stillness – smooth and serene – as far as the eye can see. Sometimes I am deep, deep within the water, gliding through it. Effortless. Moving like a sea creature. But mostly I am floating on the surface. Weightless. In harmony with the ocean, I blend into its surface. I'm looking upwards at a perfect sky, and I am at peace.

So often, I need to soothe the chatter of my mind, distract myself when overwhelm becomes too much. I attempt guided meditations, or a visualisation of some kind, and I always find myself standing or sitting on a perfect white sand beach, looking out to sea. Silence and tranquillity envelop me, they invade my soul, filling me with pure aquamarine-coloured light.

In all the dreams and visualisations, the gentle waters and dreamy shores are always those of far away, always those pristine and perfect beaches drenched in the colours of paradise. They are never the wild and windy seas of my home, with its craggy rocks and crashing tides. These visions are always about the possibility and not the reality, yet both are comforting to me in their own ways. The choppy waters of the past have mostly disappeared. But, occasionally they resurface, and battle for headspace with my fears about the future. Confuse my state of mind, put my soul out of balance and mess with the equilibrium of the day. When this happens, I need to bring myself back to a place of calm, to an atmosphere of quiet, so I sort through the memory banks of my life and find the places where I remember feeling total contentment. And instead of going back to them, I bring them forward. I bring them out of the past and into the present.

CHARTING A DIFFERENT COURSE

A random Monday morning in 2004 and a short red line appeared. A line that made the world tilt on its axis. Such a strange way to find out such unexpected and important news – at once so unassuming and yet so final. These days tests say *PREGNANT* in big letters so there is no ambiguity, but back then, it was just an innocuous little line. Only it wasn't innocuous at all.

It was miraculous.

The next chapter of the story, or more accurately the last chapter of one story and the first chapter of a new one.

Early morning and already the heat and stickiness of the day were overpowering. Intense humidity that made my already confused mind feel even fuzzier. My roommates were at work, out on the water. Alone in the apartment back on land, there was no one to tell. But I wasn't ready to tell anyone yet. It didn't seem real. I felt a strange mixture of complete surprise and gentle reassurance. The kind of reassurance I now recognise as trust. This baby was barely more than a collection of cells, but it filled an immense void. A void I used to fill with a different life, a nomadic life. A life where I never stayed in a place or a relationship long enough to think too much. Until I landed here in Queensland and knew it was somewhere I needed to stay.

I felt another feeling too, equally intense. Something like relief. Relief that finally there would be a little someone of my own to love. Yet even as I thought this, I knew of course that not all babies make it. That not all things were meant to be. But this time there was something that ran even deeper than that. A fear that the baby would be fine, the baby would survive and be healthy, but the baby would eventually leave anyway. I knew this because I was sitting on the other side of the world, far from my own family, in a different hemisphere, having spent my life running from something or to something. I knew that it wouldn't matter how much I loved this baby … the baby would grow up and find its own wings. Take flight. It might even go off to the other side of the world one day.

But for now, none of that mattered. For now, we would have one another. We would have time together.

Yes, I had the odd twinge of fear, even once the first three months had passed. Fear my body might let me down, that history might repeat itself. And yet, somehow, I had a distant, deep knowing that it would be okay. That the baby would be fine. Luckily, my intuition was right.

Much later I would wonder about fate, as I often do. About all the steps along the road that led to this surreal moment on a baking hot Queensland morning, when I had just found out I was going to be a mother. But, on that day, at that point in time, a short red line demanded a course correction. A line that existed between the past and the future.

Her father and I were heading in different directions, on different paths. We were both content to go our separate ways. Our relationship was fleeting, it wasn't serious. He was younger than I was, not even thinking about a settled life. I told him because he deserved to know, assured him I wanted nothing from him. I decided I would head home. Return to my roots and finally become a parent.

Some spiritual systems and cultures believe that souls choose to come to earth and live a human existence. That we choose our parents. I like to believe that my daughter chose me. She chose me and she came to heal my heart.

March 15th, 2021

'Here, have a cup of tea.' I set it down on the desk in my daughter's room, ruffle her hair, and kiss the top of her head.

'Thanks, Mum,' she replies. She is busy studying, surrounded by ring binders and books. Online lessons, endless hours of revising.

'Just checking you're still alive in here.'

She's barely left her room for months. Just coming out for snacks and dinner. Occasionally we watch a film together.

Did I tell you that my daughter's name is Kailani? It means 'sea and sky' in Hawaiian, though she prefers to be called Kai.

In truth, at the point in my life when I found out I was pregnant, I had given up on thoughts of commitment, of marriage, of starting a family and following a conventional life path. I heard the name years before, but I was too busy drifting around the world and so it was lost in the depths of my mind. It came back to me in the months just before the birth and seemed fitting, given my obsession with the ocean. The perfect name for my unexpected baby.

Kai took her time coming into the world, arriving when she was good and ready. I was the opposite. Born at home, I came hurtling enthusiastically into the world before the doctor had even reached the top of the stairs. A photograph was taken the day I was born, one of only a handful of me when I was tiny. Taken with a camera that was borrowed for the day, a black-and-white shot of my great-grandmother Matilda sitting in a rocking chair holding me. I am wrapped in a hand-crocheted shawl. My mother is on one side, her mother on the other. Four generations.

I was on my own with the baby, so my family rallied around. My mum held her before I did. The perfect birthing partner; calm and reassuring, with the experience of having had four babies herself. My dad brought things to the hospital, to help transport her home. I was told she would need a hat; I assumed it was for the journey home, so it was coming later with a blanket and the car seat. It turns out they put a hat on her straight after birth. I didn't know that. The midwife made a temporary one from a Tubigrip bandage with a little knot in the top. It was tight on her head and looked like it might cut off her circulation.

Later, when Kailani could talk, she would always point out things that made her laugh and she'd say, 'Look. It's funny, Mummy.' Always an observer of the lighter, more absurd things in life. Had she been able to see herself in that ridiculous hat, just minutes after being born, she'd have turned to me with a cheeky giggle and said, 'It's funny, Mummy.'

I had sold my studio flat, one I'd rented out while I travelled, and so I was temporarily back in my childhood home, about to put my baby to sleep in a special wooden crib. A crib my dad had lovingly made by hand twenty-six years earlier for Gareth. I remember watching him make it. Mum having another baby was such a surprise. Finn was in secondary school, and I was in my last year at junior school when Gareth arrived, followed by Alanna not too long afterwards. Both babies slept in the crib. A crib on rockers. A crib I had always hoped to use one day.

Before taking my own baby up to bed, we recreated the photograph. The same rocking chair. Me, my mum, and my baby. Three generations. Our family tree, constantly growing, with many more branches yet to come. Another photo that sits on the long wall in the hallway.

When it was time to go up, my hormones were through the roof. I found that I didn't want to put my little girl in the crib alone, I thought I should keep her with me. I wanted to hold her close and keep her safe. But, exhausted and desperate for sleep, I was scared that I would squash her. My mum said she would sleep in with us and she would hold the baby so I could be near her, then I could still get a good night's rest. So, on Kai's first night in the world her grandmother held her in her arms, in the space between the two of us, and I instantly fell into a deep sleep. In the morning, my whole body aching as if I had just been run over, I saw my mum fast asleep on the other side of the bed, but my baby was right next to me. She had found her way out of my mum's arms during the night, snuffled her way across the space in between, and snuggled into my side.

Kailani was attached to me like a limpet.

MARCH 16TH, 2021

HOLD MY LITTLE HAND

I remember letting go of your hand so clearly. Thinking I would hold it again soon. And here I am all these years later finally asking why the letters all came back unanswered. Why I couldn't find you each time I searched for you. I always doubted that I was enough, that anyone could love me. I drove people away, jumped before I was pushed. Or I gripped hold of them like a steel vice. I wonder if I drove you away.

I take a deep breath and click send on the email.

No one tells you that, one day, your child won't want to hold your hand anymore.

It is inevitable that they grow up and grow away from you. But knowing this and having it happen are such different things. One day they will just pull their hand away, they will run off without you and they will not always look back.

Kailani used to say, 'Mummy, hold my little hand,' as if she was acutely aware of her small size relative to that of the rest of the world. In the park she would take my hand in hers and insist we skip along. In the car, when I was driving and she was in her car seat, I would always reach behind me for her hand, and we would tickle each other's palms. It was our way of checking that the other one was still there.

We were so close, the two of us. A package deal. A good team. We were buddies. We still are. Occasionally, we will still tickle one another's hands in the car.

When she was first born, I would spend hours gazing at her, as I am sure all new parents do. As someone who is endlessly fascinated by the wonders of nature, it still strikes me as surreal that we can grow a tiny human from a seed.

Given I had always wanted a child someday, it came as a surprise that the situation I found myself in was not the one I had expected. I'd assumed I would find the perfect man and we would go on to have the perfect family. I suppose we all assume such things. Doing this alone wasn't in the picture I had formed in my mind. But that was how things had turned out. Life doesn't always go to plan, after all.

In the same way I have searched your name online over the years, I also looked for Kai's father from time to time. Scanned mutual friends on social media. Googled locations. In case she asked I suppose, but she never did. And I had no luck anyway, The truth is he was an intense brooding soul, so perhaps he never wanted to be found.

Many, many years have passed now since Kailani asked me to hold her little hand.

In my writing corner, I have a framed piece of paper on the wall. A poem from when she was at nursery. There is a handprint, where they put her hand into some bright red paint and pressed it down on the paper. The poem says it's a reminder of how tiny her hands once looked to 'make me smile one day'. It does make me smile. It always has. But, as ever, my eyes fill with tears.

The simple act of time passing by can be so emotionally intense when we look at a child. She is nearly seventeen now and yet I feel I have had her with me for so little time.

I sometimes wonder how much longer we will have …

GREAT SOUTHERN LAND

When Kai was three, before we moved to our cottage by the sea, I took her to see a different ocean. One that meant so much to me, the ocean that had inspired her name. The two of us flew to

Australia. I joked with my parents that travelling must be genetic. A thirty-one-hour trip where she was a perfect angel. No complaints or tears. Watching hour after hour of Disney films on her own little TV screen, listening via a miniature pair of headphones.

In Australia Kai held a baby crocodile, marvelled at a kangaroo, and cuddled a koala. Chased seagulls along a pier, giggling uncontrollably, and enjoyed nature walks near the beach. She collected a whole range of seashells and insisted on bringing them home, just as I used to do. She swam in a hotel pool with a jacuzzi that she called 'the funny bubbly pool.' Noticed the brightly coloured flowers and pointed at unusual birds. Through her eyes I remembered being the child who watched a procession of ants cross a dusty path, utterly mesmerised.

We spent a few days in the Whitsunday Islands, where she played in the lagoon I used to sit by; we walked to the shops I used to visit with no shoes on; we stood on the jetty observing the marina where I had loaded and unloaded the boat so many times. The days flew by too fast, and I had to prepare to leave that place again, a place I once planned to make my home. On the last day while she played on the sand, I sat and looked out to sea for what seemed like hours, tears constantly threatening to overflow. I let my mind wander back to a different time in my life, to the person I was then.

Then finally it was time for us to go. Another bus ride to another airport, a bus ride where it took all my strength not to cry once more … just as I cried when I took that exact journey once before, a few years earlier.

The last time I was carrying my surprise baby inside me. This time I was holding her little hand.

.

March 17th, 2021

True North

For many thousands of years, navigators didn't have tools; they navigated with the sun and the moon and the stars. Especially the North Star. But when there is too much cloud, you can't navigate with the stars. You can't see your true north.

I am a positive and optimistic person most of the time, but in the last few years I feel as if my guidance systems have been off. My true north has been challenged. I know that the world doesn't always make sense, but it was getting cloudier. I finally found a new therapist who seems to understand me, who is helping me to navigate my damaging thoughts. Find my way back to my husband.

Shooting Stars

Kai used to tell people that, 'the sun goes to sleep behind the post office'. And indeed, in our little French village that is where the sun sets. The last couple of hours of sun are often the hottest of the day, when we sit sipping gin and tonic, as the final rays cover the courtyard in golden light. My dad used to lift her up in his arms, point at the building across the road, and tell her that is where the sun 'goes to bed'.

So many of Kailani's childhood summers were spent in France.

She would listen excitedly for the sound of a honking horn in the morning, the signal that the bread van was driving into the church square. Holding her grandad's hand, she skipped into the square, helping to collect the fresh baguettes and croissants.

Market days always meant fresh seafood and juicy Charentais melons, and stopping for a cup of coffee in the town square. In the evenings we walked or cycled around the village and out past the sunflower fields. Sometimes we collected sloes to make sloe gin, or mirabelles from the neighbour's tree to make fruit tarts. Kai loved to forage for blackberries and help her grandma weed the garden. She followed her around in a little sun hat, carrying a tiny watering can. She learnt to ride her bike in the church square.

Nowadays Kai and I have a tradition of always going for a bike ride on the last evening before coming back to England. The last time we visited she still wanted to go, despite being a teenager. Cycling along the quiet village roads in the warmth of a summer evening. Just the two of us. Just as it was at the start.

This evening I booked tickets for France in the summer. It seems so long since we were last there. I am so content in France, my home from home. A place we try, whenever possible, to surround my parents with all their grandchildren at the same time. A place we watch the sun go down and the stars come out. We speed through our lives so quickly, things feel frenetic. Sitting and watching day turn into night, doing nothing in particular, is a rare treat.

The night skies are incredibly clear, with enough distance from the nearest town to have hardly any pollution. The evening is warm and balmy once the sun sets. We sit out all night and barely feel a chill. When Gareth and Alanna were children, the four of us would lie out on sunbeds in the courtyard for hours, hoping to catch sight of the shooting stars rocketing across the sky.

Sometimes we still do.

MARCH 20TH, 2021

I t is the first day of spring. My magnolia tree has bloomed early. Soon the flowers will begin to fall, which means renewal is on its way. Normally, I feel peaceful when I look at it, I cherish this time of year when the blossom starts to appear on the trees. Spring flowers make me feel hopeful, even on bad days when my thoughts are dark and draining.

But this morning I finally got my answer. After all these years I know the truth about you. The truth about why the two of us could not be together. A long, intense, and detailed message. Even a couple of newspaper articles.

I took the truth out along the cliff path. I walked alone for a long, long time. And I screamed into the wind.

Part of me always knew, I think. But it seems fitting to get this message today, as the cherry blossoms are beginning to flower. As a new season begins.

———

When Kailani was five years old, and the cherry blossoms flowered another season began. It was time for another change for the two of us.

One day those blossoms were tiny buds; the next they were in full bloom, a soft pink, making me smile as I looked at them. I have a photo of Kai, lying on the grass surrounded by petals. She was laughing with a school friend she adored. I had yet to tell her we were moving away, that she would need to leave her friends behind and make new ones. Blossom reminds me of new beginnings, of change, of renewal. It reminds me of looking at different horizons and experiencing a feeling of hope mixed with uncertainty. And it reminds of the giggles of two little girls who were once each other's whole world.

And now it will remind me of you. Of knowing the whole story.

MARCH 21st, 2021

THE ART OF BALANCE

My head is killing me. After yesterday I was drained emotionally. I couldn't sleep at all. My husband is banging around in the hall. Putting a picture onto the wall. The thumping is getting deep into my head. I am about to yell at him, but Kai beats me to it.

'Oh my god. You are so loud. I'm trying to revise.' A muffled shout from an untidy teenage bedroom.

'I'm nearly finished.'

He stands back and looks at the framed photograph of Kilimanjaro on the wall. It's a stunning image. He's skilled with a camera himself. Searching through all the boxes these last weeks, he's found all kinds of old memories. Safari photos from Tanzania, photos from Stone Town, Zanzibar. His old slingshot. Images from Nepal: prayer flags and a Tibetan singing bowl. Pictures he never unpacked up until now, pictures he didn't place around the house. I'm not sure why. But now he starts to put a few up in different places. A balance between my pictures and his. Interlocking paths.

When Kailani was young, she went to France with her grandparents, and I took my husband to Nepal. His first visit. The driver smashed in and out of potholes, weaved between buses and vans, veered all over the road to avoid bikes, people, and mangy-looking dogs. Nepal has similarities to Zanzibar, to Bali, to other places too. Yet each one is unique. We pointed things out to one another at roadside stalls, shouting comments over the blare of the car horns. The sounds, the smells, the atmosphere felt so familiar. My senses tingled and waves of nervous anticipation built.

On my first ever visit to Nepal I was amazed at the sheer weight a porter could carry. Seeing them with immense baskets on their backs, held on with a strap round their forehead, and piled high with trekkers' rucksacks, or bags of climbing equipment heading up to base camp, was incredible. It was hard to believe some of these men, so slight in stature, could support that much weight, let alone move so easily. They made it look as if the load weighed nothing at all.

That's the way I always felt when I travelled. As if there was no weight on my shoulders. No baggage from my life. Complete freedom.

I needed that balance again. Between the parent I had become and the person I used to be.

So many different things had happened in Nepal, a place where anything is possible. We ate dinner cross-legged on the floor in an intimate restaurant, candles on the tables and huge glasses of Everest beer. We collapsed into our simple hotel room, exhausted from the flight. That feeling of being almost too tired to fall asleep started to take over, not helped by the cacophony in the street outside – music, shouting, car horns and motorbikes. Dogs howled late into the night. Things eventually quietened down and I was just about falling asleep when the cockerels started up, then the call to prayer began at a nearby mosque.

'Yeah, because that's what we were missing, a bit of singing ...' came a voice from the other side of the bed.

We took a rickety seven-hour bus ride to Pokhara. A place where the colours of Phewa Lake and its surrounding mountains changed from blue, to grey, then pinks and purples. Colourful wooden boats floated on the lake. A lake that, in some seasons, has the surrounding mountain peaks and the whole of the sky reflected across it.

In the Annapurna Sanctuary, in addition to the blue teahouses, there were piled up rocks along many of the pathways. They are markers for hiking trails, there to guide travellers along the right path. But they have deeper meanings too. They are all about balance. Sometimes they mark sacred spaces. The physical act of stacking the stones is thought to be about patience and worship. About asking for good fortune or wishing good fortune for others. Building them is a meditative exercise. Seeing a stack of these stones along a track or near the water's edge has a kind of calm associated with it.

Sculptures created with stones. Nature and art, seamlessly blended.

Nepal, as ever, provides me with the whole spectrum of feelings. Beauty and sadness, permanence and impermanence. New memories of a special country and unforgettable old ones, mixing and blending forever.

MARCH 22ND, 2021

MEMORY BOXES

I'm surrounded by piles of printed photos and old hard disks. Chaos across the lounge.

'What are you doing, Mother?' Kai emerges from her room to forage for snacks.

'I'm looking for some old photos. Photos of someone from a long time ago. And don't call me Mother,' I say to counteract the wobble in my voice. 'You know I hate it.'

'It's such a mess. You are a nightmare. I liked it when Alanna was here, the house was tidy all time. Why aren't you more like her?'

'What's that darling?' I say, not listening. 'Everything's all over the place. Prints, albums, stuff on the laptop. Stuff on the phone. Hard disks. Utter chaos.'

'Whatever.'

When I next glance up from what I am doing she is no longer there.

Later, he returns from the farm. He too is irritated by the mess, but for once he doesn't get angry. He knows something is wrong. That something has happened to upset me. I never was any good at hiding my emotions.

'What's the matter? What happened yesterday? We were doing so much better.'

'It's complicated … it's … to do with someone. Someone from a long time ago.'

'Someone else? What are you saying exactly, is there someone else? Is that the problem?'

'No, nothing like that. It's in the past, it's just made me think about everything. About what I want.'

'Honestly, you always seem to be looking for something else, something better. But I love our life, I love what we have. It feels comfortable to me, but it's as if it's strangling you.'

'No. I just—'

'You know, when we first got back together you were all over the place – pushing me away, not sure what you wanted. I thought we were past all that. And now when we are finally getting somewhere with the therapist—'

'We are. She helps. I don't know. I've spent so long moving. Standing still scares me.'

'What's wrong with standing still for a while? You always want something new. But I can't offer you anything new, I can only offer you what we have.'

Frustrated, he leaves for a few days at the farm. Says I need to decide once and for all what I want. He's right, he's being fair. I'm the one who isn't being fair. But I can't think about that. It's too much. I try to distract myself sorting through the other boxes.

I can't think about him right now. And I can't think about you.

SANTORINI SUNSETS

I'm sipping ice-cold white wine in a bar at sunset, watching the sky change colour over the Caldera. Domes of deep blue, bright white buildings with private infinity pools. A calm expanse of azure sea. A million shades of blue.

And a photo of Bernie, laughing raucously, her hand stopping the wine from running down her chin. I place it on the pile.

INFINITY POOLS

A giant infinity pool in the middle of a jungle. Tall trees and clouds reflected in the pool as the water runs over the edge, never stopping. A continuous circle of motion. Gentle yet relentless. Much like life. Loving people is so much better than not loving people, but so much harder to handle. We cannot keep them close. Keep them safe. Ensure that we can have forever.

Tropical plants, humid air thick with water droplets. Fresh fruit on platters and sumptuous cocktails. Bali. Paradise.

A photo of Kai. An open-sided hut, cross-legged at a table, surrounded by still ponds of lilies. The sun was setting behind the rice paddies as she closed her eyes, breathing in the smell of the rain. I place the photo on the pile.

Later that evening, the three of us sat out on the porch, listening to the sounds of the insects. There were candles and hurricane lamps. I woke at dawn each day, relishing the sounds of nature and the blissful solitude of the early morning. Our own little infinity pool mesmerised me with its comforting sounds. The pure water recycling endlessly into its depths. Tumbling down, over and over. Forceful, life-giving, essential.

Infinity.

If only there was a way to spend it with the people we love most.

CHARENTAIS SKIES

France, my husband's birthday. A group of friends sitting under ink-blue, cloudless skies. The sunflowers are out, the entire village edged on all sides by sprawling fields of gold.

Champagne for brunch, barbecued tuna steaks from the market with huge bowls of salad. One evening I click the shutter as Cara and Nadia share a joke. They dip crusty French bread in bowls of moules marinière, heads thrown back in merriment, as the last of the sun's rays disappear.

A week of peace and ease under skies that are Charentais blue and another image I place on my pile.

March 24th, 2021

Circles of Rebirth

In my little corner of England, the Covid rules are easing again. They say it will be the last time, but no one knows for sure. We are currently at a place in between the old world we have lost and the new one we are attempting to navigate. Between our old lives and our new ones. Between winter and spring.

I am between worlds too. Between a world that involves you and a world where I must resolve things with my husband.

It should be much warmer now and on some days it is. But today was a day that had both the warmth of spring in the sun's rays and the slight chill of winter in the breeze.

The world is trying to be reborn, but these winter-like days keep returning. Like the waves of the pandemic, they creep back in, silently and insidiously, blighting our hopes of a kinder tomorrow.

I am back to my old self, physically at least. So today I ran slowly up the hill path and through the fields on top of the cliffs. I ran inland, away from the coastal path and through grass peppered with the beginnings of colourful wildflowers. I ran with the sun on my face and the wind in my hair.

I have still not managed to book a hair appointment so my hair is the longest it has been since I was a teenager. It allows me to time travel backwards. A comfort on the days when the face of the woman reflected in the mirror does the exact opposite.

I no longer tie my hair back when I run. I find I need that special sense of aliveness you can only feel from a strong breeze.

On my way back through the village I passed an old man, hunched over two sticks, walking slowly but with dogged determination. Trying, for even a short time, to manage without the support of his nearby wheelchair. We smiled at one another, there was a connection. A sense of knowing that we were doing the same thing. Though a few decades separated us, we were both trying to reach out and touch something that made us feel alive. We were both trying to be reborn.

And so today, in the beauty of the countryside, I stood in between.

Between the light and the shadow.

Between the past and the future.

Between the dancing sunlight of the spring and the black claws of the winter.

And I waited for the circle to turn.

STONE CIRCLES

I wake abruptly. The image of a Celtic circle in my mind, tears on my cheeks that must have started in my sleep.

I have always been drawn to circles. The sense of calm and symmetry to them that draws me in. I love the beach art that is made up of ever decreasing circles of pebbles. Painstaking works of art that exist only temporarily and are washed away by the sea. The water enveloping the beach and removing the beauty that had been created there. I am fascinated by the fact that stone circles exist. The book where my mum found my name is a story of a Cornish stone circle. Six novices who broke their vows and were turned to stone. Some see these merely as rocks in the ground, but others believe these are six young women, punished for eternity, frozen in a dance.

Like so much else, it all depends on how you see the world. If you believe in mysticism and spiritual magic. Most people agree the positions of the stones are related to the movements of the sun and the moon and their relative position to earth.

The stones, the sun, the moon, the earth. All these things are circular.

MARCH 27TH, 2021

WHEN LIGHTER EVENINGS ARE COMING

O ne of my favourite times of year occurs when I am out walking in winter, and I notice that it's almost five o'clock and it's not dark yet. It invigorates me to realise that the spring is creeping ever closer.

When I lived near the equator, the change from day to night was so fast, almost as if someone had suddenly switched off all the lights. I find a photo of me at the 'you are now on the equator' sign. Here you can literally jump from one hemisphere to another, or you can straddle an imaginary line through the middle of the world, one foot on either side. The world is a miraculous place: a place where you can stand, simultaneously, on both sides at once.

Tomorrow we will change the clocks and watch the days get longer. Lightness will start to brighten my world once more – I will let go of darker days and try to move on.

Kai wanted to see some pictures of Croatia this evening. It was a welcome distraction from thoughts of you. We went backpacking and island-hopping when she was thirteen. Kayaking around the city walls of Dubrovnik at sunset, swimming in caves, and snorkelling in clear turquoise water. Jet skiing. River canyoning – freezing cold, even in wetsuits. Rock jumping and sliding through rapids on our backs. The young Croatian adventure guides were messing about and daring the youngsters to do the big rock jumps. Nervously, I watched Kailani climb the rocks. I wanted to keep her close, keep her safe, but she rushed ahead of us, and I just had to let her go.

I had missed the thrill of adventures. Of wondering if things would work out or go wrong. I find that much as I need peace and calm, I cannot thrive in constantly calm waters. I need a powerful storm to sweep through occasionally, for the winds to rage and the water to become choppy and dangerous.

For a long time, holidays had been more family friendly. They'd been about building sandcastles and staying in places with a kid's pool. When my husband first moved in with us, we went to The Eden project. It poured down with torrential rain. We made a den and sat inside, drinking hot chocolate. Kai and my husband chased one another on the beach at Salcombe with beards made from seaweed. We had cream teas and sat watching the boats in the harbour at sunset. A glass of wine and the slight chill of a British summer evening once the sun had gone down.

Kai was now old enough to do the things I'd been missing. To take part in the adventurous holidays with me. Still, I missed that little girl who wanted me to braid her hair before she jumped in the water. The child who left me notes saying, 'I love you Mummy' round the house. The toddler who made me buy her jelly shoes that squeaked all the way to the beach. The three-year-old who spotted a strange rubber toy in a shop, like a squishy caterpillar. We walked along the seafront holding hands and with her other hand, she swung it in circles with one of its stretchy legs. I try to store all these memories up in my mind, but there are days when I feel them pulling away from me, when they seem to blur.

My memories of you are starting to blur too.

MARCH 28TH, 2021

For as long as I can remember, I haven't worn a watch. I always know the approximate time. When I was young, I loved those sand-filled hourglasses. I loved to watch all the grains slide from one half into the other, measuring the flow of time. It always seemed like it was speeding up towards the end.

This is how life feels now. Life is speeding up and the sand is running through much faster.

Age causes this to happen I suppose, but becoming a parent makes it more visible. We even like to pretend our parents are not ageing either. But that change becomes visible too, perhaps even more so. Each time I visit mine they seem a little frailer, a little smaller. We like to think that old age with its inescapable conclusion is still far away, but we all know it is drawing ever closer. What can we do but keep enjoying the motion of the waves, the sparkle of the sunlight on the water, the freedom of the breeze, and the feel of possibility.

However much I try to escape, to chase those possibilities I sense in the air, I cannot pretend that I am not watching my daughter age. My precious gift of a child went from being a squidgy, giggly baby with long flowing blonde hair, who always had her arms around my neck, to being a strong-minded, funny young woman whose hair has darkened year on year. And it happened in the blink of an eye.

And so over the years I have taken photograph after photograph of her, almost as if I will never have enough photographs of her. These pictures are not just memories; they are an attempt to freeze her in one place, to stop time from running so quickly through the hourglass.

SNAPSHOTS IN MY MIND

We are curled on the settee sleeping together. She is snuggled right next to me, like a precious hot water bottle. Only a few days old, then before I know it, a few weeks old. Time to treasure, just the two of us.

We are playing together in a swimming pool. Even though she has armbands on she doesn't want to let go. So we are jumping out of the water and back in again, she has her arms around my neck, clinging on and giggling.

We are sitting on the little wooden train in the park. She is so excited, her face full of wonder. She laughs as we set off around the track. She looks worried when my eyes fill with tears. She holds my hand and says, 'It's okay, Mummy, it's not scary.'

We are in the kitchen. I am making dinner; she is wearing a school uniform even though she seems far too tiny for one. The school years have arrived much too fast. She is drawing a picture of a sausage with a happy face – she's laughing, she loves sausages.

We are in the church square. I am sitting on a wall reading a book, she is cycling round the square. She shouts, 'Mummy, look at me' to get my attention. Afterwards she potters around picking up bits of bark. She tells me not to look and uses the bark to write 'I love you' on the wall. When it's finished, she lets me look and gives me a kiss.

We are at home. She is stair-surfing in a fluffy onesie – over and over – she thinks it's hilarious. We read a book together on the sofa under a snuggly blanket and have a tickling match, her head thrown back in fits of infectious giggles.

We are meeting our puppy Honey for the first time. Kai's whole childhood has been filled with cuddly dogs; she would always find new ones she couldn't live without. A bedroom full of fluffy toy dogs. Now she has a real one. A real one that looks like a fluffy toy. She holds the puppy in wonder – looking like she is about to cry.

We are at the beach. It's not a specific beach, but many different beaches. Blending. Beach after beach, spread across the years. Years that have passed in the blink of an eye. She jumps in the sea, swallows some water, and comes up half coughing, half laughing. The sound carries on the breeze.

Now she is jumping through the waves, laughing ...

I am jumping through the waves laughing ...

I am coming back from a day at the beach, feet covered in cuts from the pebbles and rock pools. Finn and I have dinner with our grandparents. The two little ones are already in bed, and I fall asleep on the sofa, in front of the fire, exhausted from the sun and the sea.

I am sitting on a settee. I have Gareth snuggled one side, Alanna the other. I am reading them a story. We get to the end, and they want to hear it all over again.

I am in a small boat on a lake. My brother and dad have fishing rods, Finn catches a huge fish, and we bring it back with us, flapping about in the bottom of the boat. He wants to show it to Mum when we get back. He's so proud he caught it.

I am toasting bread on a long skewer in front of the fire in the lounge. I have it for tea with a mug of hot chocolate and we all watch a Sunday night TV programme together. We are excited; the programmes are in colour now, not black and white like they were last week.

I am jumping from stone to stone across a river in a wooded glade. The sun is glinting through the trees. It's magical. My mum says I am sure-footed, like a mountain goat. She looks a little worried as I go running on ahead, totally fearless. She calls out to me to be careful and looks as if she wants to grab my hand to ensure I don't fall. But she lets me go.

I am being lifted into a huge tree in the woods behind our house. My dad almost throws me up there with his big arms, as if I am weightless. Then I walk along the big branch holding onto his hand for a few steps before letting go, because I can do it by myself, even though it's high up.

271

We go for a walk: me, my dad, and Finn. We kick up leaves and we make a den. We are outside for hours, then when we get home, it looks like Mum has been busy and the house smells of cake baking.

I am building sandcastles and swimming in the freezing sea; my brother is there too. For now, there are only the two of us. We assume it will always be that way, but a few years later when we do this, there will be a little brother and a baby sister in the picture. They will be running and laughing in the sunshine with us.

We are in our new house, it's exciting. We go to the park next door. It has a river and canal. I pick some flowers for my new flower press. There is a little wooden train in the park. It has a proper engine, and it goes around a track like a real train. Excited, I drag my mum over to it. I am desperate to have a ride on it. She smiles and we both get on board.

Now I have my arms around my mum's neck. I am holding on tight – it's bedtime, the story she was reading to me is finished – but I won't let go …

MARCH 29TH, 2021

THE PASSING OF THE SEASONS

Alanna called last night. Mum was taken to hospital; she had a high temperature. She was incoherent and almost fainted going to the bathroom.

Initially they feared it might be Covid, but it turned out to be an infection. We were all relieved, but it gave us a fright. Reminded us that life is fragile. Time is moving quickly, and the seasons are changing.

'She's fine,' Alanna reassures me. 'On antibiotics now. The nurses were all brilliant. They let Dad go in with her.'

'I feel so far away when things like this happen,' I reply.

'I know, but honestly, she's home now and she's fine.'

THE WARMTH OF TROPICAL RAIN

The images from different countries are building up now. The way the exhibition will look is much clearer. I select certain pictures from the boxes. A young girl in Bali, carrying a box of colourful paper fans on her head, her eyes locked onto the lens, a gentle smile. That trip broke something in me. It felt like a release from somewhere deep inside. I couldn't figure out the cause. A reminder of more carefree days, perhaps. Days of travelling, relaxing, of looking out over palm trees towards tropical sunsets.

Perhaps it was the sounds and scents of a place that felt intensely familiar. Different countries have different fragrances to them – almost like their signature scent. In Bali this is the scent of rain-drenched tropical flowers. It is the smell of incense. Small curls of exquisite, aromatic smoke rising from the offerings that people place across the island.

My home country, of course, is famed for its rain, grey rain. Rain that often feels unremitting and endless. That always amused you, coming as you did from somewhere bathed in so much sunshine. Warm tropical rain feels so different to our own rain, but it is all still rain. It is all just water being released from the clouds. It should all feel the same, yet it doesn't. Warm rain feels joyful. It makes you want to throw off your clothes and dance naked. To twirl in the sudden downpour, in a tropical garden filled with exotic plants and a bath decorated with rose petals ...

Sometimes in life, nature herself, through a simple act will lift a weight off your shoulders.

DOLPHINS

Years ago, I visited Janelle and we swam with dolphins in the cold and choppy sea off the coast of New Zealand. Complex creatures, who balance their animalistic nature with their emotional intelligence. Highly trusting of their instincts, they live peacefully with many other species, including us humans.

As symbols or spirit animals, dolphins have many meanings attached to them. They represent peace and harmony, inner strength, cooperation and joy. Ancient seafarers saw dolphins as a sign of protection, and a reassurance that land was close by. The Greeks believed they carried the spirits of the dead into the next reality. For other cultures they symbolised rebirth, reincarnation, and renewal. In my mind they symbolise both freedom and joy. They are strong and carefree, playful, and smiling – human characteristics. I select a photo of Janelle. Usually carefree and playful too, this was a moment where I caught her off-guard. A moment of reflection by a campfire, her face illuminated by the flames in the black of night.

In another memory, I am standing on the bow of the boat, and we are sailing fast across the turquoise waters. It's baking hot, the skies are clear, and the speed is covering us in a constant salty spray. Music, chatter, passengers sitting along the side of the boat, legs dangling, laughter lost in the sound of the swell.

We have just spent a few hours moored up at Whitehaven Beach for lunch. People go ashore to swim and sunbathe. It's beyond idyllic. The perfect clear water, the pristine white sand. Before lunch we dropped people at Hill Inlet, and they walked up to a viewpoint that looks right across the bay towards Whitehaven. When the tide gets a little lower, bands of the white sands appear, and they swirl in flowing shapes through the turquoise of the water.

As we move through the water we are joined by a pod of dolphins. They surf the bow of the boat, their sleek bodies gliding into the waves. Nature writes its own lines of poetry across the surface of the water.

The Sound of the Sea

2019. On the sands of Bingin Beach. We have been back together for ten years now, he and I. Something I never pictured.

We take a trip to Bali to celebrate. Kai is almost fifteen. Spending her days swimming in mesmerising infinity pools at stylish beach clubs and throwing herself into the ocean. The sea water comes right up to the base of the building and cuts us off from the rest of the beach at certain times of day. The sounds of the waves fill our nights, crashing onto the beach and lapping up against the wooden stilts of the building lulling us to sleep. It reminds me of when I used to sleep on the boat. I was doing this long before I was pregnant and then I continued all through the first trimester, until it was safe to fly home.

Kai is asleep on a beanbag on the deck. Her face softens when she sleeps and she resembles her baby self. Soon she will go away with friends, start her own adventures, spread her own wings. The sea air comes in through the doors from the balcony, the room smells of incense where we've had it burning earlier in the evening, and I sleep soundly at night, listening to the melodies of the ocean.

We drift down to one of the little cafés on the beach for breakfast: purple dragon fruit smoothie bowls and fresh pineapple. We pass two people meditating peacefully on a rock and surfers heading back in from a busy morning on the waves.

In the evenings we sit at tables in the sand at the water's edge with no shoes on. Fresh fish cooking on barbecues, straight from the sea to our plates. The smell of the salt water blends with the barbecue smoke, the cooked fish, and the incense floating down from the bar above.

The sound of the sea is hypnotising in its own way, but there is also music coming from another place along the beach. Some youngsters are dancing freely on the sand, spinning, and laughing under the clear star-filled skies ... just as I did in another life.

March 31st, 2021

Tales Around the Firepit

Kai was five years old when my husband came back into my life. So much was different. He had changed. I had changed. Despite how things ended, despite the years between. We had an unshakable bond. The past didn't matter. We had both had relationships that hadn't worked out. He was divorced and I'd had a child in the meantime. We knew each other so well because of the past, and yet ... we were entirely different people now.

Sometimes when we've been hurt, we think we have used up our allocation of love. But it's not true. The truth is, if we allow ourselves to trust, then we mellow over time. We expand to allow more love into our hearts. Inevitably, it will be different love but love all the same.

One weekend not long after I had moved, Kai went to stay with her grandparents, giving me a whole week alone. Walking by the water, relaxing in the garden. Glass of wine at a beach restaurant. Leisurely lunch for one. Days curled up, reading books on the sofa. At the end of the week, just before collecting her, I went to a weekend house party, a fortieth birthday celebration, with some old friends.

And there he was.

Manning the firepit, keeping people's drinks topped up, talking about mountain climbing, and dishing out big, warm hugs. It was so unexpected.

During the weekend there were flashes of missing my little girl and yet I adored the freedom of not worrying where she was. If she needed food, if it was time for her to go to bed. Most of all I loved sleeping in, having a lazy morning, still in pyjamas, sitting on sofas drinking tea, and slowly starting the day. A day containing no parental responsibilities. Another day of laughter, wine, and firepits. Of people telling stories to entertain one another.

Our sense of humour was still so similar. And he had lots of new stories – stories I didn't know from the intervening years. Adventures, drinking antics, and trips to distant mountain ranges. He entertained the crowd and his green eyes danced.

I remembered how he was a wild adventure and a safe harbour. Someone who would both protect me and let me go. Keep the nest warm but allow me to fly.

So unexpectedly, we had another beginning ... a beginning around a firepit. A tentative beginning. We'd been down this road before, so part of me was nervous, but it was time for a change. After all, the only unchanging things in life are the constants of nature's seasons and the relentless passage of time.

But now that I had a young child, the stakes were higher. I needed to think of her, not just myself, so we took it slowly. Self-protection kicked in, the seeds of doubt, and we both held back at first, wondering if we could take a leap of faith. He would come for the weekend. We'd take her to play in the park, spend hours on the beach, and walk along the cliffs. In the evenings we would watch comedy programmes in front of the fire with a glass of wine.

Strangely, the years just fell away. He took away some of the heavy baggage of the past. Like one of those porters in Nepal, he came back into my life and lightened my load.

Slowly and gently, we decided to trust in new beginnings. To roll with the tides.

GUIDING LIGHTS

When things end you must start over. Heal. Move forward. Sometimes we choose a totally different picture to piece together, one that we hope we will be much happier with. Or maybe we choose one that looks very much like the last one ... and so the cycle continues.

Round and round.

The same choices followed by the same mistakes.

Walking the same path, over and over.

Rinse and repeat.

Maybe. Or maybe not. Maybe we don't know what we want to create. I thought I knew and yet, a year into the relationship I was so sure I wanted, I tried to blow up my life. To rip apart the jigsaw. Much like I am doing right now.

He'd moved to Cornwall quickly. There seemed no point in waiting and it was a long way to drive for weekends. He got lucky with the job at the farm. Of course, he was an outdoors person, loved the fresh air and the way of life. We were happy – all three of us.

But my default setting is often to tell myself stories. Get out all my old armour in the shape of past remembrances and tell myself things that aren't true. I panicked that our baggage would get in the way, that it wouldn't last. So, I did my best to mess it up, to make things difficult so he wouldn't stay.

I pushed hard and self-sabotaged. I picked fights. He went to stay at the farm for a time, a special staff cottage. Said it would allow me time to think. He was gone for a few weeks and then just came back one night. He knew exactly what I was doing.

'Look, this is insane. You are not going to push me away this time. You are so convinced that you don't deserve to be happy, but I'm not going to fall for it. I'm back and I'm staying.'

So, he stayed. Some people genuinely are lights that you can see through the storm. They rise above the waves, show you the right direction through the wind and the rain. They don't participate in the storm; they only guide you home.

And the jigsaw remained intact.

APRIL 2ND, 2021

THE COLOURED SAND

My husband comes for dinner. The therapist's suggestion. She wants me to tell him all about you, talk about the past, but I'm not quite ready. So, she suggests we go back in time. Talk about *our* past instead. Our wedding, the happy times.

He is staring at the creation from our Sand Ceremony. It sits on a shelf in the cottage. Shades of blue and turquoise and white. Blending and swirling together, like an abstract version of the ocean in a vase.

A simple wedding. A day filled with laughter, music, and dancing. I wore the wedding ring my great-grandmother had worn, almost exactly 100 years after she herself got married. I don't have an actual engagement ring – there was no dramatic proposal, no getting down on one knee. Kai made me a loom band ring. A craze amongst children at the time. Little multi-coloured rubber bands I would find all over the house. I kept that green rubber band ring, but I wear a diamond ring given to me by my Welsh grandmother. She was engaged before she married my grandad, to a man with whom she only spent a week. One week before he left for the war. A war he didn't fight in because he caught pneumonia and died before he had the chance. Before they could build a life together. A story of love from deep in the past, buried amidst the memories of my family.

Alanna was my witness, just as I'd been hers. Bernie performed a comedy ceremony as our celebrant, embracing her inner actress. Friends travelled from far and wide. Ellie grabbed me after too much champagne, and said, 'About bloody time, Kerensa. This is my third marriage and you've only just got to your first one. Three times is a charm, as they say ... but frankly he's getting on my nerves today.'

A sand ceremony usually happens at beach weddings, but we didn't get married on the beach – it was autumn. Too unpredictable. The couple take turns pouring separate vials of coloured sand into a vase. These represent you as individuals. Then you both pour more sand into the vase, but at the same time. This blends and represents you as a couple. Instead of just the two colours, we decided to pour three different colours, from three different vials. Myself, my husband, and Kai. A symbolic way to join the three of us as a family. Of course, by then we were a family anyway, but it still meant something special.

Not long after the wedding, the vase was smashed by accident at a party. Broken glass, sand scattered across the rug and between the old floorboards. We saved as much as we could. I forgot about it completely for a couple of years, then came across it one day and bought more sand and a new vase. We put some of the original sand in the vase and the three of us added new individual layers on top.

So, a few years on, the wedding sand is at the bottom and the sections that represent each of us, as we are now, continue afterwards. I think I prefer it. The first version felt as if our lives as individuals belonged to the past. As if marriage had made us into an indistinguishable whole and we had ceased to be separate people.

The way it is now feels much more authentic. We continue as distinct people. There is a solid, supportive foundation, binding us all together, but ultimately, we are all on our own personal journeys.

Broken things cannot always be fixed, or they can, but they are never quite the same. Sometimes, a breakage is a catalyst. It can give us a chance to do something differently. To look at life differently.

I trust that I haven't broken us.

That we can still transform what we have into something completely new.

APRIL 4TH, 2021

ON THE SHORES OF LAKE COMO

We talked about the wedding and the honeymoon last night. It helped. It created a closeness between us. A long-forgotten intimacy.

A small table at the edge of the lake. Water lapping near our feet, fairy lights in the trees above our heads. The pastel-coloured buildings that look so pretty in the daytime, are muted in the darkness of the night. The lake is still and calm: a deep, dark, inky blue. The waiter has just handed us both a complementary limoncello.

Prosecco in the autumn sunshine, a ferry across the water to wander round the shops of Bellagio, a few hours in our room, with its picture window that overlooks the lake. Our honeymoon.

Neither of us are that young anymore, so it is tempting to fall into the trap of thinking that over a certain age you won't find someone who wants to share your life. That isn't true, of course, but you do have to be willing to risk your heart. The longer you stay alone, the easier it becomes to remain that way. The walls get slightly higher year on year. Letting someone in can be such a scary prospect. Pushing someone away is much, much easier to do. Relationships are different when we are older. We understand how to choose our battles, we understand how to let things go. We know it is possible to love someone deeply and yet not lose the person we are in the process. We understand that no matter what has gone before, we all deserve a second chance.

CREATING A MOSAIC

Barcelona. September sunshine, little tapas bars, eating seared scallops drenched in fresh lemon juice in the food market off Las Ramblas. The festival La Mercè is taking place. A festival that bids farewell to summer and welcomes in the autumn. At dusk the carnival begins. Musicians play, cathedrals are illuminated. Processions of devils dance in the streets and wave sparklers at the crowds. Fireworks burst across the sky all over the town, filling the night with flashes of colour and sparkling dust.

I select a photo taken on the terrace at Park Güell. Two girls clinging to one another on the long-curved mosaic bench. One has her head on the other's shoulder. She is weeping uncontrollably. The other girl strokes her hair, whispering softly, eyes looking out at the horizon. Designed to resemble a sea serpent, the undulating curves of the bench snake all the way along the plaza, providing seating for groups of friends and stunning views across the city. All the individual pieces of glass and tiles have been pieced together in a style called Trencadís. They form a riot of colour that glints and shines in the late afternoon sun. This style does not require the pieces to match in colour nor in pattern, but many sections seem to have been carefully planned and so they match perfectly.

Whenever I see mosaics, I think about how long they must have taken to create and what a special artform it is ... after all, someone decided to take all the little broken pieces and turn them into something beautiful.

April 7th, 2021

MALA BEADS

Somewhere in my mind I can see you playing with your prayer beads on the beach. I have my own set now made by a local artist. I love the way the beads all thread together and form a circle, just as our memories thread together and come back around.

They are made of turquoise, a colour I love, a stone which represents tranquillity and hope. They have a white tassel, attached to the guru bead holding them together. White sand and turquoise sea. I give myself the time and space to sit quietly with my thoughts, counting the 108 beads to focus my mind. It feels like I am holding the colours of the Indian ocean in my hands.

I am fascinated by the way that life connects, how people connect, how paths cross. Many believe, as I do, that there are no coincidences in life; some things are meant to be, there are people you are meant to meet, books that are meant to find their way into your hands. I am convinced that this is true.

The artist asked if I had a mantra to put into the beads as she made them. I didn't so she chose one especially for me.

The beads arrived in the post. Her message said,

When I was threading the beads, I used the mantra:
I flow from chaos to calm

She doesn't really know me, but it's fitting, don't you think? As I try to make sense of past chaos and replace it with present calm.

APRIL 10TH, 2021

MANDALAS

I select a photo of a young monk, in maroon robes, focussed and tranquil, a beatific smile playing around his lips. Nepal 2002. At the bottom of the door was a message saying *please the shoes is out* – so I walked barefoot into the room where some young Buddhist monks were learning how to paint Mandalas. Mandalas are circular; they are about balance and calmness. They represent the universe. In Nepal they call them thangkas. The maroon robes follow the Tibetan tradition. In Cambodia, the colours were different: monks in robes of saffron and ochre. Colours from the original dyes that were used on the cloth, shades created from the materials that were available. I bought a highly detailed black and gold painting. A Kalachakra, a Sanskrit word meaning 'Wheel of Time'.

Mandalas have geometric patterns, symbolism. They have layers of meaning. Buddhist monks often create sand mandalas. They work together as a team, taking weeks, even months to create incredibly complex designs. The sections are filled with coloured sand as the image takes shape, from the centre to the outer edge. Forming a circle, connecting all the parts.

The sand mandala represents a journey. After all the work, after all the artistry that has been poured into the creation, it is destroyed. Destroyed intentionally. Destroyed symbolically. This destruction is significant: it is done to highlight the impermanence of life. The importance of not becoming too attached. It honours the fact that nothing in our lives lasts forever. The sand is swept to the side, and it is often returned to the water. To a river or the sea, where the coloured sand disperses completely, and all the beauty of the art disappears forever.

The impermanence of life is on my mind today. I walk the cliff paths and picture a sand pattern disintegrating to nothingness.

I recall our last hours together on that beach ... and the moment when our seemingly indestructible reflections evaporated away.

APRIL 12TH, 2021

The bluebells have come early this year. The seasons are changing. The climate is starting to break down rapidly, yet so many are still in denial. Bluebells have a special place in my heart and so my spirits lift when they flower.

A photo taken in a wood full of bluebells not far from where my parents live. It's the most stunning wood I've ever seen, solid purple as far as the eye can see, rather than just a healthy scattering of flowers across the forest floor. Kailani is laughing and looking around in wonder, as am I. We haven't been here before and cannot believe the density of the flowers, the vibrancy of their colouring. This day is something we always do together, she and I. We go to the bluebells annually and I photograph her. A ritual of ours that shows so clearly the passage of time.

I can see her in different woods at different ages, ever since she was tiny. I can see her dressed in navy the year we took Honey and tried to get her to stay in one spot. Predictably, Honey was uncooperative, so there was lots of laughter. I see her in blue jeans and a white top, long hair blowing in the wind. Bluebells are protected and shouldn't be picked, but she finds a little damaged handful with broken stems and carries them for a while.

I see her at around two-and-a-half years old, in a lilac fairy dress given to her by her cousin. Her hair is still blonde and curly, with ringlets on the ends. Her cheeks are flushed. She is running along through the carpet of blues and purples, laughing with sheer delight. She coordinates perfectly with the flowers.

At one point, she stops and twirls round and round, her laughter spiralling up towards the sky. She is tiny ... like a magical pixie.

I put this image into the exhibition selection, and imagine it hanging alongside the one of the dancing child in Tanzania.

MATRYOSHKA

I believe that we become many different people throughout our lives, one after another, morphing into someone new as we move through time. Just like all those individual wooden dolls I had inside my largest Russian doll as a child. Each one a version of the outer doll. They all resembled one another, but each was bigger than the last. I would unpack them and line them all up. Pretty maids all in a row, just like the children's nursery rhyme.

I believe the dolls are different representations of ourselves, as we age and as we learn. Some are created by the passage of time and others by the things that life throws at us: its blessings, its challenges, and its pain. People often say they wish they were still the person they were in their twenties or their thirties. But I don't think they really want to be that person again. Most of us are grateful for the lessons we've learned and the people we have become through the love we have received or the storms we have weathered. I suspect what most of us mean is we would like to look like we did in our twenties or thirties. We'd like to avoid the visible onslaught of time and we'd like to have more years ahead of us.

It's funny when we see pictures of our younger selves and think back to how we thought, even then, that we were so flawed, so in need of improvement. Most of us, given the choice, would take the outer shell of our younger selves, but retain the wisdom we now possess, the experience we've gained, the amazing friends we've kept by our sides. So rather than mourn who we used to be, we should embrace each new incarnation of ourselves.

On the last day of a retreat I attended in Bali, we each collated all those parts of ourselves we didn't like, all the negative damaging beliefs we'd been harbouring for years. We symbolically placed all these thoughts into Chinese lanterns, lit the flames, and let them go.

And they floated away, out across the rice fields just as the sun set and the sky transformed into an enormous canvas of orange and purple.

April 14th, 2021

Only the Ocean

Life is such a strange thing. We spend so much time striving, searching for the things we think will make us happy. Things to complete our world. I searched for so long. I believed if I had a child and a husband my life would be perfect, that I would settle down, stop looking for answers. After all, that is the message I'd been given my entire life. That is the perceived wisdom.

Now I have those things, but, inexplicably, the world hasn't changed.

My belief that there must be more out there hasn't changed.

I am still looking outwards. I still need to be alone at times. I still need just myself and the ocean.

'Solitude. Peace. I still need those things,' I tell the therapist. 'I need them when my mind has been dealing with a constant flow of ideas. It's like water. If the water is still, it stagnates and so do I, you know? But at the same time it feels as if the world is spinning too fast. Do you remember those old funfair rides?' I ask her. 'You were strapped inside a huge metal circle and it lifted on an arm and spun around at top speed.'

'I remember. The ones with centrifugal force,' she replies.

'Yes. they kept us pinned to the sides, like a massive hamster wheel. Only the hamster couldn't even run around and around. It

295

was frozen in place, spinning constantly. That's kind of how I feel. Especially when I have to do the same thing all the time. When I'm surrounded by endlessly grinding noise ... pinned to the walls of my existence.'

She looks at me for what seems like a long time.

I think there are times I exhaust her. Or perhaps have I annoyed her.

It turns out to be neither. Instead her next words are very gentle, 'Kerensa, I am going to recommend you ask your GP for a referral. I think you need to see a psychiatrist; I suspect we are dealing with some sort of neurodiverse condition here.'

My ideas come at inconvenient times, so I am here again, in the middle of the night. Almost in a feverish state, wrapped in blankets, words pouring onto the screen. Thoughts moving too fast to be written by hand. Creations begging to have life breathed into them, determined to take flight and go out into the world. The world has changed over this last strange year. I don't know if it will be as it was before. I am not sure it can be. I fear the world we all knew is now in the past.

The sand is speeding faster and faster through the hourglass.

I am not sure if the chaos in my mind this evening is caused by the therapist's words or the news about you. It seems that my brain may be wired differently. This comes as both a surprise and an enormous relief. Perhaps this is why I have felt uncomfortable in my own skin for so long. Why my mind is never quiet.

Not all my days are as frenzied as this. As ever I leap from one extreme to another. Days of gentle tranquillity, where I bask in the sun. Reading in my favourite spot in the garden, or strolling the cliff tops, looking out across the headlands. On those days, the days when life feels calmer, I write by hand. I imagine putting a letter into an envelope for you. I picture you reading it, I picture us talking, sharing travel plans. Laughing together. A picture that has always existed somewhere in my mind. A picture amongst many others.

A picture that is pure fantasy.

April 15th, 2021

The Connections Between the Pieces

And so sometimes I speculate on the whole of that picture. On the order of the pieces. I realise, after all, that there are many, many pictures. Perhaps life is more of a montage, composed of overlapping memories, moments, and dreams. Arranged together in a pattern, in vibrant colours, like a Gaudi mosaic.

All the moments somehow link. The threads of the stories bind together. Some moments created others, some only happened in spite of others. People were instrumental in forming certain moments, whether they knew it or not. I speculate about the fact that if I'd have left Rhys and gone to Australia the first time, I would not have been there the second time. If I had not decided to go the second time, then Kailani would not exist. Another daughter or son might, perhaps even several children. But not this one. Not this ray of sunshine. I suspect I would always have ended up in Australia at some point, but not at that exact time, with those exact people.

These are the pieces of my jigsaw.

And had I not gone to America and met the people I met there, I would never have ended up in Kenya.

And of course, I would never have met you.

If that path had been different, who knows what else would be different. My impulsive nature has taken me down so many roads I may not have walked down had I been a different person. Had I been wired more conventionally, been more reticent or less daring. I wonder what would exist now and what would not? Which pictures, from which continents, would fill my photo albums?

Or maybe, if I hadn't left the first time, I may never have left at all.

April 17th, 2021

We Were Born Before the Wind

E arlier this evening, I sat on the rocks above a small cove not far from my home. Wildflowers covered the grass around me as the twilight stretched across the beach, throwing hues of pink over the grey slate rocks.

The flowers are plentiful now. Bright yellow alexanders and gorgeous pink sea thrift cover the clifftops. Some days I scramble down the rocks onto this cove to sit in solitude – it's not popular, as it's quite inaccessible. People occasionally get stranded at high tide. Often, I bring a notebook and a pen, but today I am joined only by music. Wanting the poetry of lyrics to fill my mind and take away the deafening noise of the water. It is at these times I am most reminded of the extent of its power – the danger it possesses and the havoc it can wreak. So today my ears were filled with songs from the past, songs that helped soften the fierce, crashing waves.

Van Morrison's 'Into the Mystic' washed over me as the water smashed against the rocks and droplets of the ocean splattered over me, despite my distance from the beach. In the song, a foghorn announces a homecoming. A sound I wish I could hear, even though I know that no such sound will come. It reminds me of the legend of the widows along the coast. Those women waiting, day after day, for the men who never returned to the village.

For a Short Time

Two free birds in flight.

Years ago, 1999 I think, I took a road trip in Australia with Brett, one of the Free Birds. We headed away from Perth, away from the stunning shoreline, away from Rottnest Island, and inland to see our friend Mick on his farm.

There we met Mick's family, his wife, two little girls, one just a few months old, another yet to be born. Beers, laughter, and endless sunshine … the inevitable reminiscing about old adventures from the big party house in Earls Court and days at summer camp, now long gone.

On our way there songs blared on the car stereo – as always there were songs which were new to me. Unfamiliar Australian bands. Brett would tell stories, recount tales of seeing these bands live. A song came on. A band called Weddings, Parties, Anything. Lyrics speculating on what constitutes 'too short' a time with another person – is it a day? A month? A lifetime?

Brett was perplexed at my reaction to the song, the fact tears erupted from nowhere, spilling over into the sunshine of the day.

This was a long time after your letters stopped, in fact it was during a time in my life where I hardly thought of you anymore. Yet one song on a random day catapulted me back there. To the campfire on the beach, moonlight, stars, and dancing on the sand. Talking all night long, as time became meaningless. As the golden sunrise glinted across the water.

Back to that unexpected invite to a beach party, to our chance encounter. To that serendipitous moment in time.

APRIL 18TH, 2021

GREEN EYES

My husband has waited long enough. Time to tell him about you.

The boxes have been brought down from the loft. Boxes with the letter 'R' on them. There is a whole box of mixtapes alongside. I take some out and look at them, smiling to myself at some of the memories.

'Do you remember when I made that tape for you before I went to summer camp?' I smile at him. 'You loved that song, the one by America ...'

'Yeah, 'Sister Golden Hair'. I remember.' He runs his hands through his hair. He's pacing. 'You made a playlist on your iPod, almost identical, right before we went to Tanzania.'

Not long after we got back together. I wanted to go back to Africa again so I pitched a feature to *Wanderlust* magazine. Part of me was desperate to go to Kenya and part of me wanted to just leave the past in the past, untainted. To leave my nineties self in Nairobi with all its happiness, its wild adventures. All those evocative memories – the pleasurable ones as well as the wistful, melancholic ones. All those messy, flawed, angst-ridden rows and love dramas that characterised my twenties.

He said it was entirely up to me. Understood there was so much emotion attached. So, we compromised. We went to Tanzania and Zanzibar. We camped in the wild. He climbed Kilimanjaro while I did some shooting for the feature. We strolled hand in hand around the Old Stone Town and watched the sun set over the Indian Ocean.

'Don't get distracted' he says gently. 'You promised to explain.' He looks worried. My husband's eyes lock onto mine.

Those sparkling green eyes.

My husband.

Peter.

My first love. The man who unexpectedly came back into my life in the last months of university. The one who threw my plans into turmoil. The person I may have stayed with, had I not booked a flight and decided to travel to America …

THE SOUNDTRACK OF MY LIFE

Our lives are made up stories, of moments, of memories. But they are also made up of photographs, songs, and fragrances. Things that can whisk us straight back to places and people in the past. Conjure up another world instantaneously.

Especially songs. Songs are like time machines.

Songs that take me back to meeting an old flame and sitting around a firepit.

Songs that take me back to dancing barefoot, on a beach, in the moonlight. A clear night, with only a slight ocean breeze and a host of incredible stars.

Songs that take me back to long road trips, sun beating down on dusty roads, CDs playing on car stereos.

Songs that take me back to my home, to my childhood, making up dance routines, vinyl records on an old-fashioned record player.

Songs that take me back to university, getting ready to go out. Dancing in a bedroom with a drink in my hand.

Songs that take me back to lying on the deck of a racing yacht, music loud in the otherwise still space, the milky way overhead. The water around us black and silent.

Songs that take me back to crazy house parties and noisy nightclubs.

Songs that take me back to long coach journeys. Old songs recorded on cassettes, played on an ancient Walkman.

Songs that take me back to sultry evenings and buzzing beach bars.

Songs I remember singing softly, as I rocked my baby girl to sleep.

And new songs. Wonderful new songs my daughter loves. Songs she discovers and makes into playlists to share with me.

Songs you will never hear, but I think you'd have loved.

Songs that live in the present ... but you are not here.

Buried Treasure

In the end they never found you. Apparently, the boats searched for days.

I tell Peter that the email arrived out of the blue, from someone called Luis Perez. Your brother, it turns out. He was clearing out your mother's house after she died and found all my letters packed away in a box with those photos of us. He didn't know she still had them. He remembered her ripping some of them up after you died. Sending others back. Writing 'return to sender' through angry tears. He didn't agree with her, tried to say I deserved to know. In the end he honoured her wishes. She was hurting; she didn't understand our relationship. She knew I was not to blame for what happened to you, but in her grief, she needed someone to hate.

I wasn't hard to track down. Luis managed to find me easily. My name and so many of the photos I've taken over the years are plastered all over the internet.

He took photos of the images, emailed them to me. Attached all the newspaper articles that covered the story.

A huge storm.

A sailing accident off the coast of San Luis Obispo, California in 1989.

Two dead.

One missing.

So now when I think of you, I think of you out there, forever returned to the ocean.

I think of you as a natural part of the water. A fundamental part of nature. Perhaps that is why, when I quiet my mind, I always find myself on the same shoreline looking out to sea.

I think part of me knew years ago that you had died. The returned letters never made sense.

I take a photo out of the box: two people on a beach looking out to sea. Another: two sets of feet in the water. Moonlight across the waves. A busy beach bar. Then a photo of a tattoo ... a Celtic circle ...

And I tell Peter the whole story. He sits and listens, then he takes one of the photos out of my hand. Staring at it for a long time, he's silent.

'I never understood why you went so quiet. You never answered my calls. Never explained anything. You just let what we had disappear.' He gets up, paces the room, drops the photo into the box. 'Is this why we never picked up where we left off?'

'I ... I didn't know how to tell you that I'd met someone else. It was too hard. It would have been complicated anyway ... you were going back to Edinburgh Uni—'

'But what about later?' he interrupts. 'When we were both single again? We could have talked about it, at least. Met up for weekends ... we could have tried.'

'I couldn't think about anyone else to start with. When the letters stopped I was a mess. I couldn't make sense of it. I know it wasn't fair to you. I'm sorry.'

'I was always there, you know. In the background. All those years you were in Kenya with that Rhys guy. All those times you were unhappy but you still went back. Even after that, there were times we could have tried.'

'You were going through a divorce; I'd just had Kai. I didn't think you'd still be interested. It didn't seem fair to contact you. I didn't think that you would still want me ... that I would be enough.'

He stops pacing and stares. Those eyes that usually sparkle look confused.

'Of course you were enough,' he says in a defeated tone. 'You were more than enough. I adored you – didn't you realise that? I've always adored you. But you keep acting as if you think I'm like Rhys. As if you think I'm just waiting for an excuse to leave. I've never wanted to leave, Kerensa. You are the one who has pushed me away. Every. Single. Time.' He slumps onto the sofa and puts his head in his hands. 'I can't keep doing this. It's too hard. You have to decide what you want.' He pauses. 'We need to leave the past behind us for good. We *have* to move forwards now.'

You captured my heart, blew me away. Then disappeared without warning, destroying my heart for anyone who came afterwards.

The end of us was the beginning of all the things that followed.

Just over a year after we met, and you were gone. Gone forever, as it turns out. I still remember my letters being returned from overseas. Pushing them away as if distance from the words would prevent them from being true. I remember the endless calls I made to a phone number that always went dead. Then Rhys came along, and I forgot you for a time. Forgot how I felt when we were together.

But I hope you know that you have always been my inspiration to live a fulfilled life; to seek out those adventures, to hang on to my dreams. I think you always knew you would not have many years. Not make old bones. You certainly existed that way, moving at top speed, grabbing life with both hands. Loving everything and everybody ... you had such a thirst for knowledge and fun. Such a childlike sense of wonder. It was utterly contagious.

I think you worked out before the rest of us that life is a game we came here to play.

THE COMPLETED JIGSAW

The process of building pieces of life, and pieces of ourselves, is different for each person. Some do it logically, precisely, section by section. Others do it chaotically, moving around, a piece here, a piece there. And so it goes, back and forth, as time moves on. The easy bits and the bits that won't come together.

The dull, ordinary parts and the totally extraordinary ones.

A lady I knew for most of my life passed away not so long ago. A good, long, happy life. She had been in the middle of a puzzle when she died and the unfinished puzzle, just as she left it, was put on a table after the service. People shared their memories, told stories, and had the chance to put in some pieces if they wished. And so, the puzzle was finished for her. There is something rather poetic about that.

You were always my secret. I never told anyone about you. About those few incredible days. I am not sure why … I didn't want to face questions, I suppose. Go against people's expectations. Have anyone judge me or not understand me. Or worse, I didn't want to feel I was living the wrong life.

After a time I tried so hard to forget you. I buried all evidence of you into those boxes and hid them away. Threw everything I had into the next person I loved, tried to lose myself in him, and I did it with such force that I suffocated him in the end. After that, I held a part of myself back from every single person I ever loved, apart from Kailani. Kept a section of my heart just for you and never gave the whole of it away again.

Not even to Peter.

I always believed that I wouldn't be happy unless I kept moving – creating a new jigsaw every few years, but I realise the longer I stay here by the sea, the more I am beginning to root myself down. As if I have tendrils reaching deep into the soil, soaked by the saltwater. I am finally creating a home. A place to stand still.

I wish that we'd had longer, you and I. But however long we spent together, I don't think it would have been enough. Even an entire lifetime isn't long enough with the people we love. Not really.

'I have to let you go,' I hear myself say. It sounds like it comes from far away.

Peter lifts his head from his hands. I glance at him. His green eyes are slightly shiny as if tears could start at any moment. Then he realises I am not looking at him; I am looking down at a photo of someone sitting in the shallow water on a beach as the tide comes in. The sun glare is hiding part of her face. She is laughing and splashing water towards the camera.

'I have to let you go now,' I say to the photo, and I put it back in the box.

April 30th, 2021

The Hut in the Woods

Off the grid. A few nights in the middle of the woods in a simple shepherd's hut. Nothing here apart from a table and chairs, a cosy bed, a basic kitchen, and a bathroom. We are taking time out to just be. To sit and absorb the quiet of the forest. Cook on the BBQ outside and light the firepit in the early evening.

The firepit reminds us of where we began … the second time around.

We watch the flames dance and observe the shadows in the woods, shadows which move and shapeshift as the brightness of the day turns to dusk. A deer wanders past, its hooves crunching across the broken branches scattered on the floor of the wood.

The owner has left us some raw honey. We eat it on pieces of toast that taste of wood smoke. There is nothing here apart from the silence of the wood, my feet in the dust and a clear night sky. Here in this pocket of silence, sitting by Peter's side, comforted by the warmth of the firepit, I remember once more that we are made of stars and dust, and realise I am keen to explore the world once more before the last grains of sand fall through the hourglass.

I have finally accepted the truth; the truth is I must let you go. I must put my thoughts of you into one of those lanterns, release it into the sky and let it fly away across the landscape. I have spent too long looking backwards and wishing it could have been different. You have been gone for such a long time now. Almost a whole lifetime. I must turn to the present instead; spend the time I have on the precious people who are still with me. Here in the now. My rock of a husband and my own dark-haired free spirit. No longer a child, I need to hold on tightly to the last scraps of time that I have with her. She is changing so quickly now, and I see such clear flashes of the adult she is becoming. Someone who, now and again, reminds me of someone else.

A vibrant, dazzling, wildly beautiful girl I once met.

A girl with eyes the colour of the ocean.

A girl I met quite by chance one day. A long, long time ago, on a sunny beach in California.

THE OCEAN

Crossing the ocean means we will eventually hit the land. The water and the shore are destined to meet. They meet gently or they meet violently, but always they meet. The journey we take may end, but the oceans themselves never do. They are all connected to one another, as all the individual fragments of our lives are connected to one another.

The oceans flow together, mix together and eventually, they come full circle ... and they begin again.

I realise that I do not have to choose certain versions of myself. To choose from those many, many different people we are throughout our lifetime. I realise I don't have to choose between the mask of comedy and the mask of tragedy.

I can be chaotic, and I can be calm
  I can be the mighty storm, and I can be the mild breeze
  I can be the light, bubbly shallows, and I can be the dark intense depths
  I can be wild, and I can be gentle

I am the chaos and the calm
  I am the storm and the breeze
  I am bubbly and I am intense
  I am dark

THE POINT WHERE THE OCEAN ENDS

I am light
I am gentle
I am wild

I am the Ocean

Dangerous
    Calming
    Mesmerising
    Powerful
    Serene
    Stormy
    Hypnotic
    Choppy
    Peaceful
    Refreshing
    Invigorating
    Astonishing
    Wild

And seemingly infinite

MAY 1ST, 2021

My darling Riva,
All these years after you died, I discovered that your name has two meanings. From the French it means 'the shore', and from the Hebrew it means 'to join or to bind'. Despite my sadness, this made me smile, because both make perfect sense in their way. I also discovered that Riva wasn't even your real name.

No wonder I could never find you online. No wonder all my google searches for California didn't find those old newspaper reports about your death. You weren't called Riva Rodriquez at all. Luis told me that was a name you invented, a name that sounded like a film star or rock singer. Your real name was Maria Perez. But that makes sense too – Maria can mean 'rebellious' and it can also mean 'of the ocean.'

When I first began to write this diary to you, my words were filled with the love I had kept hidden for a lifetime. Diary entries that read like letters. Letters that could never be sent. And so they began to form themselves into something else, to weave themselves into a book.

E. B. White, the author of *Charlotte's Web* (that book I loved as a child), said he thought books were actually people. People who stayed alive because they hid inside books. And so I have tried to keep you alive, by hiding you between the pages of this book.

But in the meantime, I have a second chance. An opportunity to start again. And so, this will be my last letter to you.

My new life is beckoning now, so I will end here. I will end at the beginning.

All my love,

Kerensa x

Epilogue

January 26th, 2022

Into the Blue

I am floating in the Blue Lagoon. Steam rises into the freezing air. Shadowy shapes are visible through the mist, silhouettes of people in the ghostly vapours where the heat of the water hits the cold of the air. The sky is a bright, crisp blue; black rocks form edges around the milky blue of the water.

I am not alone. The three of us are here embedding our toes in smooth silt, applying mud masks to our faces. Arriving just as the lagoon opened means it's still peaceful. Despite the early hour, we get a beer from the swim-up bar and drink it immersed in the warmth of the water, watching our breath become visible in front of us.

Kailani will be eighteen this year. Such an effortless beauty. She is posing for Instagram shots on the rocks. Filming TikTok videos. Serene and smiling, amidst a canvas of misty blue.

We think of the earth as solid. Immovable. Something to ground us, give us stability. And yet it moves around continuously. We can't always feel it, but much like other things in life, turmoil can exist beneath the surface of a seemingly calm place. Here in Iceland, we drive across the line where two tectonic plates meet. Where hundreds of tiny earthquakes happen every day. A place where we are sandblasted in the freezing wind on a beach surrounded by lumps of ice that look like diamonds – huge clear diamonds resting on black sand, against a backdrop of pale blue glaciers. A land where people believe human-like elves exist alongside them each day, populating a parallel dimension. We encounter no elves, but we see waterfalls, geothermal springs, and boiling mud pits. Wild, empty landscapes and rock formations that are thought to be petrified trolls, towering over a desolate expanse of black sand.

My arms wrapped tightly around Peter's neck, in the buoyant salty water, I look at those familiar green eyes and we melt into one another, he and I. Fully present, blissful, content with what we have.

The trip is a celebration of sorts. My exhibition was a phenomenal success, some of the images purchased by collectors.

I realised, as I was working through my feelings about Riva, that if we could all just see beyond the superficial, and bypass the highlights reels, then we would see one another's souls. I selected some famous images that people had seen before – images like the dancing toddler. After all, she was my version of Steve McCurry's *Afghan Girl.* But I included others too, simple but powerful images the public had never seen. The picture of Riva as she turned to look at me, sitting in the surf holding her board. The Canadian snowboarder, backflipping off the back of the boat in a neon pink bikini, her long dark hair forming a perfect arc. The kiwi farmer, sitting cross-legged on the blinding white salt flats in Bolivia, brushing her dark curls out of her eyes. The Aussie poet looking up from her journal by the side of an infinity pool, laughing. Peter wrapped in a duvet, toasting me with a glass of champagne, in a freezing little hotel room in the Cotswolds where the heating had stopped working, and he'd just washed my hair for me.

I called the exhibition 'Souls Revealed.' It was a celebration of stripping back all the distraction, encouraging people to love whoever they want to love without worrying about definitions or labels. After all, people are just people. We are all souls disguised as humans.

Back in Iceland, the three of us spend a couple of hours floating around in a calm oasis of tranquil blue. The world feels normal again and the future spreads out ahead of us.

My psychiatric assessment is coming up soon so there may finally be an explanation for my chaotic mind and my mental health struggles. The last time I travelled home I ran around the park. Everywhere I looked, there were magpies in pairs.

Life continues for us, for my family, for all the people I love. In the end that is all that matters.

That is the truth of it. Anything else is just noise.

Later that night, sitting on a small patch of this volatile planet, I lean back against Peter. He supports me, wrapping his arms around my shoulders like a favourite blanket. I lift one hand to ruffle his hair, reach out the other hand to clasp hold of Kailani's hand. We tickle one another's palms briefly, smile at one another and we both let go.

Nature has been silent for a while, but as we look upwards, she begins to awaken and perform magic. The Northern Lights. The Aurora Borealis – named for the Goddess of the Dawn. The signal of a new day. A new beginning.

Green and purple light patterns blaze across the skies. They do not seem to be of this earth, and yet they feel as if they are just for us ...

Glowing
Dancing
Translucent
Endlessly circling

Particles of stardust flow around us and the ethereal lights illuminate my daughter's features. Curiosity, wonder and awe radiate from her entire being as I press the shutter.

Then, I put the camera down and I take Peter's hand.

The End

ACKNOWLEDGMENTS

To my family and friends who were early readers – thank you for the gentle feedback, encouragement to keep going and your endless love.

To the people I met on the road – cheers for all the good times.

To a small selection of friends (you know who you are), thank you for letting me fictionalise some aspects of you. To those I turned into the villains of the piece – an extra thank you for letting me do this in name of art.

Thank you to the people who helped me out, showed me kindness, and taught me the beauty of simplicity. And to all the adorable children around the world who captured my heart.

I am enormously grateful to Bryony my editor for helping nurture the story from draft to finished article and for being such a fabulous cheerleader for this novel. To Mila, my cover designer, for interpreting all my ideas so perfectly and Cate for her patience with last-minute changes.

Finally, some of my travels inspired parts of this story, but I would like to acknowledge that my visits to some countries took place many years ago. Much will have changed, therefore other peoples' experiences and impressions of certain places will differ entirely from my own. As a relatively well-off Western traveller, I am aware of the privilege this has afforded and I do not take this for granted.

I would love it if you could leave me a review on Amazon or Goodreads, and share on social media if you enjoyed this book. I am on most platforms as @siobhanmurphywriter. My website for further information, to sign up for newsletters and hear about future books and giveaways is www.siobhanmurphyauthor.co.uk.

Printed in Great Britain
by Amazon

21738095R10178